THE SOUNDS OF RESCUE, THE SIGNS OF HOPE

THE TEXAS TRADITION SERIES

Number Twelve

THE SOUNDS OF RESCUE THE SIGNS OF HOPE

A NOVEL BY

Robert Flynn

with an Introduction by the Author

and an Afterword by

FRED ERISMAN

Texas Christian University Press

Fort Worth

First published by Viking Penguin, Inc., 1970.

Library of Congress Cataloging-in-Publication Data

Flynn, Robert, 1932–
The sounds of rescue, the signs of hope : a novel / by Robert Flynn ; with an introduction by the author and an afterword by Fred Erisman.
p. cm. — (Texas tradition series ; no. 12)
"First published by Viking Penguin, Inc."—T.p. verso.
ISBN 0–87565–039–2
1. World War, 1939–1945—Fiction. I. Title. II. Series.
PS3556.L9S6 1988
813'.54—dc19

89–4809
CIP

Cover design by Whitehead & Whitehead

For Mother

Foreword

I was a child of the Great Depression, although I didn't know there was a depression. We were farmers; we owned our own land. Except for salt, pepper, coffee, and sugar we were almost totally self-sufficient—my father's revenge on Roosevelt. We were considered fortunate by sharecroppers, laborers and storekeepers. I didn't know that either. I didn't know any bad people, any deformed or emotionally disturbed children. In the two-room country school I attended there was a child that our parents referred to as "not right," but he went to class and recess with the rest of us. He wasn't popular, but he wasn't shunned either. A few years later when I heard that a child in the community had been abused, I refused to believe it.

What I knew was a benevolent world, a close-knit community of mutual trust. We never locked our doors. We never slept in fear. We expected everyone to be honest. When Dad was cheated, he expressed more disappointment than anger. Neighbors ought to be better than that.

In this garden of eden there was a small serpent. In school, church, and home we were taught the virtue of hard work. But the hardest working people I knew were the poorest, the hungriest, the first to be forced out of their homes and off the land. Hoboes came to the house and asked for food or work, and they were treated with pity, not contempt. But they brought fear into the heartland because they were workers who couldn't find work. In the school, the church, the home, adults knew something was wrong, but preferred to believe that hard work would save them, while children walked to school without shoes or lunch.

In that benevolent world we feared only strangers. People with peculiar names, different accents, foreign ideas. There was violence in our familiar world, but people were beaten, robbed or killed by friends, neighbors, or relatives. Bad people lived in another world, at least in another part of the state. And to be born male in that benevolent world was to grow up knowing that someday the call would come to defend the familiar from the unfamiliar. Some would answer the call as soldiers, some as preachers, teachers, or lawmen, some as politicians, but all would hear the call.

Our preparation began early. The bad people I killed in war games were sometime Indians, or robbers, or Yankees. More often, I was a crusader and I killed hordes of infidels, my heroes and enemies chosen not by movie magnates, or even by Sir Walter Scott, but by preachers and Sunday school teachers. It was a small world and its verities grew from the land, the rain, the Bible, the love of family, the goodwill of neighbors, and the fear of change.

That world was shattered by Pearl Harbor. I think my father's brother drove to our farm to tell us about the Japanese attack. I'm sure my parents discussed it, but not in my presence. My first clear memory of Pearl Harbor was being told about it at the rural school my sister, brother and I attended. The teacher pointed to Japan on a map, showed us how small it was, and announced that the war would be over in a couple of months. In a couple of months the country was on the ropes and in a northwest Texas rural school more than four hundred miles from the gulf—the only place from which an attack could be launched—we were taught to crouch under our desks for protection during air raids. And no one laughed. Suddenly there were bad people in our community, rumors of spies, and saboteurs, and loose lips that sank ships.

I think those rumors started at the picture show; it's hard to imagine why a spy or saboteur would wile away his days among northwest Texas farmers. But the picture show had become a force in the community. Before Pearl Harbor not even children took movies seriously. Parents put their children in the movie house so they wouldn't be underfoot while the adults talked about crops, and weather, and gossiped about neighbors. After Pearl Harbor some adults, mostly women, went to the picture show without shame. And the picture show became our introduction to a world outside geography and history textbooks with newsreels about people and events that affected our lives, and with movies that gave us heroes we could adore without reservation and villains we could hate without guilt.

The movies prepared us for fire-bombing and saturation bombing, for Dresden and Hiroshima. "They" were not just our enemies, they were enemies of the human race, and we gloried in the death of each of them; it mattered not whether they were man, woman, or child. And we didn't really care if we had to bomb French and Belgian cities, and Dutch and Polish citizens to get at them. We wanted them dead. But the newsreels also showed us Japanese-Americans being taken from their homes and put in camps. It was hard not to feel pity for them. Nothing in my fragmenting world had prepared me to cheer the screaming death of each treacherous, scheming Japanese soldier, and a few minutes later to see the puzzled faces of Japanese-American children behind barbed wire.

It was in vain that our parents, teachers, ministers warned us that putting an American uniform on a man did not change him, and that some soldiers were Yankees, foreigners, criminals. They were our heroes and we heaped on them an adulation that would be known only by a few athletes and a host of rock stars. I can remember waving at troop trains and following soldiers down the street to stare in awe at their uniforms and run errands with gratitude that they had smiled upon me. But some of the men in uniform were black, a contradiction that must have seemed as strange to them as to me.

I wasn't aware of black people before Pearl Harbor, although I'm sure they lived in the community and I must have seen them. After Pearl Harbor, white men who were not drafted could get jobs at defense plants in the cities, and suddenly there were black people on our farm as farm laborers. They were honest, cheerful, hard-working, and we liked them. But they weren't heroes. They weren't patriots. They were barely citizens and shouldn't be permitted to vote, to hold office, or to fight, although they were superbly equipped to carry the packs of others.

My little world was bursting at the seams with evidence that what I had learned and what I had been taught by those I honored and loved was in fact a lie. Then I learned of Dachau and Auschwitz. Millions of God's chosen people were systematically killed while they begged God to rescue them. And God didn't. And neither did the United States. I saw the atrocities in movie newsreels, and the monsters who had committed them. But they didn't look like monsters. They looked like patriots. They looked worried, and sad, and puzzled that no one could understand that they had just followed orders like good soldiers.

About the same time I discovered things that no one ever talked about although they were in the schoolbooks. That

Muslims had killed Christians who begged God to rescue them, and Christians killed Muslims who begged God to rescue them, and Christians killed Christians who begged God to save them. For reasons I could not explain, I believed that God loved me more than He loved any of my two billion contemporaries; nevertheless, it became increasingly difficult to believe God would rescue me when He didn't rescue the Jews, or the Armenians. He didn't rescue Joan of Arc or Jesus of Nazareth. The serpent had become a cobra. The genie-God, who waited for my call to rescue me from the calamities I had gotten myself into, died.

None of this was apparent to me at the time, of course, although I was aware of a contradiction between the world as I experienced it and the world as it was interpreted for me by all the sources of information I had—parents, teachers, ministers, newspapers, magazines, movies, even books. I was still a few years from the discovery of Faulkner and Kafka, Van Gogh and Picasso. I would have liked some company, but almost everyone I knew preferred to deny the evidence, preferred to believe that the monsters were unique, an aberration limited to a specific political belief at a specific time for reasons that could be explained, and had been destroyed forever in the triumph of goodness. And had nothing to do with lynchings in the South, race riots in the East, Indian reservations in the West. And was categorically different from war-profiteering, fire-bombing, Hiroshima.

I wasn't consciously aware that I began to reconstruct my world, bigger this time, and more complex with lots of strange angles and incongruities, a world that did not deny reality and that made some kind of temporary sense. It was years before I realized that as a writer I wrote about men and women who discovered that their training as human beings was not only inadequate and flawed, it was false. In

North to Yesterday, Lampassas tried to be a success by following a code that was as outdated as he was, in a West that had never existed outside the minds of its fanciful creators.

Pat Shahan, in *In the House of the Lord*, tried to be a prophet in a church that allowed only managers, to be a voice in the wilderness to a church that had all the answers, to succor the oppressed when he and his church had chosen to support the oppressors, to perfect the world in a society beyond redemption.

I don't remember where *The Sounds of Rescue, the Signs of Hope* began. The first clear image I remember of the book is of a man standing in an incredibly beautiful world and blaming God because the air is not clean, the rivers not clear, because children die of disease, of hunger, of neglect, whining in self-pity at how hard life is, and seeking something—drugs, sex, astrology, diet, health foods, television—to rescue him. It is an anti-utopian book but I have never thought of it as a pessimistic one.

I created a man, Gregory Wallace, and through him tried to experience the physical and spiritual extremities of life to see if he–I could endure—not just survive but live meaningfully under those conditions. Gregory is no Lancelot, no Robinson Crusoe, no Mister Roberts. He is a non-heroic everyman who finds that the world he lives in is not the world he was trained for and is almost killed by his equipment for survival. He finds he can live on the island if he is willing to accept his present condition, but he is unable to forget the past and ignore the future. He explores his past for signs of hope and discovers that his family, his history are without significance if there is no future; his present struggle is meaningless if there is no hope. He changes the island to meet his present needs, and reconstructs his past to conform to his present condition.

After the publication of *The Sounds of Rescue, the Signs of Hope*, my own reconstructed world was shattered. Within a few months I went to Vietnam as a reporter, my wife was diagnosed as having multiple sclerosis, and our youngest daughter died.

My wife has had no further symptoms and although doctors never admit a mistake, their predictions of blindness and life in a wheelchair have not happened. We no longer believe the diagnosis and we no longer plan for that kind of future. Nevertheless, I am still trying to construct the kind of world in which Vietnam could happen, in which a family's life could be irrevocably altered by someone else's mistake, in which my daughter could die. In this long and painful process, *The Sounds of Rescue, the Signs of Hope* has been a strength I cannot explain. But that book prepared me for a world that falls to pieces, for happy memories that turn sour, for certitudes that turn to dust. A world in which tears are sounds of rescue, in which death is a sign of hope.

Others have kidded me about the title of the book, calling it, *The Signs of Rescue, the Sounds of Hope.* I have never believed such confusion. Rescue is a sound, whether it's the sound of an airplane, the telephone, the mailman, a trumpet, or a child. Hope is a sign. I am certain that the world as I am reconstructing it will crack and perhaps shatter and I will have to begin again. But in that world, hope is a sign. Sometimes it is the only sign.

Robert Flynn

THE SOUNDS OF RESCUE, THE SIGNS OF HOPE

1. DON'T PANIC. RELY ON TRAINING. 2. THINK THINGS OUT. 3. SET DEFINITE GOALS. 4. ENUMERATE CHANCES. MUST WRITE INSTRUCTIONS DOWN BEFORE I FORGET THEM. THINGS I WAS TAUGHT. MY BEST HOPE NOW.

I am alive. On land. Lying under thick tangled shade. Maximum concealment. Plane was hit while attacking Jap carrier. Ducked into clouds to avoid Jap fighter cover. Disoriented. Lost bearings. Engine failed. Got out okay. I'm alive.

Think things out. I was in the water. My chute barely opened and I was in the water. Tangled in parachute. Mae West around neck. Drowning. Felt something grab me. Shark. Kicked at it and arms pulled me free of the chute. Pulled me into the air where I could breathe. Passed out after that. But I am on land. Under concealment. He brought me fruit and water.

Definite goals: 1. Avoid capture. 2. Regain strength. 3. Persuade rescuer to guide me to Allied lines. 4. Watch for rescue. RESCAP will be out looking for me. Must let them know I am alive. 5. Gather information for Navy Intelligence.

Chances: 1. I am alive with only minor cuts and bruises. 2. Am on land. 3. RESCAP will be making intense search for planes lost in strike. 4. Task Force will be chasing Jap fleet. 5. Island has fruit and fresh water. Natives friendly. Can live here for a while. However, I was off course. Am in dense vegetation. Will be difficult to spot. Am on Jap island.

What else? Keep log. Supposed to keep log. Last known position and time of bail-out. Name, serial number, physical condition of personnel. Wind direction and velocity, times of sunrise and sunset, weather, rations used, condition of personnel, inventory of possessions, information of value to Intelligence and Survival officers.

T/O 1812
Grndspd 200k
Course 242°
Wind 305 at 20k
Ship course 330 at 21k

Target 1938
Time over target approx. 8 min.
Track after damage ?
Est. Grndspd after damage 200k
Time in air ?

I don't know where I am. Don't know how far I am from target area, what direction from carrier recovery rendezvous, what time I bailed out.

Lt. Gregory L. Wallace 015323. Weak from shock and near-drowning. Sore from fall into sea. Superficial cuts from shrapnel. Coral abrasions. No signs of panic. Mind clear. Memory good. Have encountered no other Allied personnel.

Wind appears easterly at about ten knots. Sky clear. Towering cumulus in northeast. Lost shoes and survival gear in water. Had to get rid of Mae West and parachute to avoid drowning. Don't know how I lost my watch. Stainless-steel band. Unable to get chart board out of airplane. Have flight suit, three pencils, waterproof case with paper and codes, operating channels, recovery time, IFF and notes on survival. Also six packs of cigarettes in beeswax. Had some matches in waterproof case but Willett borrowed them just before we were launched. Not much of a loss, since my rescuer has a fire.

Survival Instructors should note that a man can be killed by his equipment for survival.

Something else. Some other instruction. Don't be afraid of the jungle. Fit self to country. Travel not recommended.

LOSS OF AIRCRAFT REPORT

Aircraft was hit by explosive shell while in low-level attack on light carrier of Zuiho class. That must have been yesterday. I managed to release the bomb on the target and flattened out to keep airspeed, hoping to get out of range before ditching. The controls were working, and as soon as I cleared the Jap field of fire I made a quick damage estimate. The shell had knocked out the radio, compass, electrical circuits, shattered the dials, and frosted the shatterproof windscreen. Most instruments were out, but I could read the needle ball and airspeed indicator. My arms, legs, and face were stung by slivers of glass and metal but I was able to operate the airplane. Although I was unable to read the power indicators, I believed the engine had suffered damage and loss of power.

Due to the loss of engine power I was unable to keep the running rendezvous with the rest of the division and being under attack by the Jap CAP I ducked into ragged low-lying clouds. It was my intention to keep the plane in the air as long as possible to get as far from the Japs as I could. Without the compass I had no idea where I was or what my heading might be, but I hoped after shaking the Japs to break clear of the clouds and follow returning planes back to the carrier. If not, I hoped to get close enough to the Task Force for them to pick me up on their radar. Without IFF they couldn't identify me but might vector out the CAP to intercept me and I could follow them back.

However, I was unable to break out of the overcast, and flying only by needle ball and airspeed indicator I had difficulty controlling the damaged plane. I kept it straight and level as long as I could but when the engine began smoking and throwing oil I knew I'd had it. I tried to remember what I had been taught. I disconnected the headphone, pulled on my goggles to protect my eyes, opened the hatch, nosed up to kill airspeed, rolled over the side and dove for the trailing edge of the wing. I had my hand on the ripcord as I bailed out, since I was certain I was very low. As soon as I had cleared the plane I pulled the handle and the chute opened. I only swung once and was drifting backwards when I hit but had no time to turn around.

I hit the water hard and must have been stunned, because the next thing I knew I was under water, all tangled up in the parachute, thinking how I had to remain calm and at the same time remembering how our last briefing indicated that the waters were infested with sharks. My Mae West must have been cut by shrapnel because it wouldn't inflate and was tangled around my neck and arm, choking me. In an effort to get free I dropped my survival kit, pistol, and knife, and worked out of the Mae West. I must have lost my shoes and helmet when the chute cracked. I don't know how I lost my watch. I would have drowned had he not saved me, pulling me free of the shroud lines and dragging me over the reef.

I followed instructions to the best of my ability and under the circumstances know of no way I could have saved the aircraft. I suggest pilots receive more actual practice in escaping their survival gear.

I have tried to remember and record what the manual says about natives. Never show fear. Respect their customs. Entertain with tricks. Treat as equals. Avoid physical contact. Be good sport, as natives love practical jokes. Learn native words to win friendship. Learn their tricks of survival such as trapping, fishing, hiding, etc. I regard my memory as evidence of the excellent training we received.

I am fit now, rested and well, and reasonably well fed, although the fruit is more filling than nourishing. Although I have remained constantly on watch for search planes I have seen none. In fact, no planes of any kind. I am not certain how to interpret this, but I believe it means that the island is occupied by a strong Jap force and RESCAP has been avoiding it, assuming that if I came down here I would have been killed or captured. My best course of action then is to persuade my friend to take me to his village, where I may get information and assistance, perhaps a guide and a boat to take me to a friendly island or to one that is not occupied by the Japs where I may be picked up.

My friend saved me from the sea and he has been very generous in bringing me food and water, but he has made no effort to guide me to safety or to assist me in escaping. Captain Willett said all you had to do was tell the natives you were an American and they'd give you their house and favorite wife, as they hate the Japs worse than we do. I have tried this repeatedly, telling my friend that I am an American, USA, and a killer of Japs. He stares at me as though he doesn't understand a word I say. Either he is extremely backwoods or he knows something I don't know—like where the Japs are, maybe. He seems friendly enough and he did save me from the sea and he brings me food, but I don't trust him entirely. He has a way of looking at you—docile and eager to please, and at the same time cunning.

I don't see how I could have lost my watch unless he took it. Not that I mind his taking my watch. I'd gladly have given it to him as a reward for saving my life. But when I ask about the watch, pointing at my arm where it was, he pretends he doesn't know what I am talking about and stares at my arm with great interest. He can be understood only if you assume he has lived his whole life on this island and has had no contact with outsiders. But, then, what's he going to do with the watch? He can't tell time. Maybe he took it because it is shiny and makes a noise, or maybe it has barter value in his village. Or he could have taken it to the Japs as evidence that he knows where I am and is going to turn me in for a reward.

I am going to keep a close watch on my friend, but pretend I suspect nothing. Nevertheless, I am moving at daylight tomorrow. If the Japs capture me it won't be because I sat here waiting for them. I just wish I had my .45 to make it a little harder for them. And my friend is going with me just in case. I'm not leaving him behind to guide them to me.

Captain Willett said for a couple of cigarettes you could buy anything you wanted—from a meal to a piece of ass. Certainly the cigarettes are worth more than the extra mike and vitamin pills, or the condoms and candy bars that some of the guys carried in their survival gear. I gave my friend a puff and he was like a kid—poking about half of it in his mouth and then choking on the smoke. But eager for it, wanting more. Maybe he thinks it's some kind of magic. I'll bribe or persuade him to take me to his village and if everything is on the beam—straight and level—I'll buy a canoe and a guide with the cigarettes and get out of here with as much information on the Japs as I can obtain.

NOTE TO SURVIVAL INSTRUCTORS: Pilots should be alerted to jungle noises. Especially at night. There is constant rustling, whistling, and snapping of twigs, which sounds like a Jap patrol sneaking up on you. This has an unnerving effect and causes loss of sleep. However, most of these noises are from harmless sources—the wind in the trees, falling coconuts, birds, insects, small animals.

There are no Japs here. No villages. No one. Nothing. Just the two of us. Alone. On a very small island. No other islands in sight. The island is very small. Not over four miles long, maybe a mile wide. In other words, it may be unknown. I'm certain it was not on our charts. Alone. Without an airplane.

No sign of rescue. No sign of life. As far as the eye can see, the sea, the sky are empty. I am unable to sleep. To think. Scarcely able to eat. The Task Force could be anywhere by now. No ships, no planes, no other islands. The whole war has disappeared, passed me by. All hope.

Mother must have gotten the word by now. DEEPLY REGRET TO INFORM YOU THAT YOUR SON LT. GREGORY WALLACE 015323 HAS BEEN REPORTED MISSING IN THE PACIFIC. FURTHER REPORTS WILL BE FORWARDED AS RECEIVED. Wonder who will deliver the telegram? Probably old man Blevins has come out of retirement with all the young men off to war. Proud to be of service to his country. Aware of his newfound importance. The first person in Wonder Springs to get the word. KIA. Probably wears a coat now and a felt hat. A man carrying important messages must have dignity. Moving slowly along the street, aware of the long shadow he casts. Hesitating before he turns up the sidewalk and pausing at the door to give those waiting inside time to prepare themselves, set their paws and grab their throats.

"Telegram, Mrs. Wallace," he'll say apologetically, simultaneously ringing the doorbell.

Mother will come to the door, probably still in a house coat, or maybe a pair of overalls and one of Dad's shirts, her hands grimy from digging in the flower pots, a smudge of dirt on her cheek. She won't be surprised at first. If it's old man Blevins he probably goes by the house with every telegram—"Looks like a death notice for the Lockharts. Thought you might want to do something"—so she can cut some flowers for a bouquet, or maybe make a wreath for the door.

But when she sees his face, she'll know it's different this time. "I'm awful sorry, Mrs. Wallace. I'd rather give this to anybody than to you," he'll say. That's what he says every time. Mother will say, "Come in, Mr. Blevins," and he'll go in and sit down, stiff with respect, placing his hat on his knees. Mom will stand there holding the telegram with both hands, staring at it. He'll say, "Why don't you sit down, Mrs. Wallace," and Mom will sit down uncertainly, as though after all these years she has forgotten the height of the couch. Frantically she will tear open the telegram and look at it, her mind refusing to comprehend what it says. Slowly its meaning will become clear to her and she'll place the telegram on her lap, carefully smoothing it with her rough hands. "Gregory is missing in action," she'll say.

"Oh, that's bad," the old man will say. "But it could be worse. It could be lots worse. I delivered a telegram to Mrs. French just a day or two ago. She knows Marvin is gone. Knows it for sure."

"Will you have a cup of coffee, Mr. Blevins?"

"Well, thank you, Mrs. Wallace. I don't mind if I do."

Mother will carefully place the telegram on the dining

room table on a stack of unopened newspapers and unanswered mail, and while the stale coffee is heating, she will absentmindedly try to pick up the cluttered living room. "I just can't seem to get my work done any more for worrying," she'll say. "All day I had the feeling something was wrong."

"Gregory was the youngest wasn't he?" Mr. Blevins will ask politely and Mother will say, "Yes, he was my baby." And for the millionth time she will tell how Dad used to take me to the grocery store when I was small, and how, when the customers asked who my father was, I'd say, "Mr. Walrus."

She'll tell how when David started to school I used to run away from home so that I could be with Dad in the store, and how I used to help with the housework when she was busy with her garden, and how I delivered the flowers when people were sick or there was a death in the family, and said, "Compliments of the Wallace Grocery Store."

After she's had her cup of stale coffee and her bouquet of happy memories, she'll admit that this wasn't the first time I had caused her pain and tears, and Mr. Blevins will nod sympathetically. "Let her talk," he'll think. "It's good for her." And she'll tell how I didn't get along too well in school, and how it broke her heart the way I felt about Dad, and about the time Mr. Watson caught me trying to steal a box of candy from my own father's store. And of course she remembers that tragic affair with poor Ruby Watson. And just recently she has gotten a hotel bill from San Francisco that I neglected to pay.

"Poor woman," old man Blevins will say as he leaves to spread the word through town. "Poor Mrs. Wallace," he'll say in the corner drugstore. "That boy always caused her a lot of grief. And now this." And all over town, at the Busy Bee Café, and the Ice Cream Parlor, and Hill's barber shop they'll be deciding my chances for getting back. "Well, if it was David, my guess would be that he'd come through all right," they'll say at the grocery store. "That David always took care of himself pretty well. But you'll have to admit that Greg was different. People didn't seem to take to him as well. Naw sir, if it was David, I'd say he'd come through all right. But Greg I don't know about."

I wonder if Mom will close the store. Not for long. Mr. Watson will say it's detrimental to the war effort. A disservice to our loyal customers who have been hoarding food and swapping sugar stamps. I wonder what he'll say about me with everyone in town knowing about his daughter. Will he say he hopes I don't come back? No, Harry doesn't have the guts for that. He'll say, "I guess I've got as much reason for hating Greg as anybody in Wonder Springs, but I hope he gets back for his mother's sake." And he'll hang on at the store thinking that after the war David will be grateful enough to keep him on as manager.

They'll have to change my star on the church Honor Roll Banner. From blue for service to silver for missing. Poor old Harry, that's his job, too. Licking the stars and applying them to the white silk banner. Very careful to keep them in straight lines. Sucking his lip in concentration as though he were weighing T-bone steak. Ignoring the women who would prefer that the stars be arranged in a "V" or "USA" or some other attractive design other than straight lines. Fretting because some of the even rows of blue are now interrupted by red and gold stars. And now he will have to remove another blue star and replace it with a silver one. And what does Mr. Watson think as he licks the silver star? Does he wish it were a gold one instead so that he could forget me? Will he tell Ruby that I am missing? Or, to spare her the excitement and worry, will he just tell her that I am dead? Or will he tell her nothing at all, believing that she is incapable of caring, beyond remembering?

Mother will believe the worst. She always has. I never had a stomachache in my life that she didn't think it was appendicitis. She won't hold out hope for long. But maybe Captain Willett will write her, or Major Ebaugh, to indicate how much hope she should hold. They won't want her to hope for the impossible. At the same time they won't want her to give up too soon if there's a chance of my being rescued.

What will they tell her? That I failed to return from an attack on Jap shipping. That after the attack they received no radio contact, spotted no parachute, sighted no one in the water. That the waters were enemy-controlled and shark-infested, the Japs inhospitable toward downed pilots, and no friendly islands in the area. Will they also say they believe it best that she accept the sharp but brief pain of the inevitable and spare herself the unrelenting torture of unavailing hope?

Or will they extend a straw of consolation? That I might have been picked up by friendly natives, kind Japanese, or that in my Mae West I might drift to Australia. Will they say that hope is worth whatever it costs to hold it? Or will they say that hope is the ransom cowards pay? Major Ebaugh is too kind a man, too much the optimist to abandon hope entirely. But Captain Willett is a realist. He calculates the odds, even his own chances, without sentiment. He will advise Mother to consider me dead.

After Mr. Blevins leaves, Mother won't do anything but drink her wretched coffee and stare at the telegram, unwilling to think. Then she'll remember that she must make a wreath for the door. And one for the store. And a special flower arrangement for church Sunday. For a while she'll be happy that she has something to do and then she'll remember David. She has to call David. Even for an emergency it'll take hours to get through to Washington, but she won't cry until she hears his voice. Then she'll go all to pieces, crying uncontrollably, unable to talk. But David will know that something has happened to me and that he must go home to Mother. But David doesn't take anything for granted. He'll ask for verification. He'll write to the squadron. He'll want to know my last known position, my last radio transmission, possible courses of action. He'll investigate my record. He'll go through every ADC Intelligence Summary, Periodic Report, war diary, and squadron muster. He'll make a personal sweep through the area. David likes to be sure about things. And if there is reason for hope, he will hold that hope forever. And if he sees no cause for hope then I'm as good as dead.

Mother won't think to call Helen. Not until the whole town is talking about me, and Helen's folks call to find out if it's true before writing her. Then Mom will call. Maybe she'll just read Helen the telegram. I hope to hell she doesn't just call and say, "Helen, Greg won't be coming home. I thought you should know." Helen would stop writing. And she wouldn't wait for me either.

But Helen will want to know the details. She'll write and ask her folks. Maybe she'll come home from college just to talk to Mom. But if Mother gives up hope, Helen will too. Maybe Helen will be home while David is. David has been overseas. He has the word. If he says I have a chance she'll believe it.

Bunny will never know I am missing. Neither will Lisa unless Willett writes her. But he'll be sure to write her so he can go see her when he's rotated back to the States. He may even write Helen. I gave him her address in case something should happen to me. He might even go to see her. Tell her how much I used to talk about her. How I used to read her letters over and over. The dreams I had. The memories. The time she kissed me in the park, and the time she came to the base to see me, and how she looked in the white organdy dress. So proud and beautiful—

Mother, I am alive. Helen, wait for me. Bunny, for God's sake remember me.

I must not panic. Think things out. Rely on training. Enumerate chances. Determine goals. According to our last briefing these are Jap waters. All islands enemy. All submarines enemy. But friendly PBY's may be sighted in the area. And if these are Jap waters, then our planes and ships will be in here to root them out. Unless they intend to bypass these islands. Even so they will have to neutralize them and keep them under surveillance. The Task Force may even have chased the Jap fleet in here.

I've got a chance as long as guys like Captain Willett and Major Ebaugh and the rest of the squadron are up there flying. As long as they're out here they'll look for me—I've got that hope—until they're rotated back to the States.

At least the Japs will have air and sea patrols, and if things get too bad I can always surrender. Even being captured by the Japs is better than dying. At least folks back home would know I was alive. But, hell, I could probably live here for years. There's food, water—and if I'm rescued I'll be sent back to the States for a medical survey and get survival leave. Helen and I can get married. There's nothing wrong with this island. Too much jungle, but most of it's fruit. My friend has been able to live here for—how long? What the hell is he doing here, anyway? There are no natives on this island. Who is he? And how did he get here? He came from somewhere. Probably somewhere close. And he has some hope of escaping this island or being rescued, and that hope is my hope too.

My best course of action is to remain on this island, fit into the jungle, avoid capture, and wait for rescue.

Generally clear. High cirrus. Wind east by southeast at about 9k. Unable to verify time of sunrise.

My physical condition is good, although I have been troubled with diarrhea due to a diet of fruit and coconuts. I have adjusted to sleeping on the ground and island noises and rest much better, although the mosquitoes are troublesome. Every morning my face and ankles are swollen from their bites, my lips puffy and my eyes almost closed. Not only are they destructive of sleep but I am weakened from loss of blood and fear they may carry malaria. That means I cannot live here long without medical supplies or attention.

The best defense against mosquitoes is to stay fully clothed, let hair and beard grow, cover exposed parts with coconut oil, sleep in the open where there is a breeze, go to bed before sundown, and cover yourself with leaves. However, one mosquito will find its way through the leaves and it is all to do over again.

My friend does not seem to be troubled by the mosquitoes. Either he has gotten used to them or his skin is tougher and thicker than mine, because he is completely naked. He seems unable to understand why I zip up my flight suit, turn up my collar, roll down my sleeves, bathe my face, hands, and feet in coconut oil, lie down in the breeze where it is cool, and cover myself with leaves.

As best I can understand, his name is Kay Yap or Kee Yop, something like that. Sometimes it sounds one way, sometimes another. He does not speak distinctly. Mostly he mumbles. Maybe because he has been by himself for a long time with no one to speak to and has forgotten how to talk. At least when I point to myself and say, "Gregory, American," he points to himself and mumbles, "Kee Yop." Of course that could be the name of his village or something.

Beyond that he is a mystery—who he is, how he got here, where he came from, how long he has been here. He is over six feet tall, perhaps an inch taller than myself and probably about the same age, although he looks older and taller because he is so thin and bearded and his hair is long and wadded up on his head. Also his forehead is high and deeply lined, and his teeth are very long—probably due to poor diet and lack of brushing.

He has wrinkles on his shoulders. Maybe everyone has them but I've never noticed them before. Or they could be caused by some activity like paddling a canoe or something. His buttocks seem to hang down rather flat and appear to be callused. I don't know whether this is normal or not. And he has the largest fingernails I have ever seen. His hands are large and the tips of his fingers seem to be square rather than tapered. The nails cover almost the whole end of the finger. Generally he seems to be less hairy than myself. He is not circumcised.

Where he came from is a puzzle. Is he from a nearby island? A survivor of a torpedoed ship or downed airplane? Then how did he get here? Certainly he couldn't have swum. And why can't he leave the same way? Surely he doesn't stay by choice.

His language sounds Asian but it is not Japanese. He is much too tall to be Japanese. He could be a Chinese sailor or airman. However, he doesn't look Chinese. He is dark like the Chinese but this is possibly due to exposure to the sun. His hair is dark but curly. I don't remember exactly, but I think Chinese hair is straight. And his eyes look just like ours. But very large. In fact, he has the eyes of authority. The ability to look right through you. What I took earlier to be stupidity is the look of command. If he is military, I would say a Captain's eyes. However, if he is a soldier he has certainly let himself go, since he is naked and dirty and exhibits neither military bearing nor discipline. Other than his language there is no clue as to who he might be.

I do not believe he is naked by design. As far as I am aware there are no people anywhere who do not wear some kind of clothing. I believe his clothing was torn or rotted away, or perhaps discarded in the act of getting here. This was my first clue that he is a stranger here, for if he were a native wouldn't he know how to make clothing out of leaves, or bark, or something?

It is impossible to know how long he has been here because there is no trace of him. The island is unmarked. No campsites. No trails. No shelters. Nothing. Just the ashes from the fire, as though he always kept the fire in the same place and did nothing but sit beside it eating fruit. It's as though he arrived here the same time as I, but that's impossible, because he pulled me out of the water. He looks as though he has been here for a long time—no clothes, no shoes, his hair long and unkempt. If so, he has certainly been idle and made no attempt at improving the island. Not even clearing off a place to live.

I tried to communicate with Kee Yop in the pointee-talkee the manual says is so effective. The universal language, it says. "Island," I said, pointing at the ground and then with my finger tracing the outline of the island. "How long," I said, pointing at the sun and opening and closing my fingers. "You," I said, tapping him on the chest with my finger. "Been here," pointing again at the ground and tracing the outline of the island.

He understood none of it but was eager to please and agreed with whatever I said. "How long?" I asked, pointing at the sun, and he would point at the sun and nod his head and try to say "how long." This little game went on for a while until I lost my temper and jerked his hand down when he pointed at the sun and told him to listen. After that he stopped trying to be so agreeable and watched what I said. But the most I got out of him was a gesture, holding one hand parallel to the ground and wiggling the fingers of the other hand beneath it.

I interpret this as being rain—the open hand indicating clouds, the wiggling fingers indicating falling rain. He means he has been here since the rain. Since it rains here almost every day he either means that he has been here since the rainy season began, or since a severe storm. Maybe a tropical storm or hurricane washed him overboard, or drove his fishing boat out to sea and he escaped here.

Or the flat hand could represent airplanes and the fingers falling bombs. He has been here since the bombing. As there is no evidence of bombing on this island he must mean bombing elsewhere. He is a refugee from an island or ship that was bombed. It would be helpful to know whether it was bombed by us or the Japs.

But no matter how he got here, or how long he has been here, something has kept him going, kept him alive. Some secret hope of escape or rescue. "Escape," I said, making paddling motions, and then waving my arms like I was flying. "Can we escape?" At first I thought he didn't understand. "Get away from here," I said, waving goodbye to the island. He stared at me intently, narrowing his eyes, and then slowly he smiled, and winked.

~

NOTE TO SURVIVAL INSTRUCTORS: *Ally recognition*

1. Military personnel should be given courses in the identification and recognition of our allies.

2. There have been many instances of allies being mistaken for enemies and killed, wounded, or imprisoned.

3. Had I landed safely on this island instead of in the water, and had I kept my pistol and jungle knife, it is possible that I might have mistaken Kee Yop for an enemy and killed him.

4. The only evidence I have that he is an ally is that he saved my life and brought me food and water.

5. The only means of recognition we have at the present time is uniform, national emblems, and unit insignia.

6. It is impossible to identify someone who wears no clothes.

~

What am I doing here? Why doesn't someone come? They know I'm missing. Why don't they send someone to look for me? Why don't they answer my signals?

What am I afraid of? There's food here. Water. Even a

companion. There is little danger of capture. I can hold out until rescue comes. Then what am I afraid of?

Is it the waiting? Am I afraid I won't be able to hold out hope, that I will go insane with impatience? Is it because I have no airplane, no way of getting out of here, no means of escape? Am I afraid because I must depend on others to save me? Major Ebaugh, Captain Willett, Mother, David? Is it because I am afraid I will be forgotten and left here? Am I afraid I will forget my training, my friends, my family? Forget where I came from? Forget who I am? Forget how I got here?

I guess a lot of guys left on an island like this would be asking, "Why me?" That is certainly one of the great games of the war. "Why did they draft me?" "Why didn't they send me to Georgia?" "Why did they send him to Clerk Typist school and put me in the Infantry?"

I used to hear it all the time on the carrier. We were never briefed for a mission that some of the guys didn't bitch about how much easier someone else had it. And it's true. You can't split war down the middle and give everyone an equal share of it. On the carrier we had showers, and clean sheets, three hot meals a day, movies on the hangar deck, an air-conditioned ready room while other guys were fighting in mud up to their ass. Some guys would go through the whole war without ever hearing a shot and we would spend three minutes over a target watching tracers reaching for us, knowing the only difference between those who came back and those who didn't was sheer blind stupid luck, and the lucky ones who made it back to the carrier would have to return to the target again as soon as the planes were gassed and rearmed, and that no amount of skill or training or experience could save them from a stray bullet or a broken oil line.

But it always amazed me the way some guys saw everything as a conspiracy. As though there were some design or plot against them. As though the whole war was staged just to interfere with their lives. Some guys thought the Joint Chiefs of Staff sat up nights just to think up ways to get them killed. And other guys thought God diverted bullets and moved clouds around just to save them. One man sees everything as a conspiracy against himself and becomes a cynic. The next man, faced with the same circumstances, sees it as the plan of God and becomes a saint. But I know it was just an accident that it was my airplane that was hit, that it was blind chance I came down near an island, plain bad luck that I have been left here.

INTELLIGENCE REPORT ON KEE ISLAND

The island is vaguely crescent-shaped, about four miles long and a mile wide at the widest point. It is mostly flat, but near the center there is a rock hill or mound about 30 or 40 feet high. On the ocean side the mound drops off to the water and on the island side it is steep but can be climbed. The mound is an excellent place for signaling and observation. The rest of the island is a jungle of vines and creepers that grow down to the water and climb up the trees, covering them like a spider web. Where there aren't vines and trees there is high grass and brush. Except for the mound and a small fresh-water pool that seeps out of rocks, there is not a clearing or bare spot on the island. There isn't even as much of a beach as you would expect. In fact, at high tide there is no beach at all. On this side of the island—the inside of the crescent—there is a reef that forms a large, shallow lagoon. The reef appears to be a half mile or so from the island, but you can always tell where it is, even at night, because of the boom and white spray of the surf.

The island is habitable and contains all the necessities for survival. We bathe and get our drinking water from the fresh-water pool, and there seems to be fruit on every tree. I have been troubled with diarrhea but I think it is because Kee Yop will pick anything. He doesn't seem to have a very clear idea of what is edible and what isn't. Also, he is rather unimaginative when it comes to variety. I do not remember very clearly the section in the manual on wild food. Captain Willett said, "Forget that stuff. Just eat what the monkeys eat." Unfortunately there are no monkeys here so I am having to experiment. I include notes on my findings for the benefit of other survivors.

VEGETATION

1. Most of the island, except where the trees grow thickest, is covered with grass. There are at least four kinds, two of which have edible roots. A third variety bears a burr that can be eaten while green.

2. There are shrubs bearing a tough, nut-like berry. It is bitter to the taste but the oil is useful in aiding elimination.

3. The fruit trees are generally known. Coconut, bananas, a kind of wild pear, and what I believe is a hard plum. There is a gourd-like fruit that can be eaten when roasted. I believe it is breadfruit. Or maybe breadfruit is another name for coconut. I was taught none of this. Also the damn coconuts are almost impossible to husk without a knife.

4. The other trees have no value but as shelter or signal fires, except for wild potatoes and orange bush. The pulp of the orange bush draws fever and inflammation from in-

sect bites. Wild potatoes are willowy trees with bulbous roots that can be eaten raw or baked. They are tasteless but can be kept for days without spoiling. They also bind the bowels.

5. Hardened sap from the trees may be chewed to stimulate the gums and clean the teeth.

6. Leaves on the island are glossier and pulpier than leaves at home, probably due to greater rainfall. As a result, none of the leaves may be eaten. In general, the roots of plants may be safely eaten, in some cases the stems, and the thin inner bark of some trees. The leaves cause cramps and diarrhea.

7. There is a curious tree with roots that grow from the limb to the ground like crutches so that it leans toward the sun supported by the roots. There is one very old tree of this type which I have grown fond of. Because we are always together here it is nice to have a special place where you can be alone.

8. There are many tall trees with limbs only at the top. They are difficult to climb, although Kee has managed to do it. No advantage is to be gained from climbing them.

9. Hardwood will not burn while green.

10. There is something aphrodisiacal about being alone with nature. I am hornier standing under the trees or lying on the grass than I was on the carrier. I believe this is why women like to live in houses.

WILDLIFE

1. Lizards. There are many lizards on the island, most of them small. The meat is stringy but not unpleasant. However, I believe they are most useful in catching mosquitoes.

2. There are large frogs on the island and they are

easily killed. Everything can be eaten but the skin. Although they are considered delicacies back home, the flesh is limp and tasteless.

3. There are many birds on the island, some of them as large as doves. They are all edible, as are their eggs. However, few of them nest here.

4. Sea birds have a fishy taste.

5. As yet we have seen no snakes. However, where you see one snake there are two. Where you see none there may be many. They have no value unless they can be eaten.

6. There are no animals on the island large enough to be dangerous and few animals of any size. We have discovered trails made by rodents, probably rats. In an emergency they probably could be trapped and eaten.

7. There are shellfish along the tide line and inside the reef that may be eaten raw or buried under the fire and roasted. But they are so small that it is hardly worth the effort. Also it is dangerous to reach into coral or under rocks to pick them up.

8. The water inside the reef is clear and small fish can be seen, but Kee and I have grabbled for them without success. It is difficult to grab a fish in the water. The hand refuses to close.

9. In deeper water, near the reef, there are larger fish, but they hide in the coral and I have twice been bitten while chasing them, I believe by small sharks. Also I once ran into a moray eel and although it did not attack me, it refused to leave and I had to get out of the water. It is hard to put down your bare feet when you don't know what you are stepping on.

10. I have given up making nets out of vines. They are

awkward and don't work right in the water and are too heavy and clumsy to use on birds.

SHELTER

Although we have seen none, the Japs must patrol the area, so Kee and I have made a camouflage shelter that will conceal us from observation and protect us from the sun and rain. The shelter was made by weaving together the large leaves in the thickest part of the jungle. So well camouflaged is it that Kee and I have trouble finding it when we walk away a few paces, and so tightly knit are the leaves that I believe it is impervious to rain. The important thing is to use the leaves in a natural way, never leaving one turned upside down or inside out, since it can be easily spotted.

Kee helped with the shelter but he is not as skillful as I had hoped. Either he is extremely lazy or he does not understand the need for concealment or why we are putting the shelter in the densest part of the jungle.

SUGGESTIONS

1. Where the vegetation is densest, the ground is dampest, the insects thickest.

2. Some means, such as leaves, should be used to keep the body off the ground. Not only does the damp ground cause aches and stiffness but it is impossible to keep clean when lying on the ground and dirt has a damaging effect on morale.

3. The leaves should be changed every day, since insects infest the leaves in a few hours.

4. A shelter should not be built near fruit-bearing trees, since they seem to attract bugs, especially coconut bugs.

5. Although the vegetation recovers quickly the same path should not be taken twice, in order to avoid making trails. This has been hard to explain to Kee, who blunders along the easiest path possible.

6. Carry a stick and make a noise when moving about. This alerts the snakes and gives them a chance to get out of the way. Snakes are dangerous only when startled.

7. Thorns driven upward into the body are not so serious as thorns driven down into the body, since those driven down into the body tend to break off under the skin and become infected, while those driven upward into the body tend to drain by themselves. The most painful are thorns driven into the joints, between the toes, and into the genitals. Kee was pushing through the brush when a branch snapped back and drove a thorn into his balls. He soaked them in salt water for several hours, and although they didn't get infected, he is swollen and has difficulty walking.

8. Where to crap? Regulations insist that it be buried, but this is impossible as we have no way of digging. Kee Yop favors scattering shit all over the island and there is merit in his ideas, since beetles dispose of small amounts in a short time. But what if we don't have a short time? What if we wake up some morning and the Japs are here? Our refuse is positive proof that humans are on the island. For this reason I favor dumping in the ocean. It is quickly dissipated by the motion of the water and to my knowledge has never washed ashore. However, Kee has some superstitious objection.

SIGNALS

S and R will put eyes and ears in the area. It is our responsibility to call attention to ourselves. We have piled up brush on top of the mound, which is the highest point, and at each end of the island, to be set afire when friendly ships or planes are spotted. A fire in wartime always merits observation. Three fires in a geometrical pattern on a small island can hardly be considered routine or accidental.

Insofar as is possible we will take every precaution to avoid making signals that can be intercepted by the Japs. But an even greater problem is how to let the Allies know we are friendly. All Allied forces are aware of the treachery of the Japs and if the spotters think we are decoys they will avoid the area. If they think our fires are bivouac fires they will bomb the island.

Probably they will first send over an SBD at about 10,000 feet. If he receives no fire he will probably circle and come in at a lower altitude. He might even make a simulated bomb run to see if he draws fire. This is the crucial moment. If we can convince him that we are friendlies then he will send back a P-boat, but if he has any doubts they won't risk a plane to pick us up.

1. The most effective signal by day is smoke.

2. The most effective signal by night is fire.

3. Signals can be received at greater distances than we can detect help. Our sight is limited by the horizon, but there is no reason to assume that our rescuer's vision is similarly limited.

4. My training included means and methods of signaling, but I was not taught what was an acceptable sign or how to properly identify myself as friendly and worthy of help.

5. By breaking and killing twigs and branches at the tops of low bushes and trees it is possible to create for a short time a brown signal against a background of green.

Because we have no tools the sign will have to be small and will be visible only at low altitudes.

6. To write "US" or "V" in dead leaves would be too obviously a Jap trick. To write my name or serial number would be too long. To write the name of my ship would give information to the enemy. A cross would be mistaken for the mark of a missionary. The Japs would bomb it, the Allies ignore it. Therefore I have decided to write a short obscenity that will be recognizable to Allied airmen and will identify me as an American.

DEFINITE GOALS

It is apparent that we are going to be here longer than I had expected. While rescue may come at any moment it would be foolhardy for us to be idle. We must work to improve our living conditions on the island, and we must do everything possible to increase our chances of getting off the island.

1. Burn out a clearing where we can breathe. Where we can see out. Where we can move around. The jungle is stifling. It smothers you. We could be seen in a clearing. We could prepare a strip where a disabled plane or injured pilot could land. I could patch up the plane and fly us out of here. Get us back to our own lines. At least to another island.

2. Common language. In order to avoid Jap patrols and to make the most of our chances of rescue, Kee and I must work together in the closest kind of cooperation. For this reason we must have a common vocabulary of essential and fundamental words such as mine, ours, come, go, help, hope.

REASONS FOR HOPE

1. The war. As long as the war lasts ships and airplanes and men will be searching for targets, and in the search we may be discovered.

2. The record. Even if I am presumed dead, even if I am believed dead, I must be carried on the records as missing until six months after the war is over, unless my body has been recovered or eyewitnesses can declare certain knowledge of my death. That's the book.

3. Coast watchers. Coast watchers may have seen me go down and reported my position. Or they may have seen our smoke and fire from a distant island we cannot see.

4. Routine flights. SCAT planes may spot our signals and report activity on the island.

5. Routine patrols. Surface vessels or submarines on routine patrol might see our signals.

6. Routine searches. Other men will be lost at sea. In searching for them, S and R may discover us.

7. Accidents. An accidental ship or plane can save us as well as one looking for us. A ship or plane avoiding a storm or driven off course by enemy attacks could discover us.

8. Long shot. Because of minor damage or injury to the pilot, a Jap float plane might land in the lagoon. Kee and I could kill the pilot, repair the damage, and I could fly us out of here.

9. The enemy. The enemy will naturally be where our forces are not.

10. Peace. When the war is over common decency will demand the recovery of the men who risked their lives and are waiting for rescue.

11. Memory. Although I am no longer carried on the

duty roster, Major Ebaugh, Captain Willett, and the other men of my squadron will remember me and watch for me as long as they're in the area. Although I can no longer write to them, Mother will keep my memory alive with flowers, I will be a silver star on the church Honor Roll, David will search the records to verify the facts, and every night as she kisses her pillow, Helen will remember me. When Willett goes to see Lisa they will talk of me. When Bunny Jensen looks at her baby she will think of me. When Sister Mary Martha prays, she will have to pray for me.

12. The hope that is in others. Kee Yop has been here longer than I have. Something, some secret knowledge and hope, has sustained him. That secret is also my hope.

God, the days are slipping away. Running through my fingers and I can't stop them. The Task Force will leave. The squadron will be rotated back to the States and I'll be left here. Left here to die. I'm almost insane from shouting, waving, burning the signals, calling for help. And they won't notice. They won't come. What do they want? What else can I do? I'm afraid to sleep for fear a ship will pass unseen. When my eyes close from exhaustion I jerk awake thinking I hear the sounds of rescue, afraid they will pass before I can signal them. When I sleep I dream that a plane is passing low over the island, but no matter what I do, no matter how I shout and wave they will not notice. They will not help. Sometimes I dream that when rescue finally comes I have exhausted the firewood and there is nothing left to burn, or that I am too weak to signal, unable to call out, to make myself known.

There is so much here—more on this island than I will

ever know. More of peace, more of beauty—yet it is slipping away and I will never know it. Time is too important, too precious, it must be held too tightly. I have no time to enjoy the island, to know it, because time is slipping away, running through my fingers and I feel lost, overwhelmed, confused. If only I could make it stop for a moment—until I could get my bearings, until I could think things out. Then I could take hold of something—cling to a moment of peace. Of beauty.

To Major David Wallace, Army Air Force Training Command, Washington, D.C.

David, I'm not coming back. I know that now. There is a war on, and there are so many missions to fly, so many targets, that they have no time to look for me. I have done the best I can, more I think than could be expected of me, but they are not coming and I will never get off this island.

In a way it seems like everything was against me. That the whole mission was snafued. We were briefed for a predawn launch to put us over the Jap fleet at first light and catch them by surprise, but our scouts lost them in darkness and bad weather, so we sweated it out in the ready room until somebody could find them again.

We spent all morning waiting and then settled down for the afternoon. Finally our scouts spotted them. They had given us the slip and were steaming away. Even under favorable conditions we were barely within range. There wasn't enough time to hit them and get back before dark, the weather was marginal, and we had to turn away from them to launch into the wind.

But nobody said anything. We just tried to copy down

the new data off the board. Winds aloft, intended course and speed of the carrier for the next few hours, operating radio channels, call signs, IFF. Nobody wanted to take a chance on his memory when he was scared and maybe wounded. We barely had it down when we were ordered to scramble all ready rooms. They were trying to get us off fast so we could find the Jap fleet and hit them before darkness and weather hid them again.

I was worried about the ordnance I was carrying. A thousand-pound instantaneously fused bomb in addition to the normal warload of 50 cal ammo. I had never taken off with that much of a load before. While I was sweating over that the bullhorn blared. "Fifteen-minute delay in take-off."

That unnerved us all. We were ready to go and every minute into the wind put us farther from the Japs, and every delay diminished our chances of getting back with any visibility left. But there was nothing to do but wait and wish you had time to take a leak.

Fifteen minutes stretched to thirty. They couldn't decide whether to risk the weather and distance and hope for success, or let the Japs go, because by morning they would be completely out of range. And all this time we were turned into the wind, steaming away from the Japs. Finally they ordered immediate take-off, and we started the engines and ran through checklists while the plane handlers held up boards giving last-minute instructions and changes in wind, course, and range.

The handlers rolled me into position and the Flight Deck Officer gave me the two-finger turn-up. I stood on the brakes, revved up, and made a quick check. Fuel pressure was marginal and that could be trouble on a trip like this, but I knew if I signaled I would be out of the strike, so I gave him thumbs up. The flag whipped down, I kicked off the brakes, and rolled down the deck. I couldn't seem to get any speed but I lifted off and banked slightly to starboard to clear the ship's path in case I went in.

The plane seemed to hang barely off the water until I got the gear and flaps up and began to climb. I orbited and joined up with my division and we tried to climb out of the weather. Tried to hold formation in the scattered clouds, checking the fuel gauges, thinning the mixture, and plotting the return trip. We spotted the edge of the Jap formation and Willett reported their position. Our time and fuel were running out, but Willett bored on in looking for the carriers. We were down to 6,000, trying to see through the clouds, and the flak was heavy. Finally we spotted a carrier of the Zuiho class and Willett ordered an immediate attack.

I went in, kicking the rudders and yawing the airplane to throw off their aim. That's when I was hit. At first I was stunned by the explosion, but I kept the nose of the plane below the horizon to hold my airspeed and I headed out to open water. The controls handled okay but I was afraid I might have a punctured fuel line or shrapnel in the cooler. The Jap fighter cover was all over us and I knew I had to ditch fast and hope I wasn't strafed in the water or picked up by the Japs, or try to duck in the clouds and follow someone back to the ship.

There was a Zero on my tail and I could feel slugs hitting my stabilizer, so I ducked into a cloud. I don't know how long I was in the clouds. It was all I could do to keep the airplane in the air. There was turbulence in the clouds and my stabilizer was shot all to hell. Without the compass

I was lost. The turbulence was tossing me around like a ball, it was getting dark and the dirty gray muck was spinning around. I had vertigo so bad I had to duck my head and stare at the needle ball to level the wings, and watching the airspeed indicator I tried to get down out of the clouds.

When I broke out of the clouds I couldn't have been more than fifty feet off the water. Visibility was less than a mile and not another aircraft in sight. I didn't know where I was or which way it was to the carrier but I figured the longer I stayed in the air the better chance I had.

I tried to stay just off the water, out of the overcast, but the ceiling was dropping and it was getting dark fast. I flew that way as long as I could and then I knew I had to climb out on top because I could no longer see the waves.

I was scared shitless, because the only way I knew I was climbing was by the airspeed indicator and the sound of the engine, and then the wings would begin shuddering, ready to stall. I was near panic. My mind was spinning and all I wanted was for one minute to have my feet on the ground so all the motion and spinning would stop and I could think. I tried to remember what I had been taught.

I thought of how Major Ebaugh said, "When you're in clouds, keep your eyes in the cockpit and trust your instruments." But the artificial horizon and climb indicator were out and I didn't trust the airspeed indicator because I didn't know how many rpm's the engine was turning.

I thought of how Captain Willett said, "When you think you're lost don't be afraid to hesitate and circle. Get out your plotting board and plot. A little high-school math has saved more pilots than all the prophylactic kits in San Diego." But I was afraid to try to turn in the clouds, afraid

I would get even more mixed up, and not knowing where I was it was useless to plot.

I remembered the story Dad used to tell about how he was in a patrol surrounded behind the German lines and how everyone was in a panic and the Lieutenant was so scared he couldn't do anything but run off at the bowels. Then Dad realized the only reason they hadn't surrendered was because the Lieutenant couldn't get his pants up long enough to raise his hands. That struck Dad as being funny and he started laughing, and the other men started laughing too and they forgot their panic and fought their way back to their own lines, and the Lieutenant recommended Dad for a Silver Star. "Boys, when you're in trouble," he used to say, "just stop a minute and think how funny it's going to seem once you get out of it."

A crock of shit, like everything else he ever said. I had reached the end of the line. It was either bail out or spin in. I didn't know how high I was but I knew I'd never be able to ditch in the darkness and overcast. I rolled back the hatch and went over the side, damn near breaking my neck because I forgot to unplug the headphone.

I don't know why of all the shells fired that day it was my airplane that was hit, or why of all times to lose the radio and most of my instruments it was in ragged weather, or why of all the islands in the Pacific I came to an unknown, inhospitable one in the middle of nowhere, or why of all people to find on an island I find a man who is as much a stranger here as I am, who cannot tell me how he got here or where he came from, or build a shelter or make a fishing net.

Accident. Mere chance and circumstance. There is nothing I could have done to have changed things. I obeyed orders, I followed SOP with a damaged aircraft insofar as was possible. I followed standard jump procedure. I was as good as my training. I did the best I could. The rest was chance.

I am resigned to my fate and I am determined to die with dignity and with all my debts paid. I have written some letters and I wish you would see that they are delivered for me. You will notice that one of them is to Sister Mary Martha. I thought that might be better than writing directly to Ruby.

Dear Mom:

This is the last letter you will ever get from me. It never occurred to me that I wouldn't be coming home, but I know it now so I am writing this letter. I always thought that when the war was over and I was back home I could straighten things out, make a fresh start, but I know now I won't be coming back and there's nothing I can do to change things except to say I'm sorry.

I guess you got the record I made in Honolulu. I know it sounded silly. Childish. There was so much I wanted to say to you—the way I felt about home, and the grocery store, and Dad, and going off to war. How sometimes at night I could see Wonder Springs just as though I were there again. The trees, the garden-club park, the high curb in front of the grocery store where the farmers used to sit on Saturday evenings, the bank across the street with its cupola and high, barred windows, the one-window post office where Helen's dad sold stamps, the old brick schoolhouse with the dome and the fire-escape slide from the third floor to the ground. How sometimes at night looking out to sea I could smell it again—the hot camphor smell of summer, auto exhaust, burning leaves, the oil-covered dirt streets, the rugs and flowers and bread smells of the house. Sometimes I could hear it all again. All-night traffic on the main highway through town, the ten o'clock whistle at the gin, the blast of the Silver Zephyr passing nonstop on its way to Denver. I could hear the wind in the cottonwoods, dogs barking on the other side of town, the muffled sounds of children crying, the tinkle of iced-tea glasses, and snatches of music from a distant radio. And I would think—that's what I'm out here for. So folks back home can sit on the curb in front of the grocery store, smell the dusty, oiled streets, lie in bed and listen to the rumble of the Silver Zephyr outward bound. And it would make me happy, Mother. Even when I was afraid I might die.

But when they closed the door of the little booth and I was alone with the microphone I knew I wouldn't be able to say what I wanted to. So I told you those corny moron jokes and bragged about what I was going to do to the Japs. I hope you'll throw the record away, Mother. I don't want you to remember me like that.

Mom, the waterproof case you gave me to carry a Bible and your pictures and letters in is great. I carried it on every flight. They told us on the carrier that it would be best on missions over enemy waters if we didn't carry anything personal that the Japs could use, so I had to leave your pictures and letters on the ship. I wish I had them now, but I guess if I did I wouldn't be able to write you because when I took out the pictures and stuff I filled it with paper to write down codes and instructions in case I was downed in the water. The paper is running out now but I wanted to use the last of it to write you. I'll put this letter in the case and pray that some day you'll get it. I don't want to just fade away with no one knowing what happened to me. I want to be alive someplace or dead someplace.

I know you never understood the way I felt about Dad.

I wanted to explain but I didn't want to hurt you. I loved him, Mother. I used to run off to the grocery store just to be with him. I wanted to grow up to be just like him. The way he walked through town waving and smiling at everybody, calling them by their first name. The way people gathered around him in the grocery store, listening to his stories, laughing at his jokes. But that was before I started working in the store after school.

It wasn't the work, Mother. Dad thought I was lazy, but I didn't mind working in the stock room uncrating goods, or helping Mr. Watson butcher the meat. It was having to work out front. Watching Dad patting everyone on the back, playing the big shot, playing the fool, playing everybody's pal, joking about what a hero he'd been in the war, cussing F.D.R. to the businessmen and the W.P.A. to the farmers, talking church with the ladies and dirty jokes with the men, waving his hands to keep their eyes off the scales, telling them the punchline so they'd laugh as they signed the charge slips; "this is twenty-three cents instead of twenty-one. Greg must have marked it wrong." All for a two-cent overcharge on a box of soap or a head of lettuce. "I don't sell groceries, I sell happiness," he used to say. Well, the happiness he sold was overpriced.

I was ashamed, Mother. Can you understand that? You never went to the grocery store. David and I always brought home the groceries. Vegetables that had been bruised and picked over, meat that had turned brown with age, eggs that had been in the store so long you had to break them one at a time into a cup to be sure they weren't rotten, stale bread, potatoes taken a few from each hundred-pound sack so the customers would never know the difference. I was ashamed, Mother. Because he was so small.

They laughed at him, Mother. He's dead and I'm sorry, but they laughed at him.

I used to go up to the attic and look at his moth-eaten uniform hanging there and pretend that he really had been a hero, and that some day everyone would know it and stop calling him "Wally," stop laughing at him behind his back.

Dad could never understand why I wasn't the most popular boy in school, but he wouldn't let me play football, and I was ashamed for my friends to see me working in the store. Dad wouldn't let me have the car, and in Wonder Springs you don't date popular girls without a car, Mother. The only time I ever dated Helen in Wonder Springs was the time we doubled with David and his girl because Dad let David have the car.

I tried to get along with Dad, but I couldn't laugh at those corny jokes and I couldn't pretend I believed all those tales about what a heroic clown he was in France. David didn't believe it either but he laughed and kidded Dad back, and ragged the customers. "Better get some of this bread, Mrs. French. Not over ten days from the oven." Anything to get along. I know I hurt Dad. I know that's why he came home upset. But I think he would be proud of me now, proud that I splashed a Jap plane.

My insurance is made out to you. Take it and buy some new furniture, get rid of those old rugs, brighten up the place a little. You don't have to live like that now—never going anyplace, staying home and taking care of your flowers. Buy yourself a new dress. An expensive one. I know David is planning to take over the store after the war but I think you should sell it and be done with it. Get yourself a new house.

I guess they will send my sea bag home. Don't open it. There are a lot of things in there that should be thrown away and David can take care of it. You can send my wings and ribbons to Helen and any of the pictures of me you don't want. Tell her she can have a bracelet made out of the gold wings. There are some 50-caliber shells in there but they are harmless, since the powder has been removed. Any of the flying stuff that David wants—flight jacket, gloves, helmet, extra mike, plotting board, manuals —he can have. I don't know how much of it they will send. Also any of my civvies that he can wear. Do whatever you want with the uniforms. Give them away or hang them in the attic with Dad's stuff. You can keep my log book, Mom. I'd hate for it to be thrown away. And whatever back pay I have coming.

Mom, if you think Ruby would like to have any of my stuff—if you think it would be good for her—whatever you think.

Please don't cry for me. I did my job and I did it well. My only regret is that I cause you sorrow.

Your son,
Greg

Dear Helen,

I don't know if you'll ever get this letter, but I hope you do because I want you to know how much you meant to me. I think of you all the time, wishing you were here, thinking what a paradise this island would be if you were here with me.

It was the thought of some day coming back to you that kept me going through all the waiting in the ready room, the 0300 reveilles, briefing, flight schedule for the day. It was you I thought of while checking the status board for speed, course, anticipated recovery time, while trying to find the damned plane in the middle of the night, when dropping off the flight deck in the dark without being able to see the horizon or how far off the water I was and only the truck lights to show me where the other ships were, on the long haul back with my controls shot all to hell, having to circle with the gas tanks registering empty because someone had crashed the barrier.

But I did it, Helen. I kept going because I said each day brings me one day closer to the time I come back to you. Every minute waiting for "start engines," every pre-dawn take-off, every mission, every patrol, every bomb or bullet was one step closer to you. When I shot down the Jap plane I said, "That one's for Helen." And when my plane was hit and I was hurt and lost and scared all I could think of was, "Helen, I've got to get back to Helen."

If you get this letter it will mean that you are free to make whatever kind of life you can for yourself. You'll get my wings and ribbons. I earned them and I want you to have them. Something to remember me by. And because you earned them by waiting for me. You didn't write as often as I wished, as often as some of the other guys' sweethearts wrote, but the mail is so fouled up out here I don't really know whether you wrote or not. But I realize that being in college you didn't have as much time to write as the women who had nothing to do but go to the beauty parlor.

Helen, I've spent a lot of time thinking about our last night together. I understand why you thought it was best to wait until after the war to talk of marriage, and I've tried to understand how you could send me off to war without even a kiss. I know you are modest and have a lot of self-respect, and I know it was embarrassing to have

Miss Manning standing there watching. But your rule about waiting until the fifth date for a goodnight kiss seemed kind of silly when I was sitting in the ready room waiting for what might be my last mission. Sometimes at night it used to drive me crazy to think that you cared what that old bitch thought when it was our last night together. Every time I was vectored out to intercept Japs or launched on a fighter sweep I would think what a vain and heartless thing it was. How could you do it, Helen? I'm dying. How could you leave me with a memory like that? Our last time together you refused me a kiss. I hope you waited for me, because if you didn't you don't deserve my wings.

Love,
Greg

Dear Bunny,

I hope you will read this even though you may hate my guts. A lot of things have happened to me, Bunny. I've changed. I understand a lot of things that weren't very clear to me before. But I won't be back now, and all those things I was going to do differently will never be done. It's too late now. Too late for anything.

I used to think of you a lot during those days on the carrier. Especially when they were showing movies on the hangar deck. It's hard to think of you or the war without remembering the movies. I was in Primary and you were in high school—both of us full of the glory and excitement of a country at war. The movies were so close to us then, so close to the way we felt. I was a young hero and you were my true love. We saw our destiny, the truth of our lives written on the screen. But I guess the movie ended for both of us on your porch that night after the U.S.O.

dance. Because in the movies the hero knows what to say, and his true love cries without pain, and in the movies love never leaves scars or bastards.

That's what I tried to say in the other letter, the one I wrote when I was in Intermediate Flight. You never answered, so I always figured you threw it away unopened. I didn't know the words then but I tried to say what I should have said that night on your porch, after I had played the young hero going off to war and you proved yourself to be the true love who gave herself in trust to a man who might never return.

I tried to say that it wasn't you or me—it was the war that was at fault. Movies, and uniforms, and songs, and knowing that every moment was very important because all about us were death and change. I tried to explain that the foot soldiers still had death and glory ahead of them, across the ocean somewhere, but that we took a piece of it with us every time we climbed into the cockpit. That I was afraid of failing, afraid of bilging, afraid I would miss out on the glory and excitement. And you wanted to be part of all the music and poetry, the big blowout, the great escape. I tried to say that the movie ended that night on your porch. Because in the movies death and love are never inconsequential or without glory.

You helped me when I needed it and I have always been grateful for that. I never thought of you as a chippie or furlough wife or anything like that. And I hope you will remember the good times we had—the record shop, the U.S.O. dances, and all the times we talked of love and flying.

I guess your folks don't think much of me right now and I'm sorry, because they were swell to me. I know you may hate my guts and I don't blame you. I hope you married the football player and that he's 4F and that everything works out for you. But if you want to tell people we were secretly married, and if you want to tell the kid his father was killed in the war, it's all right with me. I don't know anything else I can do.

I sent you a scarf from Honolulu. I hope you liked it.

Sincerely,
Greg

Dear Sister Mary Martha:

I never thought I would be writing you, but I'm not coming back and there's something I have to do before I die. I have to make you understand about Ruby. She wasn't wicked the way she thought she was. She wasn't even bad. She was just a plain, fat little girl who wanted to be noticed and loved.

Do you remember what it's like growing up in a small town like Wonder Springs? The whole world is inside the city limits. Your parents are so wonderful, and grownups are so wise, and no where else in the world are people so good and patriotic. And you want to grow up to be just like them but no one will ever take you seriously. You're always little Greg the grocer's son, Ruby the butcher's daughter. And no matter how pretty you are you will never be as pretty as your mother was. And no matter how hard you work your father was the sole support of his family at your age. And no matter what you do you'll never measure up to the family standard.

Then one day you discover that the family standard isn't much. That being the son of a grocer or the daughter of a butcher isn't so great, but you're stuck with it. That a grocer isn't interested in the happiness and well-being of people, he's just interested in gouging the customers for two cents. That a butcher isn't really an artist who gives shape to a formless carcass but an expert who turns fat and bones into dollars. That a grocer is the town clown and the butcher is his hired help. That outside the city limits is a world that is bigger and better and more honest than anyone in Wonder Springs ever dreamed.

So you dream of going away for a while and doing something that nobody in Wonder Springs ever heard or thought of—like being a nun or a fighter pilot—so that some day you can come back to Wonder Springs and people will see you as yourself. Not Wallace the grocer's son, or Harry Watson's daughter—and isn't it a marvel the way that poor man has raised her without a mother to help.

Ruby just wanted to be noticed. She just wanted to be loved for herself. If you could just forgive her, Sister Mary Martha. If you could just love her. Please don't hate her. Try to understand.

Sincerely,
Greg

David,

I hope you can read this. I have to write it small and on the inside of the cigarette packs because I'm out of paper. I guess if I had to I could write on leaves or strips of bark.

David, do something for Kee if by some miracle he survives. He saved my life. At least he prolonged it for a while. Long enough for me to write. There is nothing I can do for him here. I made him some clothes but he won't wear them.

When you go through my sea bag you will find some books, pictures, and other junk that Mother need not see. Please throw them away for me. If they send the brandy it's for you. Probably my buddies will drink it. It's worth a lot of money on the ship. Also you will find a bracelet with my name on one side and "Bunny" on the other. I wish you would return it to her. Bunny Jensen. You'll find her address in my stuff. Return her letters to her also. I guess they should be burned, but they meant a lot to me. I'd like her to know I kept them. Send them to her and if she wants to destroy them she can. If you would write her a letter telling her how I died I would appreciate it.

Also I wish you would notify the squadron, or at least Major Ebaugh and Captain Willett if the squadron has been broken up. You get very close to some people out here and these guys were swell. Just to set the record straight, if I had been recovered I wouldn't have accepted survival leave, even if it meant not getting married. I would have asked to be sent back to the squadron.

David, when I said that you kidded with Dad and the customers and tried to get along, I didn't mean you demeaned yourself. I just meant that you were the popular one. People respected you. Your friends didn't try to sneak stuff out of the store just because you were checking out. And I wasn't trying to cut you out when I told Mother she should sell the store. I know you plan on going back and getting rid of the country-store atmosphere and setting up a chain of stores. I was just trying to think of what was best for Mother. So she wouldn't have to be sorry about it and wouldn't have Harry Watson coming over all the time to go over inventories and orders and things. He's planning on taking over the store, David. It's better if Mother just sells out and you can build your own store wherever you want.

David, it is possible that an unscrupulous person named Lisa Burto may come around asking Mother for money. Don't give her anything. She is nothing but a common whore. I paid her and paid her well, but she had her hotel bill sent to Mother. I owe her nothing and neither do you. She was just a piece of ass. You understand, David. I was alone and drinking and there was a party. For God's sake, keep her away from Mother.

~

Ceiling and visibility unlimited. Wind at three or four knots. Just enough to rustle the leaves. I wish to God one of those damned PBY's would come over. They could see for a hundred miles. A great day for flying.

I know the other guys in the squadron are up there somewhere. On station over the Task Force, splashing a few meatballs, or maybe sweating one of those long over-water missions where you keep listening to your engine and checking your compass, keeping track of wind drift on the waves, and elapsed time, watching the manifold pressure and fuel supply. Maybe sick, lost in the overcast, scared, shot up. Searching for some sign of the picket ships, praying to get down safely. I'd trade places with any of them. No matter how sick, or scared, or lost. Just to be in the air again. To be free of this island.

I'm just not ready for paradise. It's too quiet here, too safe, too simple. When we are hungry we take fruit from the trees. When we are thirsty we go to the pool for a drink. When we are tired we lie in the shade. At night we sleep under the stars. When I'm restless and can't sleep, I lie awake and listen to the pounding of the surf, and the wind in the palm trees, and watch the stars move across the sky, caught up in the peace and beauty of it all.

It's not like trying to go to sleep on the flattop. Trying to shut out all the hammering and creaking and rumbling of the ship. Trying to shut out all the past fears, trying not to think about tomorrow, trying not to dream of being lost in sudden storms with no top or bottom, of facing a Zeke with your guns jammed, of hanging in the air with streams of anti-aircraft pouring up at you.

Here there are no Japs. No throbbing of the ship's engines. No clanging of alarms, no sirens, no bullhorn or crackling radios. No shouting of frightened and excited men. No blast of airplane engines being started. No whir and thump of the catapult and the roar of the engine below the flight deck. After the shouting and noise of war, a reprieve. And it seems a shame to waste even one such night of peace in sleep.

When I wake in the morning it's like another world. The wind and the waves. Flowers, and birds, and trees. The sky all pink and silver and the ocean blue. From the mound near the center you can see the entire island and the ocean on every side. Great piles of coral beneath the water. White spray along the reef. The water, which is almost green inside the reef, and then blue, and then dark blue marking great holes in the bottom of the ocean.

Sunset is the greatest art show I've ever seen. Every color. Sometimes the sky is clear with only a pencil smudge above the horizon. Sometimes the whole sky is tinted the color of rust, or lemon, creamy white, or rich red wine. A cloud may be royal blue trimmed in silver. Last night the sunset was the color of an old orange plus the purple black of a deep bruise. I've never been much for art galleries, but I know if some artist painted the sunsets here the way they really are no one would believe it. They are too perfect. Too beautiful.

An island paradise. But I would trade it all for one cigarette, to hear one bomb, to see one ship, one airplane. It's so damn quiet. The war is so far away. We haven't seen a single ship or plane. We'll never be discovered this way. If only we could be a little closer to the war. Close enough to see the ships and planes, even hear the guns. But out of range.

Early morning CAVU. Very light haze to the southwest. Wind about 6 knots gusting to 10. By noon there was some cloud build-up in the west. Towering cumulus. Fantastic shapes. I never was one for watching clouds back home and I never saw anything in them the way some people said they did. But I can see them here. Icebergs and islands. Lemon meringue, heaps of ice cream, tall buildings, whole cities with gleaming streets, a row of fat naked dancers. There was a cloud looking perfectly like an arrow with the arrowhead pointing northeast. Nearby was a figure resembling Santa Claus on a sled, with one hand flung backwards over his shoulder as though he were either pointing the same way as the arrow or had thrown the arrow over his shoulder. I was afraid I had fever and delirium and I called Kee Yop and asked him what he saw.

I pointed to a cloud and said, "What do you see, Kee? What do you make of that?" He studied the cloud intently while it changed from a big-hipped woman to a puff of smoke. "Nuka vulavicki biru," he said, which is an expression that seems to mean "Balls," or "Who gives a shit," or "What the hell," depending on how you say it. I pointed at another cloud I thought might look something like the kind of house he grew up in. "Nuka biru," he said. I pointed out clouds that looked like food—ice cream cones, hams, chicken drumsticks, baked yams—he recognized none of them and I was beginning to think it was my imagination when Kee saw something. "Mali ku-see," he said matter-of-factly, as though he were saying, "That looks like an elephant." All I could see was a kind of dark veil across the sky.

I spent the day on the mound, watching the sea and the sky. But the ocean is so big and the sky so empty. After a while I began to get what the Dumbo pilots call "island eyes." I was looking so hard for an airplane, or ship, or island that I began to see them everywhere. Specks in the sky that looked like a formation of airplanes, until I blinked and then they were gone. Every shadow of a cloud on the water looked like an island. Every swell looked like a submarine. Everywhere I looked I saw visions of home and signs of rescue until I had to turn away and close my eyes. That way is madness. There is nothing to do but wait.

It wouldn't be so bad if I had a cigarette. In war you expect to spend a lot of time waiting. Time that is going to be interrupted, maybe forever, so that you can't do anything or think about anything important. But you can light up a cigarette and it gives you something to think about when you don't want to think about what happened yesterday and what might happen today.

Sometimes you want to go home so bad—you want to talk to a girl and touch her hand, or walk down Main Street and look in the window of Brock's store so bad—that you can't think about it or you'll go crazy. So you light up a smoke and it helps. It gives you something to look forward to. From the first puff in the morning to the last slow drag before hitting the rack. Something you can hold on to. Something you can plan on.

Here there is nothing you can look forward to or plan on without going out of your mind. Nothing to do when you don't want to think. Nothing to wipe out the smell of this place. The rotting vegetation. The hot, spicy smells of growing things. Musk and decay and stink bugs. The sickening sweetness of flowers. If I just had one of the cigarettes I wasted on Kee. If I could just smell the smoke from a burning cigarette. Flat, stale, but full of memories —noisy bars, crowded cafés, fraternity parties, hangar dances, horseplay before training flights, a break from meteorology lectures, a victory drag at the end of a mission, a shared cigarette after a tumble in bed.

Nothing is so monotonous or so changeable as the sea. Nothing so restless and hypnotic. Always in motion, yet it always looks the same. All we can see. Just watch the ocean and wait. Watch the waves rolling in. On every side of us. Hemming us in. Separating us from all we love.

Everything I want, everything I love is on the other side of the water. The ship, the squadron, Helen, home. If I could just walk down Main Street again the way I used to walk home from the store. Past the Busy Bee Café, Hill's barber shop, Brock's Five and Dime, the green-tinted windows of the post office where Helen's dad works. Cut through Hugh Stanley's service station, through the gap in the hedge, along the alley and beneath the trees behind Ruby's house and come out on Mesquite Street. Dogs will be playing in the street in front of the Weirs' house. Mr. Johnson will be mowing the grass and Mrs. Johnson will be burning the leaves. Across the street Martha Bailey and a couple of her girlfriends will be gossiping in the porch swing, pretending to study. Music from phonographs and radios will spill out into the street, and already you can smell stews and cabbages and liver and onions.

Behind the hedge, between the cottonwood trees I can see the house. Picked especially by Dad to be our home. Old enough to be established but not old enough to look shabby or run down. Large enough to be comfortable but appearing smaller than it is, for no one must suspect that the money that buys the milk for baby buys private bathrooms for the grocer's sons. With a yard big enough to keep Mother busy potting and planting and to keep David and me out of the street, but not so big as to set us apart from our neighbors. Surrounded by a neat hedge and a white picket fence with a little swinging gate that discourages casual callers without being rude or insistent about it.

Mother will be digging in the front flowerbed in an old dress or maybe one of Dad's shirts over overalls, and one of Dad's old hats on her head. "Hi, Mom," I'll say, and she'll turn around, annoyed that her quiet world of flowers has been interrupted. "Why, Greg," she'll say, surprised to see me, her joy at knowing I'm safe incomplete because of her anger that I have caused her so much grief and worry. "It looks like you could have let me know you were coming." Almost whining. Torn between crying for joy and crying in helpless rage that the answer to her prayers is not full delivery from pain.

She will wipe at the corner of her eyes with the back of the cotton glove, smudging her cheek, and crossing her hands over her breasts she will stand for me to embrace her, and lay her head on my shoulder, not wanting to hold me too close for fear of soiling my uniform and being completely overcome with emotional confusion.

All the way into the house she will fuss about the way she is dressed, and in the house she will apologize about the way she looks, and she would have cleaned and straightened up if she had known I was coming. While she is washing and putting on a clean dress and rearranging her feelings, I will pick up the living room and clear off the dining room table so she won't be embarrassed.

"What would you like to eat?" she will ask first thing. I'll suggest that we go to the Busy Bee Café. But no, we can't go out to eat, not the first night I'm home, not with all the food there is in the house and no one to cook for, and what would people think? She'll open the refrigerator door and look at the confusion of bruised and wilted vegetables, watery dressings, dried cheeses, and discolored meats trying to decide what to fix until I suggest scrambled eggs and bacon.

She will be relieved, and we'll discuss David and Helen and Mr. Watson and the grocery store while she's breaking the eggs one at a time into a cup before pouring them into the skillet. I'll wash the pot that has been sitting on the stove all day and make fresh coffee. By the time the food is ready we'll have talked over everything and I'll ask about her flowers, and she'll ask if I've changed. I'll compliment her on her cooking and she will apologize because she's out of practice, not having anyone to cook for but herself. Then we'll try to talk about Dad. How he did it for us, so that she could have the house and solarium and her flowers, so that David and I could have a room of our own and money to go to college. How if I had understood him, believed in him, he wouldn't have come home nervous and agitated every night so that he couldn't eat dinner without having to run to the bathroom to throw up.

"Are you all right, Dad?"

"I'm all right, Sugar. I must have eaten too fast."

While Mom's clearing the table I'll drink another cup of coffee with my cigarette and then I'll walk downtown to look around, past the old school, maybe stop at the fire station and tell the boys where all I've been and about the Jap plane I shot down, stop at The Corner Drugstore for a malt, walk by the Pictorium and look at the pictures on display—stills of some movie that has been around for a while. *Spring Parade. Gone With The Wind. My Favorite Wife.*

I saw that with Helen. The way Cary Grant looked when he stepped out of the elevator and saw his wife. Irene Dunne I think it was. He thought she was dead and he had married again and there she was and he just stood and looked at her. Helen caught my arm and put her head on my shoulder she was laughing so hard. I told her it really wasn't funny. That could happen in war. A guy could be lost at sea, or captured, and still be alive although everyone thought he was dead. Helen said that's why people shouldn't get married for the duration.

I might walk down to the train station and look in on the little canteen the American Legion set up for boys passing through. Have a cup of coffee and a smoke with some of the Legionnaires and talk about what it's like.

The war wasn't so bad. Dull as hell. Reveille at 0300. Waiting for flight quarters. Checking the status board. Checking the Intelligence and Aerology Reports. Plotting and replotting course. Checking the board for last-minute instructions. Standing to. Waiting for "start engines." Waiting for launch. Combat Air Patrol over the ships. Waiting for something to happen. Waiting for recovery time. Waiting to be taken aboard. Acey-deucey. Listening to the scuttlebutt about the next day's mission. Bitching about the weather, the ordnance we were carrying, the Intelligence Reports. Waiting to be secured. Most of the time it was routine as hell. But that's what we enlisted for.

Back in the States it was great. You were a hero even if you had never been overseas. All you needed was a uniform.

People would give you a ride, take you home to dinner, introduce you to their daughters, and give you the key to the car if they had gas and tires.

Any other time Bunny's father would have kicked my ass out of the yard. A stranger who walked up on his front porch and started talking to his daughter. Even if he had known that Bunny and her giggly friend had whistled at me as I passed by. But there was a war on and I was in uniform and there weren't any strangers any more, just homesick boys, so her parents didn't do anything but cough or rattle pans once in a while to remind us that they were there inside the house.

We must have talked all afternoon sitting there on the porch. I had just soloed and I had to tell somebody. Most of the others had already soloed so no one in the barracks wanted to hear about it. I called Mom but she had already been through all that with David so she wasn't too excited, just worried that I would be shipped overseas immediately. But Bunny really listened. As though it were important. The most exciting thing she'd ever heard.

And it was exciting. I wasn't scared when the instructor got out of the plane and turned it over to me, but I was so excited I could hardly stay in the cockpit. I just wanted to jump out and run down the strip. I believe on that day I could have taken off without the airplane. And I was worried, too, because I was one of the last to solo. I was afraid if I didn't make good on this one I'd be cut. So I opened the throttle for the take-off roll determined to do it or die trying. I raised the tail, and then when I pulled back on the stick the plane lifted off like I'd never felt it before. Without the extra weight of the instructor, it climbed like it had never climbed before, and I knew I would never feel that lift again. Climbing right up into the sky. I was so entranced that I was flying I almost forgot to get into the pattern, but I came around and set it down so easy the instructor sent me around again so I wouldn't get overconfident. But the second was just like the first and so was the third, so he waved me in.

I guess I must have looked dazed, because he reamed me out for being cocky and getting careless, but just the same I could tell he was pleased. God, I was excited. I would have taken on the whole damn Jap Air Force with a .45. But nobody at the barracks wanted to hear about my perfect approach or how I greased the wheels onto the runway. They wanted to talk about women and shallow eights and gripe about the chow. I couldn't stand it, being cooped up with all that noise, so I went outside and wandered around for a while until I found a quiet place behind the base chapel. I just lay down and looked at the sky. God, was I pleased with myself.

I guess if the M.P.'s had come along they'd have picked me up for being drunk. And I was drunk, as high as I've ever been. But I knew then I was going to make it. There was still a long way to go but I knew I could fly. I'd get my wings. I wouldn't have to tell Mom I wasn't good enough, and explain to David why I couldn't cut it. I decided to go to the PX and call Mom. I had to tell somebody.

"Mom, it's Greg. I soloed today."

"You did."

"Mom, I flew the airplane by myself. For the first time. Mom, I'm going to make it. I won't get bilged."

"Well, don't take any chances, Greg. There's a lot of things more important than flying airplanes."

"Mom."

"David says he wishes now that he had gotten into the

Quartermaster Corps. He could do just as much toward winning the war, and after the war he would be a lot better off."

"I know, Mom. I just wanted to tell somebody. I thought you would be pleased."

"I am pleased, Greg, but I don't want you doing anything foolish. Your coming home alive is the only thing that matters to me."

Nobody really wanted to hear about my solo but Bunny, and telling her was almost as exciting as doing it. We must have talked all afternoon, until finally Bunny's mother came out to run me off and Bunny conned her into inviting me to dinner because it was unpatriotic to let a serviceman go hungry.

Fliers had it made with the girls. Just tell them how you were training for the most dangerous mission of the war, or how you were afraid of being bilged, or about the time you were upside down at 5,000 feet, or about your best buddy who was killed shooting the circle, and while they were playing the understanding girl, slip it in.

Take a girl to a restaurant and two out of three times somebody would pick up the tab. Some old doughboy who'd like to be back in it, or a mother whose only son was on Bataan, or maybe some guy who felt guilty because for the first time in his life he had money to throw around. Even the cops were nice if you were in uniform. And women like Lisa, who in peacetime would never give you a second look.

I know there are slackers back there, and profiteers. I know they sold out the guys at Pearl, and Corregidor, and Wake Island. I know that in Wonder Springs people have more money than they've ever had before, and business is so good Harry has had to hire a woman and a couple of high-school kids to help out at the store. But I sure wish I could be back there with them. If I could just get behind the wheel of one of those Pontiac Torpedo Streamliners and drive through Wonder Springs honking and whistling at the girls. Or if I could take Helen for a spin along the river, and over thrill hill so fast her stomach jumps up in her throat and she squeals and catches my arm.

If it were just the distance—I believe I could walk forty miles a day. With nothing to eat but fruit. Even through the jungle. Even in Jap territory I could make thirty miles. A thousand miles a month. Even if I were in a life raft in the ocean I would be moving. Drifting with the current, or being blown by the wind. But to sit and sweat and wait and watch the sea.

Kee does nothing. Eating. Drinking. Sleeping. Aware of nothing. As though these days could last forever. He has the primitive's way of letting time pass in oblivion. Enjoying letting it slip away. Sleeping while his moments run out, while the Task Force steams away and leaves us here to die.

Maybe Kee is smarter than I am. Maybe I should give up too. Drift along waiting for the end. Accept circumstances as they are. Do nothing to help myself. Not caring one way or the other. But people like that don't build nations. They don't fly airplanes. They don't win wars.

I wasn't taught to wait. Dad always said, "Better buy it now, it might not be here tomorrow." In school they always told us never to put off until tomorrow. The minister sometimes talked about laying up treasure in heaven, but the men who stood outside on the steps, smoking cigarettes and waiting for the service to begin said, "Better get it while you can. The government may cancel the program tomorrow."

All they ever talked about in Flight School was angle of attack and killer instinct. Keep alert, keep your tail clear, watch for Japs diving out of the sun, get him in your sights and get him good, there may not be another chance. Captain Willett used to say, "The cherry you don't pick today will be a crabapple tomorrow."

Everything was speed. Get in the air first. Climb fast. A quick strike, running rendezvous, orbit the ship, into the groove, chop the throttle, drop it on the deck, taxi off the cable, cut the switches, bail out, and report to the ready room on the double.

I wasn't trained for this. To sit here and rot into the jungle. Until everyone has forgotten me. Given me up for dead. Until I'm as naked and abject as Kee. And everywhere I look that goddam ocean.

But this is Jap territory and the only chance of rescue I have is the sea. If help comes it will come by the sea. Even if I am sighted from the air, I will have to be picked up in the water. The sea is my chance of escape, or rescue. It brings us things. Maybe a bit of the airplane will wash up. A scrap of metal. Part of the parachute. A message. A rubber raft or lifeboat from a ship. The sea is not just separation. It is our connection with the Allies. Our lifeline to hope.

NOTE TO SURVIVAL INSTRUCTORS: *Things to look for from the sea*

1. Seashells that may be used as containers.
2. Edible shellfish and crabs.
3. Refuse from ships such as wreckage, oil, life preservers, floating debris or other evidences of ship traffic and war progress.

4. Bodies bearing clothing, letters and pictures, shoes, or useful tools.

Light shower activity before dawn. Shortly after sunrise low cloud cover began breaking up and by midday the sky was broken with high, towering cumulus. Wind southeasterly at 12 to 15 knots.

For the past several days I have been working on a common vocabulary as a basis of communication. Mutual understanding is essential to our survival. But it has been very difficult to communicate this to Kee. He thinks I am playing some kind of game. He refuses to take me seriously, he fails to pay attention, and he mumbles so it is impossible to understand anything he says.

To make it easy for him, I have tried to use as many words from his language as I can. "Patu manee pakarua" for shelter or place of refuge. "Wah lala" for drinking water or the fresh-water pool. The lagoon we call the lagoon because he has no word that fits it so well. I have been unable to find a word that means "food" or "to eat" as distinct from the names of edible things, therefore we have agreed on "vulevu," which seems to mean "appetite" or "good taste." "Malihini huruhura" is his name for Jap, enemy, or anything evil or destructive. "Mali ku-see" is what he once called whatever he saw in the sky—some reminder of home or sign of hope. Evidently "mali" is sky, "ku-see" is horizon or ocean or beyond, and the combination of words means "hope" or "whatever comes to us from beyond the sky."

I would like to use more of Kee's language but it is so illogical, many-syllabled, and inefficient that it is unsuited for survival. It is essential when rescue comes to be able to identify quickly and accurately the direction from which it comes. I tried to teach Kee the clock system of locating objects but it is impossible. His mind wanders, he loses interest, he wants to go pick bananas. Maybe he has never seen a clock. A hundred times a day I have to remind myself that he is the product of a simple culture and has a short attention span. As often as I can get his attention, I drill him on essential words. North signal, south signal, signal tower—which is what we call the mound—come, go, run, hide, strike.

Kee's language appears to have no word for "weapon" or "hit." If I show him a stick he says one thing, if I show him a rock he says another. Those are the only two weapons on the island. It is hard to believe he is so primitive he does not have a word for "weapon" or "self-defense."

Unfortunately, whoever has the words of command has command. This is not a responsibility I want. Nevertheless, if we are to survive somebody must make the plans and give the orders. And staying alive is the first order of the day, our primary mission. I'm not trying to take advantage of Kee, I'm just trying to get us off this God-forgotten island. Regardless of my personal preference I am better qualified to keep us alive and get us back home. Back to the things that matter. Helen, and Mom, and getting a car, getting ahead, living again.

We have had the greatest difficulty in communicating abstract words, yet these are the most important of all if we are to truly converse. Kee does not seem to understand the concept of "mine." We have so few possessions—my flight suit, a few seashells or coconut halves we use for dishes, a few stick tools, the pencils, the tree I like to sit in—and because of their scarcity and the difficulty of replacing them, these few possessions become very precious. To lose one is like losing a part of yourself. Yet Kee will use my cup when his cup is right beside it or sit in my tree when there are trees all over the island. He will step on my shell and break it or beg for one of the pencils. It isn't meanness or stupidity and it's hard to believe he is from a society so primitive as to have no concept of private property. I can't understand him, unless he has never had anything of his own and therefore wants whatever anybody else has.

I have tried to make him understand that the island, the fruit, fresh water, fire, the shelter and signals, and hope are things we have in common and are for both of us to use as long as we do not abuse the island, pollute the water, destroy the fruit trees, or endanger the fire. I have explained that while he can't use the pencils, the pages I write belong to both of us, that it is our record, our history, our war effort so to speak. I have also explained the importance of the log, that whatever happens to me, the log must be saved and placed in the hands of the Allies. I have let him look at these pages, wrappers, and strips of bark, let him hold them in his hands, and then I have taken them and very carefully put them away in a crevice in the rocks where they will stay dry.

I have been unable to discover Kee's word for help. I know he must have one because such a word is the cornerstone of civilized society. Without mutual aid men are nothing but savages. Kee understands this concept because he helped me when I was drowning, and when I was lonely and afraid. But I can't find his word for it.

Help may be the most important word on this island. Even more important than hope. But sometimes you don't know a person needs help until he tells you. Like the gunner in Wilson's TBF who was shot in the throat. He bled to death before anyone knew he was hit.

But how are we to let each other know we need help unless there is a word for it? And even then it isn't always possible to say it. That last night with Helen I couldn't find the words to say it. I couldn't make her understand I needed help. I had to go to a strange woman to ask for help. I guess there were times when Dad was asking me for help. Tapping me on the arm, tugging at my sleeve, watching my face for some sign. Only I didn't understand.

Sometimes I get so discouraged I just want to give up. Sometimes I think there is no help for us. Kee is so impatient. Sometimes he turns away as if to say he doesn't understand, will never understand, and just wants to be left alone. But if we keep talking, keep trying to communicate, no matter how discouraged or exasperated we get, we will eventually reach a kind of understanding. Today was the first breakthrough. A very tiny one, but I believe it is the beginning of understanding. Kee said, "California."

It didn't sound much like "California" because Kee mumbles so and he can't pronounce English words anyway, but I recognized it. "California," I repeated, nodding my head. "California," he said again, getting much closer to it this time. "Yes, yes," I said, and we both were getting very excited now that we had finally broken the barrier. "California."

"California," he said, following it with a string of words I couldn't understand.

"California," I said. "I understand that. California."

"California," he said, and again he tried to tell me something, speaking slowly and breaking every word into several syllables. I tried but I couldn't understand, and he became very exasperated with me and kept speaking louder and louder.

"You have been to California," I said, pointing at him. "You, California."

He kept waving his hands and shouting at me. "I have been to California," I said. "Me, California, U.S.A. Yes, yes, California."

We both ended up shouting at each other and waving our hands, and to avoid an angry scene I turned and walked away. Tomorrow I will try again. Kee knows something that can help us, maybe even save us from this island if I can only find out what it is. Maybe he has been to the U.S., or maybe he knows California is part of the U.S., or maybe someone in California knows he is missing. It could even be that he knows how to get to California. It isn't much maybe, but it is a beginning.

~

NOTE TO SURVIVAL INSTRUCTORS: *Shelter*

1. Thatch-weave shelters are excellent camouflage but are poor protection from the rain, since water runs through the leaves. Also the shelter continues to drip after the rain has stopped.

2. The best rain shelter is an A frame covered with broad palm leaves.

3. The shelter should be built close to the ground, since rain blows under it.

~

Weather continues good. Few isolated clouds but nothing that would interfere with operations. The squadron must be up there somewhere. Even if they have given me up for dead they must be up there looking for other survivors, Jap planes, ships. Somewhere the war is going on and my job is to wait.

While I sit here in safety enjoying the quiet and sunshine, the squadron is sweating out another day. Waiting in the ready room. Trying to doze, reading the same magazine the third time, hoping time will pass. Sitting in their planes on the flight deck sweating out one delay after another while weather and darkness close in. Out over the water listening to the engine. Waiting for a break in the clouds. Checking and rechecking the compass and fuel gauges. Computing and recomputing the course, rendezvous, and recovery time. Looking for some trace of the ships as the fuel runs out. Waiting for the engine to sputter and stop. Seeing nothing below but water. Wondering what went wrong.

I guess most of the time I spent on the carrier I spent waiting. But it was waiting to do something. It wasn't waiting for something to happen to me. And with the fear there was also exhilaration. I had a chance and I held that chance in my own hand. It wasn't waiting helpless and afraid with doubt gnawing at your guts. And it was waiting with others. Being part of a group that was committed to a job.

I may not have been the leading ace in the squadron but I was a part of it and I still am. I know the other guys will do the job. I know they will look for me as long as they are in this area. Major Ebaugh promised that. And I will do my job too. I will keep this log and I will stay alive, and I will keep the watch.

I believe that all over the world there are people who seem to be doing little, who perhaps think they are doing nothing, but who are a very vital part of the whole effort. The people who keep the factories going. The women who save waste fats and grow victory gardens instead of geraniums. Men who give the bumpers off their cars for scrap iron, boys who collect paper and tin, girls who write their sweethearts, the soldiers and sailors who never fight the battles but support the guys who do. It may not look like much, but Kee and I are holding this island for the Allies.

~

NOTE TO SURVIVAL INSTRUCTORS: *Clearings*

The island can only be cleared by fire. The first fire destroys the grass and brush and strips the leaves from the low trees, but the large trees are scarcely affected. To burn them it is necessary to pile dead matter around the trees before setting them afire. The ground is fertile and the fire improves it.

~

Have been sleepless at night. Apprehensive. Afraid that help will pass while we are asleep. And every time I doze off I am awakened by strange sounds or Kee crying out in his sleep. "Killing Japs," we called it back on the flattop. I wonder what he dreams about. Does he cry out in joy between the thighs of his wife or sweetheart? Is it an involuntary cry of horror as he sees the Japs torturing his family? A cry of despair at being lost, cut off from everyone? Why does he toss and struggle so in his sleep? Sometimes I whisper "California" very softly so as not to awaken him and the sound seems to soothe him. He stops moaning and struggling and soon his breathing returns to normal.

On the carrier I would dream of Japs on my tail and I would fly farther and farther from the recovery rendezvous, unable to turn without turning into them, watching my time and fuel run out, and I would wake up wet and shivering. Or I would dream that the carrier was out there somewhere under a fog bank and I couldn't find it. I would fly, becoming more and more confused, losing my orientation, unable in my panic to read the indicators, discovering at the last minute that I was diving into the sea when I thought I was climbing, or that I was in a left bank when I thought I was straight and level.

Here I dream of help that passes us blindly by in spite of all our efforts to make ourselves known. Last night I dreamed I was on the signal tower. I was watching the sea, but not just watching; I was waiting for something. Not impatiently, but hopefully, as though I were waiting for the mail, or waiting for Helen to show up for a date. Pleasantly anticipating. And I look up and there's something there. "A gull," I say. "Ten o'clock high." Then I realize it's too far off to be a gull. It's a plane and I can hear the drone of its engine.

I stand up but I don't wave because it's too far off. I am thinking calmly, rationally, "So high he may not even see the island." But even as I think it, the airplane alters course to fly over.

"Bandit," I think as it loses altitude. I can see it's one of ours but I'm afraid to admit it to myself. I stare at it intently, unbelievingly. I know I should light the signal but I can't move. I watch as it flies over the island and slowly fades into the distance. And then just before it disappears, I see it stand on one wing, coming back for another pass.

I run to the clearing where I may be seen. I try to light the signal, but my hands are shaking so I can't carry the fire. For some reason the signal won't burn. The wood turns to black ash without flame or smoke. I begin to cry as the plane passes over again at a lower altitude, but this time I wave. I jump up and down and shout and wave.

Again the plane turns and comes back. Very low now. So low that I can read the number. Old 84. Major Ebaugh's plane. So low that I can see the open cowl flaps, the six meatballs painted on the fuselage. So low I can see Major Ebaugh, see his sharp quick little eyes looking right at me. I am saved. I am rescued. Excitedly I wave, but Major Ebaugh does not wave back or give any sign of recognition. Instead he circles the island.

He doesn't recognize me. Somehow I have aged incredibly. My hair and beard are long. My clothes have rotted away so that I am naked and wrinkled and brown from the sun and dirt. I look like Kee. Major Ebaugh mistakes me for a native.

"Gregory Wallace," I shout. "I'm Gregory Wallace." Frantically I try to think of a way to identify myself as an American, a friend, a person in need of help. I run around the clearing as the airplane circles the island. "American. Friend. Shipmate," I call, but my voice is thin and reedy. A strange voice that scarcely sounds American at all.

"Lt. Gregory Wallace. 015323. I flew in your squadron. You promised to find me." How can I make him understand? "We were together at Pearl. At Boena. Mati. Tanau. Gregory Wallace," I shout, although I can scarcely hear my own voice. The airplane rapidly climbs away. "I showed you pictures of my mother. My sweetheart. I shared my packages from home, you bastard. I looked for you when you were down, you son of a bitch, I tried to find you—"

I woke up then and at first I could hear, or thought I could hear, the airplane as it faded away. Instantly I was awake. I jumped across the fire and shook Kee. "Listen,"

I shouted, cupping my hands to my ears. "Listen. Did you hear that?" Together we listened but it was too late. The sound was gone and Kee had not heard it.

Yet something had happened. I know it had. I looked up at the sky. Light cirrus veil but I could see the stars. Something had awakened me. Had the wind changed? Quickly I checked. No, it continued the same. Was it the mosquitoes? I brushed over my arms, but I have gotten almost used to them and the breeze kept them from being troublesome. Had a plane or ship passed far away, the sound waking me? It must have. If only Kee had been awake. If only he had heard it too.

I built up the fire, and taking a torch I went up to the signal tower and set the signal afire. I kept it going the rest of the night, hoping if there had been a ship or a plane it might come back, or that it might spot our signal long after we had lost the sound of it. Sitting by the fire I waited for sunrise, knowing that the whole Task Force could be laid out on the horizon. Yet daylight revealed nothing. Could they have passed in the night while I was asleep? Could hope have gone while I was helpless, asleep? Or was it just a dream?

The truth is, there is a war on and Kee and I are missing in action. "If you're not back by the next flight quarters we'll have to scratch you off the duty roster so we can get replacements. But in our hearts we'll carry you as part of this squadron." That's what Major Ebaugh said. "And any plane launched by this squadron will count it a part of his duty to keep his eyes peeled for survivors. Personally, I'd rather save one poor bastard from the ocean than to smoke six Japs."

They may be looking for me right now. The important

thing is that we not miss our chance. We must stay alert. We must not let rescue pass in our sleep. We must draw attention to ourselves. We must show ourselves to be in need of help. We must prove ourselves to be friendly.

1. We will use fire and smoke to draw attention to us.

2. We will bathe, cut our hair and beards, and find some way of dressing Kee to show that we are civilized and in need of help.

3. We will show ourselves to be American and friendly by writing FUCK in the lagoon with logs and branches.

NOTE TO SURVIVAL INSTRUCTORS: *Fire*

It is hard to overestimate the value of fire on an island. Not only is it useful for cooking and signaling, but it affords protection from mosquitoes, snakes, and other animals, and is a valuable tool in clearing the land. At night the fire serves as a crude light by which we can find our way and identify strange sounds and calls. Also it gives a focal point to the island. A small haven where we can make our beds. Even Kee does not feel at home on this island at night.

I wish Helen could have seen the sunrise this morning. From inky black with stars to just the faintest touch of blue. And then pink and a few low-lying morning clouds turned silver and then the sun came up like a big ship burning on the water.

I am safe here. I have food. I have water. The island lies in a temperate zone so that the weather is very nearly perfect. There are no large dangerous animals, and so far I have seen no poisonous snakes. Or snakes of any kind.

There is no waking up to the clanging of flight quarters and the gut-crawling tension of pre-dawn takeoffs. No drizzly shit worrying over the flight schedule for the day, the weather, the erratic gyro compass. None of the confinement of the wardroom, ready room, hangar deck. I am free to live each day my own way without restraint or necessity.

Someday when I'm back in the fight and have to wake up each morning to briefing, low-level strafing, and estimated recovery time, I'll look back on this island as paradise. But it is not enough just to be alive, just to know that I will live. I must be alive somewhere. I must know where I am. People must know I am here.

At the time I was hit I was approximately 345 miles from the recovery rendezvous. Course to target was 242°. But when I was hit I tried to turn to the interception course of 57°.

Shortly after that I lost my bearings completely. I do not know how long I flew this way, nor my ground speed; nor can I compute wind drift without knowing my heading. But if I was making approximately 200 knots for approximately 40 minutes I could be as far as 177 statute miles from where the Jap carrier was and as close as 168 statute miles to the recovery rendezvous on the day of the strike.

I don't know how long ago that was, as I have lost track of the days. I was confused and in a state of shock. Several days could have passed without my being aware of them. Or I could have imagined several days passing in the delirium of a few hours—the way a restless sleeper thinks he has passed several hours in the tossing of a few minutes.

I should have kept a more accurate log, but I had no idea I would be here more than a few days. Also it was a shock to realize how small the island is. A man's mind reacts strangely under such stress. It seems like years since I was on the carrier, yet I don't believe I have been here for more than a month. But when I try to remember the days on this island they run together so that I can't count them. It seems as though I have been on this island for a long time and yet for only a few days.

Sometimes I fear that when I see Mother again, or Helen, or David, that I won't recognize them. I cling to their memory and yet they seem so remote, so strange. I remember the time Captain Willett came back with his airplane all shot up. He landed it all right but was unable to taxi off the arresting gear. He didn't have a scratch on him but had to be helped out of the cockpit, and when they brought him to the ready room he didn't recognize anyone. They took him below, gave him a sedative, and he slept for sixteen straight hours. When he awoke he couldn't remember how he got back to the carrier, and although he recognized us, he looked at us as though he were seeing us from a distance, or through a window, and couldn't understand what the laughing and grab-assing was all about.

NOTE TO SURVIVAL INSTRUCTORS: *Pencils*

The lead in these goddam pencils corrodes in this climate and makes it hard to write.

Low overcast. Ceiling about 600 feet. Visibility estimated one mile. Wind variable at 4 to 6 knots. Not a good day for rescue. Nothing to do but sit on the signal tower and wait and waiting is futile, since our signals cannot be seen and no ships will come close enough to the reef to sight the island. All day I waited with nothing to wait for but better weather tomorrow.

I think Kee sensed how low I felt. He came to the signal tower where I was sitting and for a while he talked to me. I didn't understand what he was saying but it was good to have someone to talk to. Just to hear another human voice, even if the words are strange. Just to see another face. I understand better now how he must have felt when he saw me in the water. Someone to talk to. Another human being who knows you are alive, who knows what you suffer. Who is aware of how courageously you cling to life. I can understand how he risked his life to save mine. Perhaps he was in a depression such as I have been in, and it was my coming here that saved him. Perhaps we are the saviors of one another.

Kee likes me. Really likes me. He cares what happens to me. He tried so hard to distract me from my despair. He sat beside me to share my pain. He brought me green coconuts still soft and milky in the shell. He touched my hand and when I looked at him he began to talk to me and sing.

I do not believe a man can live here long by himself. Yet something sustained Kee. Some hope kept him alive. I believe it was this hope he tried to share with me. As he talked and sang I began to see the home he was thinking of. An island like this one, only larger, with other islands nearby. With paths and fields and villages in the clearings where children play and women cook and tend gardens, and men hunt and fish in the clear blue waters, and a special girl waits in the moonlight beneath the trees. It seemed as though he were saying that he had been sent here naked and helpless for a special reason—to prove his manhood or to find himself and his purpose, and when he had done so they would come for him and return him to his home, to hunting and fishing and the brown-skinned girl who waited beneath the trees.

It is remarkable how we understand each other, how we communicate without words, how familiar his songs seem to me. The truth is, it's not language that is a barrier between people. It's not words that cause misunderstanding. It's something more basic than that. Some deep-rooted mistrust and suspicion. Kee and I trust each other. We share a common fate and hold a common hope.

I don't even know what Kee's language is or where he comes from but I feel closer to him than I ever did to David. David and I never really talked. We understood the words but we never said anything to each other. Sometimes David talked about how he was going to take over the store, modernize it, set up a whole chain of grocery stores—"The Wallace System." But he wasn't talking to me, he was just talking.

Sometimes he would call me "Walrus" to make me mad and I would say he was a thief just like Dad, and that would start a fight. He was bigger than me and he could hold me down and tickle me and call me "Walrus" but he couldn't make me take it back.

David was never a buddy to me the way some big brothers are. Dad wouldn't let me have the car and David didn't want me to ride around with him. When I asked him to double date so I could go with Helen it always seemed to make him mad.

We were all pretty close on the carrier. We ate together, slept together, flew together, sat next to each other on the can. I knew the guys in the Junior Officers' Quarters better than I knew my own brother. I knew the way they smelled, the way they wiped, which shoe they put on first, which ones prayed before a mission and which ones jacked off. We were a group and we looked out for one another. But no one wanted to know too much about anybody else. We showed pictures of our girlfriends, lied about our homes and prowess, and bragged that only blind luck and sheer stupidity had saved us from death and marriage. But our fear that we would let the squadron down, our hope that it would be someone else who blundered, our relief that it was someone else who died we never shared.

But I could talk to Kee. Not Greg Wallace the grocer's son, or Greg Wallace the pilot, or even Greg Wallace the hero. I could just be myself. I could tell him how I wanted to go back to Wonder Springs, how I wanted to marry Helen. I wished for Helen's picture so I could show Kee how pretty she was. How tall she was, and proud, and modest. "That's the kind for me," Willett said when he saw her picture. "Ice on the outside and fire on the inside."

I told Kee how I didn't date Helen much in Wonder Springs because you couldn't ask a girl like Helen to walk to the movies. But it was different when I was in uniform and she was in college. I told Kee about the first time I went to the sorority house to see her. How surprised she was and how pleased. How she ran down the stairs and kissed me. How she admired my uniform and how proud she was showing me off to the other girls.

I told him how she kissed me under the arch at the hangar dance while the band played and the lights flashed. And the time she kissed me in the park. Impulsively, fully, almost unconditionally. How I wanted her to come to my arms in complete trust. How I thought our last night together might be a perfect farewell, but she was stiff and unyielding, unable to laugh or cry, and when I took her back to the sorority house, Miss Manning came out on the porch and Helen wouldn't even kiss me goodbye.

I told him about Mother's flowers and Bunny's folks, and how Bunny had wanted me to give her something—some pledge or promise, but I didn't know what to say. I told him how I felt wiping my mouth with a napkin Dad had taken from a full box before selling it, and what it was like to watch a poor farmer try to figure out how his bill could be so high and how he was going to pay it while Dad laughed and joked and tugged at his drawers. How it felt to visit Ruby in that place and what it was like to have her look at me without recognizing me and watch her see children and flowers where no one else saw them.

I told Kee things I had never told anyone else and then I sang some too. "As Time Goes By"—how many times Helen and I had listened to that song—"I'm Sitting on Top of the World," "Home on the Range." Kee really liked that one. After a while we both became quiet and just sat close together staring into the fire. Then we began seeing patches of stars and for the first time realized that the overcast was lifting. Soon we could see the moonlight marking a path across the water.

High scattered clouds. Visibility unlimited.

Nothing. Nothing. Where are they? I don't understand how I can see, hear nothing. The Task Force must be out there somewhere. Planes must be up. Someone must be able to see our signals. There's no explanation, unless—The Task Force has gone back to Pearl! The squadron has been relieved. Sent back to the States. Shore leave. Women. Food. Hot baths.

Then I have been on this island longer than I thought. Or maybe the Task Force was hard hit and retired to Pearl for repairs. Maybe a lot of other guys didn't get back from that attack on the Jap fleet. It was a suicide mission. Without air cover the Task Force will have to go back for replacements. Leaving us here alone. Then why haven't we seen the Japs? There's a war on. Somebody has to control these waters.

Unless the war is over. What if the Task Force had knocked out the Jap fleet, steamed into Tokyo Bay, and the Japs quit? But that's impossible. They'll never quit. We'll have to kill every damn one of them. And even if the war were over they'd just try harder to find the MIA's. Oh, at first there might be a lot of celebrating and carrying on but the next day they'd start looking for the missing and every man would dedicate himself to finding his lost buddies.

Unless the Japs won. They'd let us rot here. Even if they knew we were missing. Even if they knew we were alive, knew where we were, they'd never pick us up, and they'd never tell anyone we were here. Bastards, they'd leave us here to die. There would be no search. All this time there would have been no search. All the time we were building signals, and waiting, watching the sea and counting the days, there would have been no one out there to see, to hear, to care. Goddam Japs. Waiting for us to die. Waiting for us to quit. I hope they kill every one of them. Buck-tooth bastards.

But they wouldn't have won the war. That's impossible. Nobody's going to win it for a while yet and we had them on the run. And even if there were a truce or armistice the Allies would insist on recovering their MIA's. That's just human decency. And they know I'm missing. A lot of people know I'm missing. They'll remember me. My hope is in them.

Mother will think the worst. Mother always thinks the worst. Dad never threw up that she didn't think it was cancer. She'll never believe that I could get out of here alive. She's never had any confidence in me. She'll give me up for dead. She'll keep a fresh wreath hanging on the door and maybe one at the store, and she'll make floral arrangements for the church in my memory. But she won't forget me. A mother couldn't forget her son. And while she's cutting and arranging the flowers, she'll remember all the bouquets I delivered for her. "Compliments of the Wallace Grocery Store," I'd say. Sitting in church listening to the hymns she'll remember the way I would fall asleep during services, and how she would make me comfortable by putting my feet in Dad's lap and my head in her own, and fan me until the services were over—not even standing for the benediction for fear of waking me. And sometimes she would even carry me out to the car, although other women would talk about what a big boy I was to carry and David would get jealous. Remembering, tears will come to her eyes, and people will say, "She's thinking of Greg. He's missing in action, you know. All this time and not a word." And as long as she weeps they will not forget.

Helen won't believe I'm dead. Not at first. And the other girls will remember me. Even that old bitch Miss Manning. They'll ask how I am and when she tells them I am missing they'll console her. They'll assure her that I will come back. They'll talk about it in their rooms at night. And Helen will dream that I show up to surprise her just as I did before, and seeing me she will run down the stairs to kiss me in her excitement. She'll be dressed in a gown, and she'll be warm and soft and yielding. And Miss Manning will go to her apartment and quietly close the door.

Helen may stop writing when Mother tells her I am missing, but she will wait. At least until she knows for sure. She won't go with anyone else. It wouldn't look right with me missing in action. And when she sits in the library without looking at the book before her, or spends night after night alone in her room, people will say, "Her boyfriend is missing in the Pacific and Helen won't laugh or go to the movies until he is safe again." And as long as Helen waits they will remember.

David will get another combat tour before the war is over. He'll probably ask for it. And he'll ask for the Pacific so he can look for me. He'll ask the other pilots if they have heard anything, seen any sign. He'll check with the coast watchers and the PT and sub commanders. All over the Pacific they'll be talking about the man who asked for the war zone so he could look for his brother. And he'll be up there in his B-17 looking himself—the best eyes in the Air Force. Someday I'll look up and there he'll be. As long as David is looking, I'm not lost.

Bunny will never know I'm missing. Not until I'm dead. Not until David gets my letter and returns the bracelet she gave me. Then she'll think of me for a while. Maybe even forgive me, knowing that I am dead. I guess she hates me. But she can't forget me. A girl can't forget the father of her child. Not if she has to look at that child day after day. Not so long as her husband looks at the child and wonders whose child it is. Not so long as the neighbors look at the child and remember the young cadet Bunny used to go with. "What ever happened to that boy?" they will ask, and as long as Bunny hates me I will be remembered.

Ruby Watson didn't recognize me when I went to see her, but she remembers because she is ashamed. And Sister Mary Martha prays for me and if she prays I may be delivered.

Captain Willett will probably offer little hope for my recovery when he writes Mother and Helen. But as soon as he gets back to the States he'll go to see Lisa. He'll tell her that he came to see her at my request. She'll ask about me. Even if he tells her there is little chance I'll ever be found they'll have to talk about me because I'm their only connection. Willett will tell how I flew on his wing, how I shared the brandy with him, how I used to talk about her. Lisa will tell how we met, all the little things we talked about, how we said goodbye, how she promised to watch for my return. As long as they see each other they will have to remember that it was I who brought them together.

Major Ebaugh will remember me. Wherever he goes. Every time he looks at the record, every time he issues a command he will remember that I am missing. He can't go back to the States and leave me out here. It'll be a mark on his record. He'll have to search for me. He promised he would. He promised he personally would make a search for anyone in his squadron who didn't return from a mission. It's a matter of pride. Leadership. Responsibility. He will have to find me to erase that mark from his record.

I don't know how rescue will come. A dumbo or float plane could land in the lagoon. A destroyer or submarine could stand off the reef and send a boat to pick us up.

It is a matter of waiting for something to happen. For someone to come. We can't get off this island by ourselves, therefore we must wait for someone to come. For a man in exile, or prison, or cast away on an island, patience is the greatest virtue. Hope is the most treasured resource.

NOTE TO SURVIVAL INSTRUCTORS: *Hope*

In war men often must face constant danger, physical hardship, and the terror of the unknown. At such times there is a tendency to give in to confusion, doubt, and despair. These reactions, perhaps natural, can be overcome by men who are thoroughly indoctrinated in the hope that is ours. Men with hope keep busy, they do not become apathetic. They plan for the future, they do not succumb to circumstance. They have the will to survive, they do not surrender to despair.

1. Hope is faith in one's country. Ours is a great country, rich in natural resources. Presently these resources are utilized in the struggle against tyranny and the destruction of the foes of freedom. Our faith is that these resources will also be used to aid the wounded, free the prisoners, and rescue those who are missing in action.

2. Hope is trust in one's unit. It is vital for the combat soldier to remember that he does not fight alone. He is a member of a unit, and the safety and success of that unit depend on his loyalty and submission to duty. Our trust is that as we devoted ourselves to the cause of the unit, even so will the unit be faithful to our needs.

3. Hope is belief in others. A man in difficult and trying circumstances should remember that no man is an island. We carry the battle to the enemy to make our friends and loved ones, neighbors, strangers, countrymen safe from harm and free from oppression. Our belief is that just as we have risked our lives and endured hardship for them, so may we rely on them to remember and to make sacrifices for our safety.

4. Hope is reliance on one's training. A man in the Armed Forces has been chosen because he is physically and morally equipped to serve. He has been taught to find hidden resources of strength and courage inside himself

and trained to perform his duty regardless of difficulty or danger. Our reliance is in our training.

David, the Task Force is gone. The squadron has been relieved. There have been no ships, no planes, no nothing. I have been marked off the duty roster, accounted as missing in action, presumed dead. There is no hope. I would never have believed I could come this far, could live under such conditions, could face such despair. I have done my best. All that remains is to face the inevitable like a man.

I am placing these scraps and pages in the hollow in the rocks to protect them from the moisture. I will pile rocks in front of the hollow to attract the attention of the curious. By this means I hope to get the book in your hands. Please present the log to the proper authorities and see to it that the following letters are delivered.

Dear Mom:

By the time you get this letter you will know that I am dead. Please don't cry over me, Mother. I have had a good life and I am not writing to collect tears. What has happened to me is no one's fault. I have done all that is humanly possible and I have no excuses or recriminations. I only want to say goodbye, and to spare you what pain I can. I only wish I could sit down with you in the breakfast nook and have one last meal. Bacon and eggs. Thick slices of bacon and honest-to-God hen eggs—not powdered, either. Buttered toast and milk. And a last cup of coffee and a last cigarette before I go. We could talk about David, and your garden, and how I used to deliver flowers for you. Maybe I could make one last delivery—a bouquet for someone's birthday or anniversary.

I've had a lot of time to think sitting here on this island. Somehow I can see things more clearly from here than I ever could back home. I can see now all the worry I caused you, and all the tears, and I am sorry, Mother. Truly sorry. If I had it all to do over again I would try to do it differently. I would try to be more like the son you wanted. And I would try to get along better with Dad.

It wasn't all my fault, Mom. Dad thought I was lazy because I didn't like to work in the store, but it wasn't that. It was the way people looked at us, thought of us. Not just Dad, all of us—as though we were the town clowns. Always good for a song and a dance as long as they would throw a few coins our way. David didn't mind. He liked it. He liked outsmarting people, selling them things they really didn't want. It meant something to him. He planned on taking over the store some day, setting up a whole chain of Wallace stores. It didn't mean anything to me.

Dad was disappointed in me because I wasn't fast enough on the scales. I couldn't weigh, distract the customer, and figure the price fast enough to fool anyone. And Dad couldn't leave me in charge of the store. Some of the boys from the football team would come in and pilfer things and I couldn't stop them. I don't know why, I just couldn't. I pretended not to notice. Dad thought I was the one taking things until one day he caught Shocky Dodson stealing gum. "You forgot to pay for that chewing gum, didn't you?" he asked, laughing the way he always did. "Greg said I could have it," the boy said, walking out of the store. And I didn't say anything. I didn't stop him or say anything to him.

I tried to explain to Dad but I couldn't. All I could say was how I hated the store and how I hated being a grocer's son. So Dad charged the gum to the Dodson's account and told me how popular David was, and how dependable he was, and how everyone respected him, and how David had caught a girl trying to sneak out a can of soup and had made her put it back and pay for it both.

Dad expected me to back him up at the store the way Harry did. "How is this butter, Harry?" he'd ask when a customer questioned him. "Oh, that's real good," Harry would say, although he had never tasted it. "I believe that's the best butter we've ever got." Just to make two cents on a pound of butter.

"How do you like this cereal, Greg? You had some for breakfast," Dad would say, although he knew I had never seen it before. I tried, Mom, I really tried. But I would just stammer, "All right, I guess," and head for the stock room.

I hated for Dad to tease me or use me to sell things. "Better get some of this tonic. Ole Greg has been taking it and he's out with a different girl every night." "I'm sorry, but I'm going to have to charge you a nickel more for this can of soup. Ole Greg must have marked the wrong price on it." Knowing that most customers would pay a nickel rather than be embarrassed by having to put it back.

But I was never intentionally disrespectful. I want you to believe that, Mom. When Dad came home from the store so nervous and upset that he couldn't eat, but would leave the table to go throw up, you thought it was because I had said something to him. But I never said anything to him. I tried to avoid him because I couldn't hide the way I felt. But you couldn't avoid Dad, you couldn't ignore him. If you looked away he tapped you on the arm or pulled on your sleeve, desperate for you to look at him, to listen, searching your face for a smile so that he could laugh with you. I couldn't do it, Mother. I couldn't laugh, and when I looked at him I couldn't hide what I felt.

Dad was a coward. I'm sorry, Mother, but I have to face it. Dad was a coward. He was afraid he would fail, afraid people would trade someplace else, afraid they wouldn't like him, afraid they wouldn't laugh at his jokes, afraid that they would find out he was a two-bit thief. That's why he came home so agitated that he couldn't eat without leaving the table to throw up. He was scared. I'm sorry, Mother, but I have to say it. I have seen more guts in a scrambled egg.

Now that I've said it, now that I've faced it I think I can understand him. I couldn't admit it before because I was afraid that being his son I was a coward too. But I know now that a man who earned his wings, who flew as many missions as I did, who shot down a Jap plane, and lasted as long as I have on this island could not be a coward. I am no longer ashamed of Dad. I understand him now. I only regret that I did not understand before he died.

Mother, I'm sorry you had to pay that hotel bill in San Francisco. You shouldn't have paid it. The clerk knew I was going overseas and he just collected for it twice. It's guys like that who are the real saboteurs.

I am sorry about Ruby Watson. If Dad had let me have the car the way he did David, I wouldn't have gone with Ruby, but you can't ask girls like Helen to walk to the movies. And Dad wouldn't let me go out for football; I had to work in the store after school. But I never had any intention of hurting Ruby and I'm sorry. I'm not proud of what I did but I know now that it wasn't entirely my fault. Ruby wanted to get pregnant. She wanted to have a baby. I just happened to be handy. It was wrong, but most of the men I know would have done the same as I did, including David.

If there were any way I could help Ruby I would do it. I know how long Mr. Watson worked for Dad and how faithful he was, and I am sorry for him, but he's the one who made her that way, always talking about what an angel she was and keeping her home. The other kids laughed at her. Maybe she never was quite right but she wouldn't be the way she is today if it hadn't been for him. The way he looked at us. Like we were dirt. Like she was filth. Something he couldn't bear to look at. The things he said to her.

I'm not bringing these things up to hurt you, Mother. I just want to set the record straight. For whatever was my fault, I'm sorry.

Mother, try to forgive me and try to be happy. Remember the good things. Life is too short to mourn the past or to remember the bad. You still have David and he'll never hurt you the way I have.

All my love always,
Greg

Dear Helen,

I wish I could tell you how I felt walking away that night, knowing that I was going off to war and might never see you again. What it was like riding the bus back to the base. I wish I could tell you how many times I asked myself what I had done wrong. How many nights I lay awake remembering, almost driven out of my mind remembering.

I wish I could tell you what it was like to wait for the mail plane and to get nothing from you, knowing how long it would be before the mail came again.

I wish I could make you understand what it was like those times when your letter came and I knew the minute I touched it that it was from you. I would hold it for a moment and just look at your handwriting, the way you wrote my name. I was always disappointed when you typed a letter, because your handwriting meant so much to me. If I had other mail I always saved your letter until last, hating to open it because your letters were always so short and in a few minutes all I had hoped for and anticipated would be over. And there would be no mention of our last moment together. No explanation. No recounting of memories. Nothing about how you loved me and dreamed about me and longed for me to hold you in my arms. I kept your letters, Helen, reading them over and over, trying to find some hidden meaning, some secret emotion. I'd hold your letters in my hand and think of you.

I would remember the times I got liberty and met you after classes. We'd walk across the campus, through the park and along the river. You'd let me hold your hand, and sometimes we'd sit on the grass and I'd just look at you, wanting you so much I couldn't speak. Sometimes you'd let me put my arm around your shoulder and we'd sit like that until you got tired. We'd walk back to the Alpha Chi house and sit before the fire and listen to records. Holding your letter in my hand I'd remember that, Helen. "Smoke Gets In Your Eyes," and "Time Goes By." How dreamy you used to look, listening. I thought that look was for me, Helen. I thought your dreams were the same as mine.

I wish I could see you one more time in that low-cut white organdy dress. I don't have your picture here but I remember how fresh and clean and thin you were. How solemn you looked when you danced with me. The way you smiled under the arch while the lights flashed and the music played. I asked you to marry me, Helen, because I thought that smile was for me.

I wanted to kiss you one time when you were mine, when you let yourself go, when you stopped wondering if anyone were looking, or caring what they thought. I wanted one time for you to put your arms around me possessively, as though you wanted me, as though you wanted everyone to know it. I wanted one time for you to forget yourself, to kiss me as though you were thinking of me.

How many times did you kiss me, Helen? Three times. The first time I came to see you at college and you ran down the stairs and kissed me. A peck really. Hardly a kiss at all. Under the arch at the hangar dance. A sweet kiss, but short. A token. And you were stiff and unyielding against me. I told myself that it was because we were in the spotlight and the others were applauding. And that time in the park. After I marched in the parade, after the music and speeches and applause were over, I went to where you were standing under the tree and you put your hands on my face and kissed me. For a moment your lips were responsive, for a moment your body pressed against mine. And then you remembered that we were not alone. I took that kiss as a pledge, Helen, that while you would not marry me for the duration, you loved me and would wait.

I kissed a lot of girls more often than I kissed you, and I kissed them better. Why did you make me wait, Helen? Your kisses weren't worth waiting for. Your kisses were as dull as your letters. And I hope as you sit around the fire on Saturday nights listening to records and rolling your hair that you think of me. I hope you remember how you sent me away. I hope you wait, Helen. I hope you wait forever. I hope you wait until you're as stiff and dry and cold as your kisses.

Greg

Dear Bunny,

I guess you still hate me and I can't say I blame you. I guess you'll go on hating me even after I'm dead. But even that's better than denying you ever knew me the way you did in front of my friends. That really hurt, Bunny. I don't blame you for being angry, but to pretend that you didn't know me when they had seen us together at the U.S.O. dance, when I had told them that you were my girlfriend, that you loved me. And not answering my letter when I tried to explain, when I tried to say those things you wanted me to say. To ignore me like I was nothing. Like I didn't even exist. You can hate me if you want to, but you can't deny me—not after the baby.

I was wrong about you, Bunny, I know that now. I thought you were just another victory girl ready to do her bit for a guy in uniform. What did you expect me to think, whistling at every uniform that passed by? You and your girlfriend. Sitting on the porch in bobby sox and loafers, your dad's shirt over your rolled up jeans, and that silly-looking sailor cap on the back of your head. You didn't exactly look unapproachable. And you were easy enough to talk to. The first person I'd really been able to talk to since I left home. Telling me about the football team and your boyfriend—whatever his name was—the football player with wavy black hair and peg trousers who thought he was Victor Mature.

And snowing your mother into inviting me to dinner when she came out to run me off. She was so funny—afraid I would get the wrong impression because of the "informality of the invitation." Afraid pork chops, baked sweet potatoes, and homemade rolls wouldn't seem like much after eating in the mess hall, worrying about how to entertain "our guest" after dinner. But your dad wasn't worried. He sat out on the porch with us and told us how he won the First World War as a motorcycle messenger, and how he was winning this one by working overtime operating a crane at the junk yard. You looked at me and smiled and pushed your cap down over one eye as he went on about how Roosevelt, Fala, and the O.P.A. were ruining the country, and how moving up the clocks to war time was defying God, and how we'd all be eating horse meat in a year. He was a great guy, Bunny. I wish I had realized it sooner. He was so impressed that I could fly, and a little envious too. I think your mother was too. Envious of us. "Now, honey, you come on in and listen to the radio and let the young folks talk."

After your father went inside we sat in the swing and talked awhile. I put my arm around you, and you pushed your cap back so I could kiss you. I didn't know what to think, Bunny. I figured you were that way with all the guys.

I was in uniform and a long way from home. When I could get away from the base you were always there waiting for me—breaking up with the football player so you could see me. You let me know from the very first that you liked me. You gave me a crash bracelet with your name on one side and my name on the other. You wrote me love letters when I couldn't get away from the base. I was young, Bunny. I didn't know anything about girls or love. I guess I believed all the movies and propaganda. I was the young hero and you were my true love. I thought all servicemen and their girls felt the same way. I didn't realize that what we had was such a rare and fragile thing.

Everything we did was wonderful—the football games when I watched you jump up and down and clap your hands, leading yells in your short skirt and the sweater that was just tight enough, the times I was broke and we went to the record shop and sat in a booth and listened to records, or spent all evening over a malt, or walked along the streets looking in the store windows and talking about what we were going to buy each other "next pay day." You were going to buy me an umbrella in case my parachute didn't work and I was going to buy you an ankle chain with my name on it and a scarf to replace that sailor cap you were wearing the first time I saw you. Everything we did was magic—even the times we pulled taffy in the kitchen or sat in the living room and looked at your family album.

The other guys in the barracks were having a wonderful time too. They had girls that were crazy about them—some of them two or three—girls who gave them presents, bought them liquor, and went to bed with them. I didn't realize you were different. I didn't know how to tell them what you were like.

And there was a war on and we all knew it couldn't last forever. For us there was no tomorrow. I guess that's what I was thinking when I came by to take you to the U.S.O. dance. I had always thought you were pretty—even the first time I saw you in the oversize shirt and rolled-up blue jeans. And I thought you were a knockout in a skirt and sweater. But when you came into the living room in your pink formal, I knew I had never seen anyone so beautiful. Your mother kept pulling at your dress and your dad was so proud of you. "That's some girl you got there, Greg," he said, and I knew he was right. And everyone at the dance knew it too.

I don't know how to explain what happened after the dance. I guess I thought the way you felt about me, it wouldn't make any difference. Or maybe I thought that time was running out on us and it didn't make any difference anyway. I'm sorry that I tore your dress. I'm sorry that I made you cry. I think if I had known what to say you would have forgiven me, but I didn't.

The time you called me and I pretended I didn't know who you were—I was just trying to get back at you for pretending you didn't know me in front of my friends after they had seen you with me at the dance, after I had told them about you. It was true I couldn't marry you, Bunny. Not until I got my wings and commission. But I would have done something. I would have tried to help. That's why I wrote you in Intermediate—to try to help. But you never answered, so I really never knew for sure whether you were pregnant or not.

I hope you made up with the football player. I hope he married you. I know you thought he was silly and immature but he's probably in uniform by now and I'll bet he looks a whole lot better to you. I hope the best for you, Bunny. I really do. I really liked you, Bunny, much more than I knew at the time, and I thought that when I got back home I would try to make amends—but I won't be coming back. So all I can do is hope you had my child.

Greg Wallace

To that 4F hotel clerk son of a bitch
at the Orpheus Arms whorehouse—

You bastard. Sending my mother a hotel bill that was already paid. You pimp. Squeezing blood out of a dead man's mother. You whore. It's queers like you that make guys like me regret dying for our country. But you had better hope I'm dead, you son of a bitch, because if I get back I'll have your balls if you have any.

Lt. Gregory Wallace, U.S.M.C.

Dear Sister Mary Martha,

I hope they will let you see this letter. I hope they will let you have it so that you can take it into the little corner of the garden where you sit all day and tell your beads and pray. Maybe as you read you will want to pray for me.

Remember when I came to see you, Sister Mary Martha? They let me visit you in the garden. I stood against the wall and listened while you prayed. You told me about all the little boys and girls who came to the garden to see you and play at your feet, and you told me how you prayed for them and loved them just as if they were your own.

You told me about a very wicked little girl you could not pray for because you could not love her, because she was so evil. Was that Ruby Watson, Sister Mary Martha?

I knew Ruby and she wasn't really evil. She wasn't an angel the way her father wanted, but that's too much to expect of any human. And she wasn't admired and respected the way she wanted. She was just a plain, fat little girl who spent too much time alone, too much time worrying about her complexion and her weight, too much time reading confessions magazines and pamphlets about how to make boys notice and respect you. She wanted to be admired because she was soft and gentle, but the other girls made fun of her because she was fat and timid, and her dresses were plain and her hair was short and straight. She wanted to be loved because she was sweet and simple, but the boys avoided her because she made cow eyes at them, because she was so strange and dreamy, because she always talked about being a nun when she wasn't even a Catholic.

I liked Ruby, Sister Mary Martha. I tried to be kind to her. I went to see her when she was lonely. But no one could like her the way she wanted to be liked. She wanted too much. Wanting me to play silly games. Always wanting me to look at her in the mirror. Always wanting me to tell her that she was pretty and how much I admired her. Always wanting me to pretend that she was a princess. Wanting me to stay when I had to leave. I tried to like her, Sister Mary Martha. I didn't mean to hurt her. I thought a lot more of her than the people who always talked about how they loved her but only pitied her.

What Ruby Watson did was wrong but she didn't mean to be evil. She just wanted to be loved like everybody else. I don't believe she thought she was evil until she saw the way her father looked at her. I don't think she ever believed she was wicked until he called her all those names. No matter what she did it was wrong for him to say all those things to her. It was wrong to send her away and make her give up the baby when all she wanted was something to love.

I know she is sorry for what she has done. I know she has suffered because of it, just as you have suffered, just as I am suffering now. I am trapped on an island and I cannot escape and no one will come and save me. So we are all the same now—all trapped. Ruby in her shame, you in your goodness, and me on my island. And we all suffer for what we are.

You are a saint, Sister Mary Martha. You love the little children as though they were your own. And you pray and do penance, and suffer with such patience. Pray for me, Sister Mary Martha, that I may suffer with patience what is to come. And pray for Ruby Watson that she may be forgiven.

Sincerely yours,
Gregory Wallace

Dear Lisa,

Do you remember me? We met at the Orpheus Arms Hotel in San Francisco. I was having a little celebration with friends before shipping out and I left the room for fresh air, or more booze, or something. There were a lot of people waiting for the elevator. We all got on—it was crowded as hell—and when it stopped, I had to get out to let the others out and the elevator went off and left me. These people, they were having a convention or something, invited me to come have a drink with them while I was waiting for the elevator to come back, and we went into a room that was just jammed with people sitting on the beds and floor and everywhere. I got a drink and sat down beside you. I don't know whether you were already there or whether you came in with me, but there was a guy with a guitar and he said, "Let's all go dance." Some people wanted to and some didn't. I didn't know what to do. I didn't know anybody there. You said, "Let's go dance." Remember?

We followed the guitar player down the hall, singing "Deep in the Heart of Texas" and clapping our hands and raising hell, and all jammed into the elevator. It was so crowded I had to put my arms around you, but you didn't say anything. We got out on another floor and went to a larger room, a meeting room I guess, because there were flags, and E banners, and victory posters, and pictures and models of ships—even a ship's bell. Remember?

Somebody started ringing the bell, and we danced the Conga and what was supposed to have been the Lindy Hop, knocking each other down, and crowding around whoever had a bottle. There were a lot of dead soldiers that night. After a while there were only a few of us left and the guy with the guitar. We sat on the floor and sang "Red River

Valley" and "Green Back Dollar" and "San Antonio Rose." Remember, he wouldn't play "Always" until you gave him a kiss.

Finally the guitarist quit and we all got on the elevator together and although it stopped several times neither of us got off until we got to the lobby. I offered to buy you a drink but everything was closed and you said you had something in your room so we went upstairs to your room and lay down on the bed. We just lay there and talked. Remember?

I told you I was shipping out and you told me your husband was a cook on a destroyer somewhere in the Pacific. I told you about Helen and how I was having to ship out without even a goodbye kiss. You told me you had been married for over ten years and that most of that time your husband had been at sea. I said I'd look him up and try to arrange his transfer to stateside duty. I said that was too long for a man to be away from his wife and you said it wasn't right for a man to go off to war without some kind of goodbye, and you kissed me. Remember? You said you wanted to make my last night ashore a happy one, one I could remember all the nights I was alone. I couldn't get your girdle off and tore your stockings but you said it was okay.

The next morning you went downstairs with me to say goodbye. You gave me your address in case I got back before your husband did, and promised to write because you knew how much letters meant. You bought me a bottle of brandy "to take to bed with me," and I gave you the money I had left. There wasn't time to buy you a present and I didn't figure I'd need much money where I was going.

I never did find your husband, Lisa, although I asked around about him, and the people I talked to said it was very difficult to get stateside duty for the duration. And your letters never did catch up with me.

I'm not coming back, Lisa. I hope that you remember me because I have remembered you. I'm sorry I couldn't get the hose and other things you asked for, but I did send a pillow and some other souvenirs from Honolulu. You should have paid your hotel bill out of the money I gave you, because they sent the bill to my mother. But maybe you did and that 4F bastard at the desk was trying to collect twice. They love to put it to a guy in uniform.

I want to thank you for what you did for me. You were very sweet and it meant a lot to me not to have to spend my last night in the States alone. I'm sorry if I disappointed you. I had never been with an older woman before and I had been drinking too much.

I guess you have heard from Captain Willett by now, maybe even seen him. I hope you didn't tell him that I failed you. I hope when you go down to the harbor to watch the ships come in that you will think of me.

Best wishes,
Greg

David, these pages are important to me, as I want people to know what I have lived through, and what I have done, and how I have faced danger and death. This book has been my courage, for who can live bravely unobserved? This book has been my hope, for who can endure suffering that is unknown? It is all that remains of me. All that remains of my life.

It is important that what I have written is not misunderstood. Due to circumstances I have not been able to write cautiously or cleverly, or to mask my deeds with virtuous words. There is no time to alter such passages as might be misinterpreted. Some will deliberately misunderstand. Some will look for the meanest motive behind every action. So that you will understand my meaning, and in order to prevent others from distorting it, I include this key for clarification.

1. I have done the best I could. I have discovered a courage and resourcefulness I never dreamed I had. I have followed the training I was given. But it has been to no avail.

2. Kee has been a help to me. We have helped each other. But I don't want to leave the impression that we sat around the fire holding hands. When I wrote that Kee touched my hand it was a ceremonial gesture. Like a handshake.

3. I mentioned that Kee had not changed or improved the island in any way and has few skills. This does not mean he is lazy or stupid. It means that he is a product of a primitive society that believes in adapting itself to circumstances rather than otherwise.

4. When I wrote that I felt closer to Kee than I did to you, I meant that Kee and I had faced death together—that we were totally dependent on each other. I always thought you and I were very close, much closer than most brothers. I never minded you teasing me and calling me "Walrus." I did think it was unfair that you could get the car when you came home from college and I couldn't get it when I was home every night. But I can't blame you for that. Dad said it was because you were older—which is what he always said when he gave you something he didn't give me. But I

know that you would give your life to save me, just as I would give my life to save you.

5. I hope my letter doesn't upset Mother too much. I don't want to hurt her, but she has to face the truth about Dad. How else can she understand the way I felt? You were different, David. You were stronger than I. You could hide your feelings better. You could joke with Dad. When Mother was upset you could tease her out of it. You could tease her out of anything. When a customer asked if the bread was fresh, you said, "Not more than ten days from the oven." When old ladies would ask where the napkins were you'd say, "Third aisle, sanitary on the left, dinner on the right." Just like Dad. I couldn't do it. It meant something to you. You were more ambitious. You had plans.

6. I wasn't trying to make you look bad to Mother when I said you would have done the same with Ruby as I did. It's just that she couldn't understand how I could screw poor old Ruby. Hell, you would have done the same thing if you could have. You know you would. I remember how you used to sneak presents out of the store for your girlfriends. So would Dad if he had been younger. You think he wouldn't? You know what he said to me after Harry told him? "I might have screwed her once myself, maybe even twice if I'd had a sack to put over her head." That's what he said. Giggling the way he always did when he was upset. "But Greg, when you screw a half-wit you've got to use a little sense. You can't knock up an unfortunate girl like that. Not if she's the daughter of a man who has worked for your father for thirty years."

7. Ruby wanted a baby. Maybe what I did was wrong, but getting pregnant was what she wanted.

8. I can't understand how Helen could have treated me

the way she did. At least she could have written more often. I know she had her school work to do and I know she had to write her parents almost every day. She also told me she was writing you.

9. I was too harsh in my earlier opinion of Lisa Burto. She certainly wasn't a whore and I don't believe she ducked out on her hotel bill. That son of a bitch at the desk just pocketed her money and sent Mother the bill. I really did try to get her husband sent back to the States.

10. I wrote the letter to Sister Mary Martha to help Ruby. I thought it would be best if I didn't write directly to Ruby.

11. It is true that there were some things we didn't talk about on the carrier, but I was very close to those guys. If I had gotten out of this I wouldn't have accepted survival leave. I would have asked to rejoin my squadron. I've never told this to anyone but I could have gotten out of that last mission, if I had wanted to. I had an excessive rpm drop on the mag check and my fuel pressure was marginal. I would have been scratched if I had reported it, but I couldn't let the other guys down.

12. It's true that I lost the airplane but I did carry out the mission and dropped my bomb on or near the target.

13. There was nothing I could do for our bombers and torpeckers when they were jumped by the Jap CAP. If my plane had been undamaged I would have tried to cover them even though it wouldn't have left me enough fuel to return to the carrier.

14. Failure to return to the carrier was not due to panic on my part. I was scared, sure, but you don't know what it's like in a single engine, single seater, over water, David. You don't know what it's like to be up there all alone with no

navigator, no radio operator, no copilot to take the controls while you try to plot your position. I didn't have any landmarks. I couldn't call for radio bearings or home in on the wheel because the electrical circuits were out. We weren't trained for that kind of flying. That kind of navigation. You don't know what it's like up there all alone in the clouds, David. Without even a radio. I did the best I could.

15. I hope I made it clear how I felt when I heard "Pilots, man your planes." It wasn't fear, it was excitement. You know what I mean. I used to think it was fear because I would get weak all over and have to piss although I'd just emptied my bladder. My heart would thump and I'd be out of breath before I was halfway up the ladder. I was ashamed until I found out the other guys felt the same way. It was the thrill of flying, that's all. The exhilaration of taking off and climbing out of it all—away from the grind of routine, above the sweat of waiting, free of the closed-in, trapped feeling of the ready room, ward room, bunk room. You've never tried to pop one off a rolling flight deck in the dark with only tiny stud lights to show you where the deck is.

16. I have been left here to die but it is by accident. There was no plot, no conspiracy against me. Just circumstances and the condition of man. Because I am human I must bear it. Because I am a man I can bear it without rancor, rage, or religion. But if I die here, who will know?

17. I have described my moments of anguish and depression with the hope that it might be of value to survival instructors. I believe moments of weakness were caused by improper diet, poor physical condition, and stomach distress. I have never at any time given up or surrendered to despair. I could wish that death would come

quickly but I will sustain my life as long as possible in order to make a final statement for use in survival training.

Greg

NOTE TO SURVIVAL INSTRUCTORS: *Sand*

Sand is the basis of our existence, for just as this island is made up of millions and millions of grains of sand, even so is life composed of . . .

NOTE TO SURVIVAL INSTRUCTORS: *Cooking pot*

Survival kits should include utensil for cooking. Monotony of food and limitations in cooking cause loss of appetite and interest in life. Everything must be eaten raw, baked in the coals, or held over the fire on a stick. Variety is necessary to sustain the will to live. A pot would allow the boiling and mixing of foods. In addition, I believe seaweed could be eaten without diarrhea if first boiled.

1. Sound is best heard at dusk and dawn.
2. The worst bites are those on the ankles.
3. SOP for removing thorn beneath the skin is to leave it completely alone for at least two days. Gentle squeezing will force thorn out. Inflammation and poison can be removed by carefully sucking the wound.
4. Solitude and loneliness produce humility.
5. The big ass moth is edible.

David, I know how the military is. Maybe they wouldn't give you a tour in the Pacific. I didn't mean that I thought it was your duty to ask for the Pacific combat zone so that you could look for me. I just meant that, knowing you, I thought it was what you'd do.

Gone. Back to Pearl. The squadron has been relieved. Sent back to the States. Willett will go to see Lisa for me. Go to see Helen. For a while they'll talk of me. Then they'll go to bed.

NOTE TO SURVIVAL INSTRUCTORS

There is no place on an island where you can hide, where you can go to be alone. Everywhere I turn there is Kee—naked, dirty, looking at me, expecting me to help him when I can do nothing for myself. The real anguish is having to endure someone else in the same condition.

If the Task Force is gone, if the war is over, if the squadron has been relieved, who will come? Who will save us?

If by fortitude I prolong my life, if by courage I die proudly and well, who will know? Who will care?

It is not enough to be alive. Someone must know I am alive.

Lt. Gregory L. Wallace 015323. Shot down at sea. I am alive. I believe I have been here for . . .

NOTE TO SURVIVAL INSTRUCTORS: *A perfect island*

1. A perfect island would contain food and water.

2. It would lie in a temperate zone.
3. It would not be inhabited by large or dangerous animals.
4. It would offer variety.
5. It would be inhabited by people of both sexes.
6. It would lie in a war or a commercial shipping zone.
7. This island can never be paradise as long as there is a horizon beyond which I cannot see, a cloud above which I cannot rise, a sea I cannot cross. If I die here, who will know?
8. Hope is a very small island.

FISHING

Fishing seems to be the best way of obtaining food on an island if a man has hooks or nets, or some way of catching the fish while staying out of the water.

David, I can explain what happened to Major Ebaugh. C.I.C. reported bogies closing in on a bearing of 280° and Air Plot scrambled all fighter pilots. The Japs had slipped past the CAP in low ragged clouds and we were launched immediately and vectored out without having a chance to orbit and form up. A dark shadow passed overhead in the clouds and I climbed up after it, losing the rest of the division. I spotted a Tony off to the left and banked hard and opened up before he could get out of range. It was a bad deflection shot but I believe I smoked him.

When he saw my tracers, he climbed, twisting and jinking, but I stayed right on his tail, squeezing off short bursts every time I got him in the sight ring. My tracers looked good but the weather was so grabby I kept losing him in the clouds. Finally I lost him altogether, but I believe I damaged him and in that weather he probably didn't get back home.

It was getting dark fast and in chasing the Jap I had lost my bearings. I was beginning to get worried when I saw a shadow above me. At first I thought it was a Jap but I climbed up and it was Major Ebaugh. He was the best navigator in the squadron so I joined up and in a few minutes we could pick out a few ships. We dropped down looking for our carrier and orbited trying to get aboard before the weather and darkness got worse.

A Jap plane dived out of the clouds, unloaded without hitting anything and disappeared into the soup. Major Ebaugh went after him. I was low on fuel, had my gear and flaps down and was in the groove. I jerked up the flaps and wheels to give chase, but by the time I recovered Major Ebaugh was out of sight. I orbited until I was sure the Jap was alone and then landed, taxied forward, cut the switches, and ran to find out what had happened to the rest of the division. They were already back and Willett had gotten a flamer.

The Air Chief was on the radio trying to guide Major Ebaugh in. He had lost the Jap in the darkness and had lost his bearings too. Everybody in the Air Group was back by then and we all stood around listening. Listening to the Air Chief trying to talk him in. Listening to Major Ebaugh grab at any suggestion.

We could hear him. We could hear it in his voice. His words were tight and his voice was deeper than usual as though his jaw were down and stiff. It wasn't panic, but he knew he wasn't going to find the carrier. He was getting more and more confused and running out of fuel. He tried to joke but he couldn't. We just stood and listened, helpless, not looking at each other. We knew time was running out on him, but there was nothing we could do. Finally Major Ebaugh said he was going in. "Don't forget to pick me up in the morning," he said. That was the last we heard.

Nobody said anything, but I knew what they were thinking—that I should have stayed with him. But Major Ebaugh was the best navigator in the squadron. If he couldn't find his way back, nobody could. It would have meant two planes lost and two pilots in the sea. The exec said I did the right thing by coming on in but I could tell he was wishing it had been me who chased the Jap and Major Ebaugh who landed. But I did the right thing, and if Major Ebaugh has been recovered he will say so. If not, then you must make it clear that I was not flying smart or playing safe. I was following the training I had been given.

David, I didn't count the plane I damaged as a probable, although I doubt that he made it home. But I do have a Jap, an Oscar, to my credit.

The Task Force is gone. The squadron has been relieved. Captain Willett has screwed Lisa. He'll go to see Helen—pretend he's doing it for me. He'll talk about me until Helen starts crying and then he'll try to screw her while he's pretending to cheer her up. I know how the bastard operates. It doesn't matter to him that I'm dying, that Helen and I were practically engaged. It doesn't matter to him that he's married. "There are happy married men and moral married men," he used to say, "but there are no happy moral married men." "There are husbands and there are fliers," he used to say. "I'm a flier."

The attack on the Jap fleet was a disaster and I don't care who knows it. The attack wasn't properly planned. We weren't trained for that kind of strike, at that range, in such weather. Due to indecision on the part of superior officers the attack was delayed until insufficient time remained for planes to return before dark. I say it was negligence. You can court-martial me for it if you wish.

NOTE TO SURVIVAL INSTRUCTORS: *The importance of a clearing*

Man's history can be told in terms of his search for a clearing. His efforts to move out of the darkness and closeness of the jungle into the open where he has the room to breathe, to grow, to plan, to fly. Out where he can see the sky and feel the sun and

Ruby's hands were square and the backs of her hands were white with freckles and stiff blond hairs. Her fingers were blunt, even chubby, like a child's fingers, but her nails were ragged and chewed off so that the flesh was puffy and bled. She also sucked her thumb.

NOTE TO SURVIVAL INSTRUCTORS: *Signs of rescue*

Survival training should include a course in the recognition of rescue signs. The first sign might be a speck in the sky, an object in the sea, a dark swelling beneath the surface of the water, a rising column or smudge of smoke across the horizon, the sound of an airplane, a flash of light, a whistle, guns firing, a voice, silence.

There is constant noise on the island. Waves, wind, fluttering leaves, groaning trees, bird cries, and singing insects. There is such an incessant whir and buzz that one would believe there were mosquitoes even if there were none. But the arrival of help might cause the birds and insects to stop singing. The first sign of rescue might be silence.

There will be dark days, despair, loss of hope, loss of faith in one's comrades, country, and personal objectives. There will be a time when the island seems strange and unfamiliar, natural events appear orderless and without meaning, the past is irreconcilable to the present, and the present is irrelevant to the future. Out of this darkness will come an awareness of change, a rising vitality, an earnest expectation. I will awake to see fire and smoke on the horizon, to hear the roar of airplane engines and the thunder of big guns—to the signs and sounds of rescue.

Gregory Wallace. The first man to screw Bunny Jensen. After the U.S.O. dance we sat on her porch. I put my hand between her legs and she told me to stop but I didn't. She said if I didn't stop she was going to call her father, but I didn't stop. I told her if she called her father he would come out and kill me if that's what she wanted but I wasn't going to stop.

I tore her dress and made her cry but I was the first one. Later she tried to deny it. Tried to pretend she didn't know me, that I didn't know her as no other man knew her. But I was the first one. No one else can ever say that. And she can't forget it either. Not after the way I stung her. She can't deny it. Not if she keeps my child.

THE PERSISTENCE OF RAIN

Some things never seem to pass away, some things seem never to end. Every morning we watch the rain begin out at sea and slowly move across the island. It is not a hard rain, and since the clothing I have is rotten, I make no effort to find shelter. We just sit and let the rain fall on us. Yet it galls the soul to know that every morning the rain will come, and that all day water will drip from the leaves, and the mosquitoes will breed.

I can remember as a child standing in the window and watching the slow, heavy drops turning Mother's flower-beds into mud. Doomed to spend all day in the house, smelling marigolds or chrysanthemums, watching Mother twist and warp and pat flowers into bouquets and arrangements. And I would envy David down at the store with Dad, watching girls jumping the rivulets of water, kidding with the people who came in to get out of the rain.

I can remember driving down the puddled streets through sheets of rain, listening to the squeak and squall of the windshield wipers and the drum of the rain on the rooftop, seeing people huddled under awnings, waiting as water streamed off the buildings, watching from behind the plate-glass windows. And I wanted to run away. Get out of the humid, clammy car, out of the wet, gray town, away from the waiting, watching faces, and the movie marquee.

I can remember standing on Primary Fly barely able to see the flight deck through the drizzle, with the ceiling 50 feet and visibility almost zero. For hours, days, it would stay like that, its persistence such that it began to seem the inevitable order of things, until gray ragged drizzle seemed man's natural condition, so that we could no longer believe in the blue skies and the white puffy clouds of good weather. And then without warning, so rapidly the eyes stung from the glare, the clouds would break up and the sun pop through until the whole sea glittered.

Some days, watching the cloudless blue sky, and seeing the sun glinting on the waves, I forget for a little while that it had rained that morning.

Some day the clouds will roll back and I will see a ship steaming for the island and it will be as though this never happened and didn't matter.

My home was not a happy home. I was ashamed to ask anyone to visit me. Ashamed to deliver Mother's flowers to some woman whose husband was dead or dying. "Compliments of the Wallace Grocery Store." Ashamed to watch the way Dad sized people up. "What's he worth? What does he want that I can sell him?" Ashamed to ride to school or church in a car with "Support Your Local Stores" painted on the side. How could I ask a nice girl for a date? How could I expect Helen to go with me?

Helen liked me. She really did. I couldn't ask her for a date because I couldn't get the car, but she asked me to her birthday party. I wanted to get her something nice—a pretty necklace, but Dad wouldn't give me any money and Mother said she would make Helen a nice bouquet for me to give her.

I tried to sneak a box of chocolates out of the store, but I'd never done it before and Mr. Watson caught me. You would have thought they were his chocolates. "You little thief," he shouted, squeezing my shoulders and shaking me. "There's nothing I hate worse than a sneak thief." He was shouting where everyone could hear him, shaking me and calling me names. "I'm going to tell your pa. I'm going to tell him what kind of son he has." But what really frightened me was his face. I'd never really looked at his face before. He always looked so blank and gray standing behind the meat counter in his white apron, only his big hands alive as he cut and weighed the meat. But his face was all changed, red and swollen, and alive, and his eyes were awful, and his mouth was twisted out of shape. I was so startled I burst into tears. Not because he was going to tell Dad or because he was hurting my arm, but because of the look on his face. I had never seen such outrage.

"What did you want with chocolates?" Dad asked. "Doesn't your mother give you enough to eat?" Trying to make a joke. How could I tell them I wanted the chocolates for Helen's birthday? How could I tell them I was ashamed to take Mother's bouquet? That Mother's flower arrangements were the laughingstock of the whole town. That every time I had to take flowers to some house where there was sickness or death I wanted to cry. Every time I had to say, "Compliments of the Wallace Grocery Store," I wanted to die of humiliation. How could I explain the way I felt having to watch people pretend the flowers were beautiful, that they were grateful, that the flowers were a gesture of thoughtfulness.

I gave Helen the bouquet of flowers, pretending not to notice the snickers of the others. And when the gifts were unwrapped, I pretended not to notice Helen looking among the scattered wrappers for a gift from me.

If circumstances had been different I think I could die without regret. If Dad had known about my kill. If I could prove to Lisa that I was better than that. If I knew that Bunny was all right, that Helen waited, that Willett talked about me, and Lisa watched from the harbor. That Sister Mary Martha prayed for me, that Mother had forgiven me, that David was up there somewhere looking for me.

Lt. Gregory Wallace, 015323. Shot down a Jap Oscar. Knocked out an anti-aircraft position at Boena. Damaged a tanker at Mati. Flew three strafing missions against ground installations at Tanaü. Attacked light carrier of the Zuiho class. Lost at sea.

Lisa Burto is a whore. She cared nothing for me. She had no intention of writing. She only pretended so that I would send her gifts from Honolulu. The hotel clerk was pimping for her. Why should I care whether or not she was satisfied?

NOTE TO SURVIVAL INSTRUCTORS: *Vitamins*

My hair is falling out, my memory and eyesight are failing, and I have lost my natural virility due to lack of vitamins.

David, Captain Willett sent us into a reverse-order attack, putting me over the target first and permitting the Japs to concentrate their fire on my airplane. Also he was negligent in not assigning someone to provide cover and guidance for me after I was hit. He may have done this so that when he got back to the States he would have Lisa and Helen for himself.

I wish I had never told him about them. I wouldn't have except that he was always bragging about his technique, and I wondered what he could do with Lisa. I bet he couldn't do any better than I did. Especially if she had been drinking. He won't get anywhere with Helen either.

The sea is empty. The sky is empty. What if the war is over? What if everyone has gone home and forgotten us? Me and Kee. Our lives here would mean nothing. The log would be worthless. But it is impossible to believe the war is over. It has been going on too long. It is so certain. The meaning and high purpose of all our work and efforts and lives. What we were trained for. We fought as though the war were something stable, something we could depend on, something to stake our future on, the most certain thing in our existence.

The war is not over. The Allies are out there somewhere. The enemy is out there somewhere. Perhaps they are watching this island at this very moment. A submarine. A dumbo. A

What if everyone is dead and I am writing to no one? And there is no one to save me. Helen and Mother. Bunny. Lisa. David. All dead. Or changed. Different. Grown into people who have forgotten me. People I don't know. But they must be alive, just as I left them. Mother plants and waters her flowers, and as she digs in the warm ground she weeps, remembering me. Helen waits for me. Five dates before they can kiss her, no matter who they are. And when they wonder why, they think of me. David is looking for me, searching the records, searching the skies. Willett speaks of my friendship, Lisa watches from the harbor,

Sister Mary Martha prays. As long as Bunny hates me I will be remembered.

Kee Yop does nothing. I don't understand how he can do nothing. I don't understand how he can sit idle, expecting me to build signals, clear the land, and watch for rescue. I don't understand how he can sleep so soundly at night when rescue might pass us by. Unless he likes it here. Unless he is a deserter. Unless he is content to remain here. Safe from the war.

Gregory Wallace knocked up Ruby Watson. She cried and prayed, and said she loved me and would never give up our baby. She waited for me to carry her away and afterward became a nun. Sister Mary Martha, pray for me.

Lt. Gregory Wallace. 0153 I am alive. I believe I have been here for at least . . .

David, I hope you can read this. I have to write by firelight. There is something out there. Off to the northwest and very low on the horizon. Blink. Blink. Blink. It is a very dim, small light and it is sending a signal, although I cannot make out its message.

At first I could not believe it and I only sat and watched. But the signal kept repeating itself, insistently, demanding a reply. I called Kee to come to the signal tower, but he could not see the signal although I repeatedly pointed it out to him.

"Mali ku-see," I said. "Hope. Something from beyond."

"Nuka vulavicki biru," he said. "Nothing. That's nothing." Or, "What does it matter?"

I don't understand how he can be so indifferent. Help, rescue was on the horizon and he refused to admit it or do anything about it. He didn't even try to read the message, unable to see meaning or purpose in anything, preferring to remain just as he is. How can I explain it? While I was trying frantically to understand the message, Kee Yop went back to his shelter and went to sleep. I could have hit him I was so furious. But Kee cares nothing about the future. He cannot see beyond the reef.

I could not make out the message they were sending, but I set the signal afire to let them know that we were receiving it, and I sent an SOS by covering and uncovering the fire to let them know there was intelligent life on the island and that we needed help. I could think of no way to identify ourselves, so when they kept sending the same signal—blink, blink, blink—I repeated it to let them know we are friendly.

It is still out there, David, and the message is still coming. I am writing this now even though it is dark, because it may be the enemy out there and I am determined to surrender. We have held this island as long as conscience and duty demand. It is useless for us to hold out any longer, futile for us to resist. At least if we are taken prisoner, Mom and Helen will know that I am alive. The Japs will give us food and clothing, and maybe Red Cross packages. Maybe we will get mail, some word from home.

Regardless of what happens I will leave this book in a

safe place on the island as evidence that we are alive, that we lived here with courage and resourcefulness, holding the island and gathering information for the Allies.

Sky overcast with ceiling about 1200. Almost no wind, making the day humid and the insects troublesome, but planes could be up.

I do not know how long I have been on this island. So many days passed in confusion. When I realized the Task Force had left and the squadron had been relieved, I gave up. I hoped to die. I lost interest in living. I couldn't eat, I couldn't sleep. I sat on the tower and stared at the empty sea. I believe I was not entirely sane. I am not ashamed to admit it. Kee tried to keep me alive by bringing me food, by talking to me and trying to amuse me. He would bring me leaves and strips of bark so that I would write on them but I threw them away unmarked. I did not care to live under such conditions. If I could not get off the island I was determined to die.

Then I saw it. A light signaling to me. I don't know why Kee didn't see it, or wouldn't admit it, or couldn't understand it, but I know it was there. It wasn't a star. It was a message. I do not know who or what was out there and I did not understand the message they were sending. But I know to live one must have hope. And I believe the message was "Hold on. Help is coming."

I do not know why we have not been picked up, why this morning we have seen nothing out to sea. I can only assume that they got our message, that they know the situation better than we do, and that if we had all the facts, we too would understand. Perhaps the time is not ripe. Perhaps an invasion force is coming and we will be picked up then. Perhaps, in some way I do not understand, we are needed here, are serving a purpose, and they were ordering us to hold on for a little longer.

One thing the war has taught me is that a man can accomplish a mission without knowing what it is or even that he is doing it. But to keep his sanity a man has to believe that somewhere, somebody knows what's going on. That somebody plans the patrols and sweeps and strikes that seem to accomplish nothing. That somebody knows where everyone is and plans what they are doing. I know now that help is just over the horizon. When the time is ripe, when we have accomplished our mission and served our purpose, they will come for us.

Clear with scattered cumulus. Wind variable at 2k.

No one has come and nothing has happened. I do not know how long I must wait but I know they have sent me a message to hold on. I know their knowledge of the situation is greater than mine. They have before them not only the present circumstances but also the plans for the weeks and months ahead. I trust in their knowledge. I await their arrival with patience.

I have given a lot of thought to what our mission might be. I have come to the conclusion that we are to study the island, discover what uses may be made of it, and how we may survive on it. Therefore the log will be discontinued so that I may record our findings. When we have accomplished our purpose, when we have in understanding reached the limits of the island, we will be rescued.

One of the earliest results of forced isolation on castaways, prisoners, and exiles is mental deterioration. Due to the lack of external stimulation and challenge they lose the mental aggressiveness that is necessary to prevail over circumstance and environment. Our proper study is this island.

1. First priority will be given to the study of the means by which we can survive.
2. Second priority will be given to an assessment of our past achievement.
3. Third priority will be given to a projection of future plans.
4. Fourth priority will be given to the study of our most immediate and pressing needs.
5. If we study the history of this island we will study the history of Kee and myself.
6. If we discover the purpose of this island we will discover the meaning of the world.

HOW TO SURVIVE ON AN ISLAND

1. Perseverance is greater than sacrifice.
2. Adaptability is more virtuous than originality.
3. The man who is patient overcomes the man who is inspired.
4. He who prepares for the worst outlives he who hopes for the best.
5. Hope seasons the food.
6. The will to survive justifies the means of survival.

RECORD OF PAST ACHIEVEMENTS

1. Explored the island entirely and the lagoon to waist deep.

2. Devised a method of signaling by day and night.

3. Discovered a symbol for recognition as friendly.

4. Found a source of fresh water.

5. Found several sources of food, including five new ones: the root of the catspaw, wild potatoes, the seed of the high grass, the leaves of the blue-gray bush after they have dried, the big ass moth.

6. Discovered three remedies for diarrhea.

7. Have adapted ourselves to the sun, weather, and insects with the benefit of minimum or no clothing.

8. Have survived despair, loneliness, and the loss of the airplane.

9. Have established the foundation of a common language.

FUTURE PLANS: *A preliminary study*

1. To sustain life until rescue comes.

2. To prevail over circumstance.

3. To discover and accomplish those purposes for which we were left here.

4. To discover meaning and happiness in our life in this place.

5. To communicate our hope and high purpose to Kee that he may share in it. He is not lazy. He only lacks motivation.

IMMEDIATE NEEDS

1. A means of preserving food against future necessity. Without the ability to prepare for future emergencies man is the victim of circumstance, the tool of chance.

2. A method of transporting water. Fresh water is available but it is inconvenient, because wherever we are we must go to the pool for a drink. We will not be free to

work, study, and travel about the island until we have found some method of piping or transporting water.

3. A permanent shelter that will protect us from the sun and rain, insects, and sudden storms. Also it will give us a place to sleep and a center around which to spend our lives.

My life on the island has taught me this—man doesn't need much shelter against the elements. The real purpose of a house is a center in which the family can be sheltered against the outside. At least I think this was true in Bunny's house—the only place I ever felt at home. It was an old frame house with big windows and high ceilings and it looked as though a puff of wind would blow it away. But when the family was all together at the table, you felt sheltered.

I never felt that way in my own home. We were never all together except at dinner, and then Dad would leave the table to go throw up. I felt we were all shut off from each other. Dad had his study where he kept his accounts. Mom was in the solarium potting flowers. David had his room and I had mine. When I was small and afraid of the dark I would tap on David's wall to see if he were there. Sometimes he wouldn't answer and I would think that everyone had gone away and left me alone in the house.

Ruby's house wasn't a shelter, it was a prison. Small and dark and there wasn't a comfortable place in the whole house where you would like to sit down. Ruby's room was like a cell. Small window. Iron bedstead. Steel springs. Calendar on the wall with lines drawn through the days. A metal dresser with a green print apron around it. Lined with bottles and jars and decorated with a crucifix. I never left that house that I didn't feel that I was escaping, that I didn't want to run before I was dragged back.

Helen's house was always so quiet and neat that no one ever seemed to live there. Helen and her mother always tiptoed around and even her dad looked as though he were afraid he was going to knock a lamp over or disturb a pillow. It was hard to imagine them sitting together at the table, laughing and arguing and talking loud. Even at Helen's birthday party all the kids were stiff, afraid to sit back, afraid to laugh.

And Lisa. Her hotel room had a single window that opened out on an air shaft. "What is there to see?" she asked. "The bay or the city. If I look at the bay I think of my husband and how long he's been gone. And if I look at the city, I think how dirty and crowded and miserable everything is, and what it's going to be like when the war is over. So I look at the air shaft. It's better than a mirror."

4. Clothing. Kee is entirely naked and I am very nearly so. All our attempts to make clothing out of bark and leaves have failed. Not only is such clothing fragile. It also chafes.

I can remember dreaming of a primitive island where I could run naked, unhampered by shoes and clothing. I can remember reading that clothing is uncomfortable, unnatural, and unnecessary, but whoever wrote that never lived where there are insects. He never tried walking barefoot through coral, or sitting on a rock without the intervention of clothing. He never tried carrying things without pockets, or living day and night with no place to put your hands. Without covering, the genital area is particularly sensitive to sunburn, thorns, and psychological stress. Maybe if we had shelter and furniture, a tent with places to sit and lie down, clothing wouldn't be so important. But when a person is in constant and immediate contact with the ground he is always dirty.

Kee, I'm sure, is an average-looking man. But it is depressing to see him day after day without clothing. To see every ulcer, every sore and insect bite. When he stands his belly protrudes and his buttocks sag. When he squats he's all hips, knees, and elbows. His finger and toenails are horny and yellow. The soles of his feet are crusty. He has wrinkles on his shoulders and elbows, his navel is lined with grit, his pubic hair is matted and gray with dust, his privates look like some unnatural and warty disfigurement.

And he could be anybody. If he had on clothing I would know who he was—soldier, criminal, student, laborer. For all I know he could be a king and speak four languages. On the other hand, from my uniform he knows all about me. An American pilot, a leader, trained in navigation, observation, meteorology, skilled in flying and gunnery. But if someone were to see me today—near naked, bearded, dirty—would they think I was a man of education and culture? When rescue comes I do not want to look like a savage. I do not want my rescuers to ask if I understand English. I do not want them to tell me what to do with soap.

If by some miracle a girl should come to this island, a nurse who escaped a plane crash or an island girl washed out to sea, I wouldn't want her to come here unclothed. I would like her to be wearing something soft. A low-cut white organdy dress. Or a loose sweater, just tight enough to mark her soft breasts and the way they move when she walks and breathes. Or maybe she could have both, and sometimes wear the dress and sometimes the sweater with a short flared skirt that showed her thighs when she jumped up and down. And she'd be wearing soft white panties and a bra—a black strapless bra. And maybe nylon stockings and a lace girdle and red high-heeled shoes. And long gloves that I could remove one at a time.

Man is the only animal without sufficient covering to be comfortable, protected from the elements, and sexually attractive.

5. Medicine. We have no remedy for headache, toothache, or bleeding gums. We have no means of relieving pain except patience. The only remedy for frequent sore throat, diarrhea, body aches, and fever is to lie down until it passes. We have only moss and leaves to serve for bedding, bandages, and toilet paper. Our only means of fighting infection is to clean our sores by licking them like dogs.

I remember Mother's medicine cabinet, filled to capacity with half-full bottles of pills and tonics for Dad's stomach. Most of them Dad ignored, but Mom tried them all. And when David or I looked tired or didn't eat the way we should, Mother would give the medicine to us, sure that it would do us good. Mother thought medicine was to help you over the bumps.

Ruby thought medicine was to make perfect something that was imperfect. Her dresser was lined with pills and bottles for relieving cramps, blues, and nagging depression, for strengthening nature's plan, and eliminating unspecified inner disturbances. Her mirror was spattered with creams and lotions for clearing the complexion and restoring natural beauty. I never screwed her when she didn't have some pain.

I never knew Bunny to be ill. Once when I took her to a movie I found she had been suffering an earache all day, but Bunny was too full of life ever to be sick, too busy to be interested in her own pains.

The only remedies for our illness are on this island. We

cannot expect help from elsewhere. The best medicine is fresh air and a vigorous mental attitude. For our purpose medicine is not to make life painless but to make it possible.

7. Work. Work is the natural and necessary condition of man. Work gives occupation to his hands, stimulation to his mind, and justification to his life. I know this now, although it used to anger me when Dad said it. But for Dad work was just an excuse for gossiping and cheating. It didn't make him happy or give substance to his life.

And I always thought there was something phony about the way David hung around the store, saying "Yes, sir" to Mr. Watson and carrying packages for the old ladies. Work was just a means for meeting girls and making an impression on people like Mrs. Harpur, who helped him get the scholarship to college, and Dad, who let him have the car. I'll bet right now David is busy meeting the people who can help him set up his grocery chain.

I know that work is necessary for man, that the difficulty and failure of the past is that Kee and I have been idle, futilely waiting for help to come. Now such an attitude is no longer possible. As long as we thought help would come today we made no plans for tomorrow, but now that we know help may not come tomorrow, or even next week, we must go to work. We must clear the land. We must find ways of cultivating and preserving food. We must make the island habitable. Work is our salvation. When Kee understands this he will no longer be idle and apathetic.

8. Relief from necessity and purpose. In the past we have had too much leisure time that was not properly utilized. Now, however, we must guard against the ten-

dency of giving value only to necessity and purpose. Happiness and well-being also require relief, relaxation, and recreation.

Dad never stopped working. Whether he went to church or lodge he was always trying to gain advantage. I think that's why he was never comfortable at home. Mother was always busy, digging, or potting, or arranging things in the house. She never stopped. She was never still, and she never seemed to get anything done.

David was a lot like Dad. Always busy, but David was meticulous. Always going on like Dad but behind all the talk he was thinking. David never missed details. I'll bet when he returned from a mission and the other guys were relaxing and tossing down a few, David was thinking over the mission, looking for mistakes, and memorizing his checklist and emergency procedures. Not like Willett. In the air Willett was serious and efficient. But when we were secured from flight quarters he turned it off and became a kid again, playing practical jokes and passing out free advice—all of it bad—on how to fake an engine malfunction, how to get rid of a wing man you didn't like, how to sit out the war on a quiet little island surrounded by naked women.

To Ruby it was all the same. She never had any leisure time because she never had any time that was different. Whatever she was doing, cleaning house for her dad or going to school, her mind was a thousand miles away, thinking of babies or whatever the hell she thought of. Helen rationed out her time as though it were gasoline. Two hours of study and then ten minutes for a coke and conversation. After her studying was done, the room cleaned, and her hair washed, thirty minutes to listen to the radio. She almost didn't go with me the last night before I shipped out because she had a paper due the next day.

Purpose and work aren't enough. The will to survive also depends on the proper utilization of leisure time. Too little leisure time leads to dullness of spirit and loss of mental acuteness, appetite, and desire. Too much leisure time causes melancholia, boredom, and masturbation.

Hot and clear. No clouds in sight after early morning showers. Wind ESE at 4–6k.

I have been busy these past several days burning away the useless brush and grass and planting and cultivating the fruit trees. Fire seems to dry out and improve the soil and also eliminates some of the insects, of which there are many varieties on the island, all of them destructive or annoying. We have also discovered by this means that many of the insects are edible when roasted.

When I have restored some kind of order to the chaotic growth, I plan to have a grove of coconut and banana trees around the fresh-water pool with other groves of fruit trees nearby. Then with a permanent shelter close at hand we will be firmly and securely established on the island.

During the past days of work and planning I have felt a contentment I had not felt since I came to this island. Having a job to do and finding satisfaction in accomplishment is the difference between hope and despair. If I could only communicate this to Kee. Man cannot be idle and happy. He cannot be useless and content.

I have tried to encourage Kee by the joy I demonstrate in doing my work. I have tried to persuade him by pointing out the results of that work. But for the most part he does nothing—poking around the island picking fruit.

Sometimes when I knock off work and go for a walk or a swim in the lagoon or sit on the signal tower and watch the sunset, he joins me, but he cannot enjoy it as I do, for without work leisure time has no meaning. If he could just once feel the joy of accomplishment, know the pleasure of seeing his plans realized.

I feel that I have failed him, because he cannot understand why I am clearing the useless vegetation. He is puzzled that I plant the coconuts, when they will sprout where they lie on the ground. I have been unable to explain to him the difference between planned and ordered cultivation and chaotic growth and reproduction.

Somehow we have lost the earlier understanding we had. I thought we had accomplished a breakthrough in communication, but if so then we have lost it. "California," I say to him, trying to re-establish that early rapport. He repeats the word. He says it much clearer than before. He even nods his head. But his eyes don't light up as before. There isn't that thrill of recognition that we once knew. And Kee goes on in his apathetic way—idly fishing or digging for clams—doing nothing.

But I refuse to be discouraged by it. I have found contentment here in work and leisure. And I know that if Kee is going to be happy he is going to have to work as I do. And the more we share the work of the island the closer we will be.

It has been a bright, clear day, the kind of day you would drive three hundred miles to see. Three hundred miles just to get in the open so you could see the sky, and feel the sun on your body and the wind in your face.

Three hundred miles just to get into the open, into a clearing.

Man always seeks a clearing—even primitive man. To get out of the choking jungle, out of the forests, out of the shut-in cities, out into the open where you can breathe and see out. An explorer plods on, regardless of hunger, until he finds a clearing in which to eat his lunch. The city dweller drives all day to get out of the city for the weekend. People who live in cities and jungles, who live in caves and cellars are little-minded and afraid. People who live in the open, who see the stars and the distant horizon dream and plan.

As a child I was scarcely conscious of the stars, or the wind, or the sky. Dad never once took me for a walk through the night or the woods. I never thought of rain unless Mother complained that her flowers needed watering or that they were being beaten down by a hard shower. I never lay awake looking at the stars. Only when I began to fly did I learn to look out the window the first thing each morning to see what the sky was like and how the wind was blowing. Before coming to this island I had never been conscious of the sounds of the night, or of the hundreds and thousands of insects that inhabit it.

Man in his artificial environments, with little frames for looking out at the sterile scenery, loses contact with life, loses the sense of majesty, the sense of mystery. What is out there? What is this life that troubles the smallest insect crawling under foot?

The sea is growing dark, yet even on its dark face there are faint glimmering lights and the sheen of the moon rippling its surface, seeming to light a pathway home.

I have flown at night and in the darkness have lost both the land and the sky, unable to distinguish between the stars in the sky and the scattered lights of farmhouses in the ecstasy of being drowned in the wonder and unity of it all. Losing all sensation of being up, losing all fear of coming down, until the moon would slip from between the dark clouds, or the radio would crackle, and I would discover that I was disoriented, and off course, and that in order to hold my attitude, in order to reach my destination, I must concentrate on the instruments and remain separate and aloof from the mystery and beauty around me.

On this island we are naked to beauty, susceptible to wind and rain, open to the night, vulnerable to the day. It has been the kind of day a man would drive three hundred miles to see. But three hundred miles is where?

What is out there? Over the horizon? Just out of sight? Sometimes in the night I will see a flicker of light, a flare, a flash. Is it a dim star on the edge of the earth? Distant lightning? A flaming airplane? A falling star? An exploding shell? Sometimes in the day I see a vague and shifting form in or above the water. An oil slick? A patch of seaweed? A submarine just below the surface? And on clear days with unlimited visibility, what is it I see just on the horizon? Is it a cloud, smoke, an island on the edge of sight? What is out there? I believe I could be perfectly happy here if only I could see a little farther.

It's strange to think, but somewhere out there right now are letters that have been written to me. Letters from Helen, and Mother, perhaps even from David. I wonder if Lisa ever wrote the way she promised she would. And Bunny, although she said she wouldn't.

There must be quite a stack of letters from Mom.

Almost one for every day I've been missing. Written at night after the flowers have been watered and the dead leaves pinched off, after clothes and papers have been picked up and stacked away in a closet. Written among the litter on the table after she has eaten her supper of chicken noodle soup and crackers and cheese. Written with a second cup of tea after she has finished the letter to David. It is only fair that she write him first, since he is oldest.

"Dearest Gregory," she will say. "How I miss you and pray each day for your safe return. How I pray that both my boys will be returned to me and that they will come back just as they were when they went away. I just told David that the war must be terrible but you must try especially hard not to let war and killing change you, and that I want both you boys to remember what Dad would expect of you if he were alive—that you follow your orders and do your job like Christians."

After her little sermonette, which seldom varied from letter to letter and which I skipped over, would come a list of local disasters. Mother didn't exactly collect disasters, but if there was a death or sickness someone was sure to let her know about it, and the first thing she looked for in the papers was the casualty lists, the obituaries, who had been married, divorced, or admitted to the hospital. And she would tell how she cut flowers or took pot plants to them all. "I heard about your boy being killed in France, Emma, and I just wanted to bring you some flowers and tell you if there's anything we can do for you at the store you just let us know. We can have your groceries sent out if you don't feel like coming in. And your credit is always good."

She'll tell how she's just run to death delivering the flowers without me there to take them, and how people don't appreciate flowers the way they used to before the war, when everyone was nicer and folks were closer than they are now. And she'll complain about how the town is changing, folks who have lived there all their lives moving away and newcomers moving in who don't care anything about the town or have any pride in themselves.

"Pruitt's service station burned down last week and the whole town is talking about saboteurs. Also only 22 people gave blood at the blood bank last month, which is way down from last year. People seem to be losing interest in the war except to gripe about it. You remember little Lonnie Weir? He got his picture in the paper. His dog was rejected by the Army because it wasn't vicious enough. I wish they had taken it, it barks all night.

"It would break your heart to see the old street. There are chugholes everywhere and everything is so shabby and run-down. No one takes pride in their yard any more, you can't get paint, and there's no one to do repairs. Everyone is going to the West Coast to work in the factories and they say the unions are taking over everything. We are fortunate that business is so good at the store.

"The Johnsons have moved to California to work in the shipyards. The Gerdens' house has been turned into a boarding house. Three girls whose husbands are overseas are staying there and there's something going on every night. Oh, Gregory, I hope you and David won't get married until the war is over and everyone has returned to his senses.

"I went ahead and paid that hotel bill in San Francisco when I didn't hear from you. I was afraid it would go on your service record if I didn't. You can do whatever you want to about it. I don't mind paying the bill but if you have the money and you want to repay me, you can.

"David writes regularly, about once a week. I sure would love to see him, but I'm just thankful that he's where he could come home if I needed him and not flying over Germany. They say that when those boys come back from bombing Germany they just put more gas and bombs in the airplanes and send them right back up.

"I heard Helen was home from school last weekend but I didn't see her in church and she didn't come by the house. I guess she's real busy with her school work."

Helen would stop writing as soon as she heard I was missing in action, but just the same I should have a couple of letters from her that didn't catch up with the Task Force.

"Dear Greg, at last I'm caught up with my school work, so I thought I would write to you." That's the way she always began, as though I were off at another college. "I got three letters from you yesterday. I don't know how you find all the time to write." As though we had regular pickup service out here. As though I had nothing to do but sit in the ready room and write letters.

"This has been my most difficult semester so far, with a foreign language and a lab science, but with a little luck I should make the honor list again. At least I have a straight 'A' average so far." As though there weren't a war on. As though I weren't risking my life every day. As though the thing that I wanted most to hear was how she was doing in school.

"You remember my roommate? Well, her fiancé came to see her last weekend and brought a friend. Al Weston. Al was on the radio before the war and when he enlisted they made him a Captain and put him in Special Services and he's already made Major. He's the best dancer I ever saw. We all went out to dinner and dancing. Luckily I was caught up in my school work because we didn't get back to the sorority house until after midnight." I could never figure out if Helen were trying to make me jealous or if she were so stupid she didn't know what letters like that did to me.

"I got a letter from David last week. It sounds like Washington is a very exciting place, but David says he'd rather be back overseas getting the war over. I hope he doesn't go back over though. He's so serious about doing his duty. I worry about him and I know your mother does too." I never decided whether it was worse waiting and waiting for a letter from Helen, or to get one and read about her roommate and her homework and how she worried about David.

I don't think David has written but twice since I enlisted. One letter from overseas while I was in Primary full of advice about how to make good in flight training and what to do in case he didn't get back. "Mother will be all right. I've made out my insurance to her and the house is clear. She'll be very upset for a while and let everything go to hell as she did when Dad died, but when things get bad enough she'll snap out of it. I guess you'll have to trust Harry with the store for a while, but as soon as you get back get rid of him. After running the store he'll never be content as butcher again and he wasn't a very good butcher anyway."

The second letter from the States, a tight-lipped letter about how in Washington you have to stand in line to get a drink, or a meal, or a promotion. How chaotic and corrupt everything is, and how he misses the simplicity and honesty of daylight bombing. "But I've been making some very important connections in Washington, people who are going to count after the war is over, people who will be in places where they can help us. I've got big plans for us, Walrus. You can stay in Wonder Springs with Mother and manage the store there while I'm setting up stores in other places. And I'm not thinking of little towns like Wonder Springs, either."

Ruby wouldn't write to me. I only got one letter from her and that was after her dad caught us. A note, really, that he was sending her away to have her baby and that he was going to make her give it away, but that she wouldn't do it. She would rather die first. She wanted me to meet her in front of the Pictorium so I could take her away and she could have the baby and keep it. But I couldn't do that. We were just kids. If I had taken the car Dad would have had me arrested before we got across the state line. And it may sound funny after what happened to her, but I think Mr. Watson was right. Ruby couldn't take care of a child.

But Sister Mary Martha might write. That is, if they let her write letters. She might say that she remembers my visit and that she prays for me. Maybe that she is beginning to understand about Ruby. By now she may even be cured.

Bunny won't write. Too much pride for that. She wouldn't even answer the letter I wrote her when I was in Intermediate. But I'd like to hear from her and how she is. And if she married that football player. But I'll never hear from her again. Unless she didn't marry him and still needs me. She might write then. But it wouldn't be the way it used to be.

She used to write such sweet letters, even though I was seeing her every weekend. Each one was different. Each one was a surprise. Sometimes it would be a joke or a little picture she had drawn with not a word on the paper but "Love, Bunny." Sometimes it would be a poem about love, or the places we had been together, or something I said to her. One of her letters was a song, "His Name Is Greg." I still remember that one. Corny maybe, but sweet. Once she wrote me a letter about a date we had, describing how she felt and what we had done as though I hadn't been there. I read that letter over and over. I kept all her letters. I suppose they're still in my sea bag.

I guess if she wrote now it wouldn't be the same. It would be about what I had done to her and how I had to help her. They wouldn't be letters I would want to read over and over. But if she would just write once to tell me how she was. Maybe that would be enough.

I wonder if Lisa ever wrote. I gave her my address, and she promised to write, although that may have just been a trick to get me to send her something from Hawaii. But she said she knew how much letters meant to guys on ship for months without seeing a woman. She sounded so sincere. She said she wrote her husband every day, always leaving a lipstick print at the bottom of the letter and sometimes sprinkling it with her perfume, even though the guys kidded him about it. But I don't see how that would work with V mail.

What would she say? Would she be shy and embarrassed, writing as though we were new pen pals? Or write a chatty letter all about her work and her friends and what she had for breakfast, as though we were buddies? Or would she begin where we left off? That we were adults and knew what we were doing, and that there was a war on and nothing was normal or made sense any more. That she had never done anything like that before. That she was drunk. That I was lonely and afraid. That it wasn't my fault or her fault, it was the war. And when the war was over and her husband came home they would start all over again. But if I came back before then—she didn't know.

At the bottom of the page would be a lipstick print—lips too full perhaps, too soft—and the barely perceptible hint of her perfume. Inexpensive, heavily sweet, overpowering. And on the outside of the envelope a little lipstick streak where she wetted the gummed flap with her red, wet tongue, and the initials S.W.A.K. Sealed with a kiss.

What will they do with my letters? Burn them? Return them to the senders? Read them and laugh, because Mother's letters are so messy and sloppily written and because she wants me to repay her for the hotel bill? Because Lisa can't be true and can't spell? Because Helen wouldn't kiss me goodbye but goes dancing with strangers? Because Dad made David executor of his will and David has such big-shot ideas?

I may even have Christmas packages from home. I've been here long enough. Oatmeal cookies from Mom. All stale and crumbled. And those bastards will eat my cookies. She'll send something else too. While I was on the ship she sent me insect repellent because she heard the boys in the Pacific needed it. As though we had mosquitoes on the ship, for God's sake. She'd never think of sending me a watch, or a razor blade, or a bottle of aspirin.

David might send something though. He's smart enough to send something useful. A pocket knife and some chapstick. That's what I could really use. Ruby wouldn't have anything to send me even if she thought of it. Unless they let her send me one of those pictures they have her painting.

I don't know whether Helen would send me anything or not. She's never given me a gift. Not even for my birthday. Not even when I shipped out. I gave her a pale green sweater and my high-school ring to wear on a chain, and a stuffed bear with a music box in its tummy to keep on her bed, but I had to write her three times to get her to send me a picture—a snapshot of her dressed for church.

I couldn't expect anything from Lisa. But she might enclose a snapshot in a Christmas card. Standing on the beach in a white one-piece bathing suit. And the bottom of the suit wet where she sat down in the surf. Standing a little awkwardly because she is not used to being photographed, her hands hanging stiffly at her sides, her smile gone dead as though she has been waiting too long for someone to snap the picture.

Her breasts are dry and beginning to sag, and in ten years she will be round-shouldered and dumpy. But standing there stiffly with her shoulders back and her breasts up, she looks good, although her legs seem heavy without high heels.

Because she is standing at the edge of the surf and the water is cold, her feet are arched and her toes are curled, throwing her knees slightly apart so that you can see the smooth insides of her thighs and the tiniest half moon of white where the sun never really reaches, just below the arch and thrust of her pelvis, and the swell of her belly.

And they destroy my mail, read my letters, eat my cookies, masturbate with my photograph. Bastards. What do they care. They have their turkey and dressing, their holiday liberty. Back on the flattop they'll have a movie on the hangar deck, and sing carols, listen to an address by the Chaplain. Maybe even mail call. And they'll read their mail and open their packages and go to sleep dreaming of beer and pussy and being home. They don't have to dream of stale oatmeal cookies and faded snapshots.

On the carrier I dreamed of sex and flying. Only it wasn't flying really, it was shooting down Jap planes—a nightmare, because my guns would jam and when I finally got them to operating the bullets would emerge slow and heavy and fall away or strike without effect, while I cursed and sweated and tossed in my sleep.

Here I dream of flying, only the airplane is so slow and heavy I can't get it off the ground. Night after night I dream that the sky is open and a plane is in the clearing or the lagoon. Escape is before me but I can't get the plane into the air. Sometimes I lift it off for a moment and desperately hold it in the air and then it dives for the ocean or the trees.

Last night I dreamed there was something winking at me, something round and pulpy, and at first I thought it was a signal or something from the sea. Then I realized it was a birthmark—but brown and almost perfectly round—on the inside of a girl's thigh. The girl was wearing white shorts and she was doing something. Playing softball or croquet. It must have been softball because I can remember the bare red earth of the mound. She was pitching, and each time she would stride off the mound I would see the mark. I wanted to examine it, it was so curious. I wanted to touch it, it seemed so soft and smooth. To touch it with my lips. But when I tried to, I saw that it wasn't a birthmark at all but a mole, and thick black hairs grew out of it like the hairs on old women's faces.

When I awoke, for a moment I almost knew whose leg it was and then I looked down and saw that the seed and promise of my life was lost and wasted—soaking into the ground. And all I had left was a fleeting memory of warmth.

When I consider the luck that brought me here, when I consider the odds that I am alive at this very moment—the shell that damaged my plane could have killed me. I could have been shot down by the Jap fighters and strafed in the water. I could have gone down in an empty sea, with no land in sight, to drift until the sun and sharks got me. I could have drowned in my parachute. I could have gotten to an island only to find there was no food or water. I could have landed among crocodiles, or Japs, or cannibals. I could have been on an island alone with no one to cheer me when I am discouraged, no one to bring food when I am sick, no one to know that I am alive.

I am unable to think of better circumstances than I now have. If I must be on an unknown, uncharted island then this must be the best possible one. There is perhaps too much vegetation, but a lot of it bears fruit and it makes us appreciate the clearings. There are too many insects, but if there were no insects there would be no birds and no bird eggs. There is too much rain, but it makes the fruit grow and it causes us to appreciate clear weather. The island is safe, it contains the means of survival, and it is abundant with the simple pleasures of life. However, the simple pleasures of life are the most difficult to enjoy.

The commonest pleasures lie underfoot, and because of their very commodity, their availability, they are overlooked. When I was a boy, catching a toad was exciting, going naked was a forbidden thrill, and what was our fondest dream during Intermediate Flight Training? To get a few hours off so we could go lie on the beach and splash in the water with nothing to do. And I have these pleasures every day.

What was it I was always looking for on the carrier that I would leave the ward room and prowl the ship, poking through the hangar deck, along the flight deck, hiding in the gun turrets, standing on the weather decks and looking into the wind? A chance to be alone, away from the constant chatter, the radio, the klaxon, the siren, the bullhorn, the roar of the airplane engines, the whir and thump of the catapult, the hammering on the hangar deck, the throbbing and vibration of the ship's screws. How many times on station over the fleet did I wish I could cut the throttle and open the hatch and just glide for a moment with nothing but the sound of the wind in my ears. What was my grandest dream and constant desire? Peace.

I have that here. When I want to be alone I can be alone. When I get tired of the lapping of the water I can walk among the trees, and if I get tired of the bird cries and the buzz of the insects, I can climb up Nellie's Tit and listen to the wind.

What was it I wanted in the service anyway? Wasn't it a challenge, an edge of excitement? A chance to test myself? A chance to triumph? For glory? For tragedy even? Here is such a place. Here is adventure and challenge. Here I am proving myself. Here is a place for triumph or even tragedy.

And when I was hit over the Jap carrier, what was it I wanted more than anything else? More than the next breath? To somehow get out of the sky, to put my feet on solid ground, to have, if but for a moment, a sanctuary. A king's x. A moment to stop and think. And I have that. Until rescue comes.

What is missing? Is it the people? No, I was sick of

them, always crowding around, standing in line, yakking in the ready room, singing over the radio the moment silence was broken. There are no women here, but there were none on the carrier either. There is waiting here, but every day on the carrier was sweat, shit, and wait. There is more freedom here, less danger. What then is lacking?

There is no variety. No change. The weather is the same every day. The same beautiful sunrise and sunset. The same pink and magenta sky. The same silver and blue water. The same leafy trees, sandy beach, quiet lagoon. The same face. The same food. Nothing ever happens here. A shark in the lagoon would be relief. A storm. A poisonous snake.

I look up and see a perfect white puffy cloud floating above the island. Along the horizon a line of pink clouds slowly fades to purple. The sky is streaked with orange. The sea turns to antique brass. The island is covered in green velvet and purple shadows, and I know that the day is slipping away and I did not love it enough and enjoy it enough, and cannot hold it. In a moment it is gone. Stars streak the sky, moonlight streaks the water, soft shadows fall over the island. And that too will be gone. I cannot hold it.

What I lack is appreciation. I do not know how to enjoy a sun that is always there, a beach that is never crowded, a wilderness that has not been planned or restored. Beginning tomorrow I will make every effort to know every moment, to enjoy every pleasure it affords, and to appreciate its meaning.

1. I shall begin by arising the moment I awake, with no lingering regrets, no trying to drift back to sleep, no attempts to recapture the dreams of the night, eager to face the day and its fulfillment.

2. I will watch the sunrise and know what it means—that this is a new day, a clean slate, another mission, a chance to prove myself again.

3. I will lie on the sand and watch the rain as it moves across the water, knowing that the rain is the promise of tomorrow, that the clouds we see today are the flowers we prayed for yesterday.

4. Get a drink of fresh water from the pool and pick fruit to eat, mindful that water is pure and the fruit is fresh and that every thing is good in its own way and for its own purpose.

5. Relieve myself with patience for the cramps because they are better than constipation, mindful that the fruit which gives life also gives diarrhea, remembering always that this quivering necessity, this cramping urge is also the lot of man, aware that I am returning to earth something of what it gave me.

6. Inspect the cleared ground, thankful for fire and the power it gives us, thankful for the fertility of the earth.

7. Walk among the trees we have cultivated and study the lesson of the coconut that springs to life, renewing itself, and grows strong and tall into the sky, bearing meat and drink.

8. Climb Nellie's Tit and meditate on the ocean that never changes and is never the same, that builds islands and destroys continents, that rocks children to sleep and lures old men to their death, that is the womb of life and the graveyard of ships.

9. Visit with Kee and share with him what I feel—that our life here is one of uncommon beauty and peace and we should rest in it—knowing that he too is troubled with vagrant memories and joyless dreams. And even though

we cannot speak in words, I can communicate to him a kinship, a pledge of mutual trust and aid.

I may be lonely, but I have a friend.

I may be lost, but there are those to find me.

I dream of the sounds and smells of home, of steaks and hams, soft breasts and warm thighs, of flying high and climbing free, but I live in paradise.

Rescue is in my heart, but heaven is in my hand.

NOTE TO SURVIVAL INSTRUCTORS: *Conveniences*

Kee Yop and I have proved that life can be sustained on this island in a primitive fashion. The following conveniences would make life on an island more than an experiment in survival; they would make life triumphant.

1. Bladed tool, heavy enough to clear foliage, chop firewood, shape trees for canoes or corner posts, open coconut husks, and delicate enough for lancing boils, shaving, cutting hair and nails, and cleaning fish. It could also be used as a weapon.

2. All-purpose pain reliever and disinfectant. When one of us is ill the other must do the work of both.

3. A permanent and reliable means for starting fire such as a magnifying glass. I think fire came here by accident, probably by lightning, and Kee has kept it going ever since. Primitive man lives by accident. He is cold when the weather is, lighted when the day is, fed when the food is. But we must have plan and continuity to our lives. Without the assurance of making a fire when we want it, one of us must always be on guard to keep it from going out. Neither Kee nor I can make a fire by rubbing sticks together. There is no flint on the island.

4. Bits of wire to use for cleaning teeth, draining wounds, removing thorns, as fishing hooks, and for picking locks in the event of capture.

5. Sunglasses. It is impossible to scan a bright sky or glittering sea for long without seeing spots.

6. Gloves to protect the hands from insect bites, thorns, blisters, dirt, and sunburn. Also with gloves we could reach into holes and crevices in the reef to catch fish without fear.

7. Snake-bite kit. We are totally helpless in the event we are bitten by poisonous snakes and would be much relieved if we possessed some remedy against them.

Dear Helen,

Kee and I have built a shelter near the lagoon under large trees. All night you can hear the surf breaking and look out and see stars. The wind is cool and pleasant and helps drive away the mosquitoes, and there is fresh water and fruit close at hand. It would be paradise if only you were here to share it with me, Helen. What a picture that would be. Helen of the island. Helen among the birds.

I wish you could see the birds, Helen. There are all kinds of birds here. I remember how you fed crumbs to the birds in the park. How you laughed as they danced and sang at your feet. "Look at them, Greg. They are so beautiful. And gentle. And they sing for us." And then you turned and kissed me.

In no time at all you could have the birds eating out of your hand, sitting on your shoulder. You loved them because they were soft and beautiful and because they sang for us. Maybe if I describe some of the island birds you will recognize them.

There are small sparrow-like birds that fly in flocks from one tree to another. They have a shrill peeping call that sounds like "sweet tit, sweet tit," and they usually lay five or six brown-flecked eggs in a nest. The birds are small but can be thrown onto the coals to remove the feathers, and eaten bones and all. The eggs are strong in taste but may have been overripe. The birds are very gregarious, always flying, eating, and mating in flocks.

Redbird. Somewhat larger than a cardinal and not so brilliantly plumaged. They have a very coarse call, "crass ass ass." After a few calls a second bird usually appears. The birds sit side by side on the branch singing to each other and pecking at each other's bills. The object of this pecking seems to be to force the female bird's head down, after which they mate.

A heavy-bodied gray bird that looks like a dove. No white meat but very good eating when baked in the coals. They can be caught most easily during mating, since they couple on the ground. The male bird puffs up his feathers and struts and hops about, prancing for his lady. At first the female keeps him away by pecking at him when he comes close. But he keeps dancing around, first on one side and then the other until she seems to become hypnotized. Then he jumps about, hopping on her and then away two or three times and then he mounts her for sure, grabbing her tuft in his beak and holding on. This is the best time to kill them with a stick, since you can come near without disturbing them.

The wagtail, a small brownish bird with a peculiar twitching or wagging of its tail that hops along the ground eating insects. The wagtail has a high-pitched cry that sounds like the cries of a woman in the pains of childbirth or love. I believe they mate in the air, first soaring and then falling together in a flutter of wings, coming apart only to miss the trees. Sometimes in ecstasy they fall to their death.

It isn't bad here, Helen. A man can be happy wherever he is if he puts his mind to it and does not waste his life with idle dreams of things he cannot have and futile thoughts of what might have been. If we could only accept circumstances for what they are. And yet it is important to me that you know I am alive, that you know of my struggles to maintain life and courage and hope. I can bear the cost if only someone knows. I want to climb to the top of Nellie's Tit and shout, "I am alive. I am hanging on. See what I am going through. Look at my hands. Look at my feet. Look how thin I am, how naked."

I am alive. That's the important thing. As long as I have life I have something to be thankful for. And life here is not unbearable. There are moments—at night watching the constellations swimming across the sky, seeing the moonlight on the water, watching the sunrise, the glowing coals of the fire in the darkness, the ocean that is so monotonous and yet so mysterious, wading in the tide, bathing in the pool—that I am overwhelmed by the beauty of it all, moved almost to tears. A blade of grass is so perfect, cracks in the sun-dried mud are so beautiful, the eye of a lizard is of such wonder that I think I would die to see a woman. Just to see your hand would be enough, Helen. The long, tapered fingers. The perfectly shaped nails. The soft cup of your palm. The curve of your back. Just to see your breast. To touch it with my tongue.

I am not afraid, Helen. I am not afraid to face things as they are. The sky is empty, Helen. There are no ships out at sea. The island is small, uncharted, unknown. The Task Force has gone and we are forgotten. There is no purpose here, no sense in our pain and effort. I know that the birds do not sing for me. I know their only value is for eating insects and for use as food. I know that you never loved me. I know that you have forgotten me. I'm not afraid to say it.

But you, Helen, are afraid. Afraid to see that birds sing for sex. That all that twittering and dancing, and showing of pretty feathers is biological urge. You are afraid, Helen, and not a woman at all. Afraid to touch, afraid to feel, afraid to love. And if I held your breast it would be as hard and dry as your lips.

~

NOTE TO SURVIVAL INSTRUCTORS: *Rain shelter*

By clearing the ground under large trees and using the trunks for support, a thatched-roof shelter can be easily and quickly built. However, we have no way of shaping stakes except by splitting them, and no way of driving them into the ground except by pounding them with rocks, which is exhausting work. All building materials must be carried on our backs. And due to lack of communication there is not a fair sharing of work. Also the roof tends to leak.

~

The peace. The quiet. The tranquillity of this place. A calm, a serenity, a lethargy comes over me, yet I dare not enjoy it for long. There is work to be done. If we are to survive until rescue comes then we must keep busy. Work. That is the answer. Clear the land. Burn off the useless vegetation. Cultivate the fruit-bearing trees. Work until rescue comes. We must be worthy. We must have something to show for our lives.

And when we are tired and may for a little while put work aside we must find other occupation for our hands and minds. Hobbies. Recreation. This island abounds in things to collect. Such as seashells. Many of these are broken by the birds or action of the waves, but others can readily be seen in the water or picked out of the coral. The best ones are those that are still alive. The soft membrane can be sucked out and the shell buried in the sand until the ants have thoroughly cleaned it.

Lisa would love the shells here. There are so many kinds. Flat and spiral and tubular, delicate pinks and blues, creamy-milky whites, deep browns flecked with gold. Lisa said she used to dream of living by the seashore, wandering along the beach, wading in the cool foamy water, gathering seashells, listening to the sea gulls, feeling the wind cleaning her face. She said San Francisco wasn't like that. She would sit on the wet sand among the litter of the beach and listen to the boat and bird sounds coming out of the haze and fog, and think of her husband out there somewhere and all those boys so far from home. And she would spend the whole time crying to herself.

I wish I could send Lisa some of these shells—one of the big ones, so she could hold it to her ear and hear the sounds of the island, the wind, and the waves, and maybe my voice whispering that I am alive, that I remember her, and how I wish I could sit beside her on the beach and run my fingers along her thigh and through her hair. Make her necklaces of the seashells and coral, lie with her in the sand and make the cries of the seagulls and the sounds of the waves.

If only Lisa were here we could decorate the shelter with flowers, and feathers, and coral, and piles of seashells that I have collected. We could lie among the flowers and feathers and I could prove my skill. I could make her fly and soar and come crashing down to earth again with memories of wings.

What's the use? It's all pointless without her. Without someone. A woman. What does Kee care if I decorate the shelter or collect seashells. What's the good of collecting when it all belongs to me. Or to Kee if he wants it. And by collecting them I don't subtract from the whole. There'll be as many again tomorrow. The whole purpose of collecting is to make the collectable objects unavailable to others.

Or maybe collecting is a kind of keeping score. Like on the carrier everyone got very excited about painting a Jap flag on his fuselage every time he shot down a Jap plane. And the carriers kept score on all the planes shot down, bombs dropped, ships sunk, sorties flown. Keeping records got to be very important.

I remember how I wanted a Jap flag on my fuselage. Just one, so that every time I climbed in and strapped the plane on I wouldn't have to look at the bare metal. Dad was like that. It wasn't the money. It couldn't have been. Not for two or three cents. It was outsmarting people. Money was just the way he kept the record. But to beat the customer and keep him laughing, keep him coming back to the store, that was the payoff.

That's why he couldn't understand me. That's what upset him so. Because after all those years he had spent playing the lovable and bumbling town crook, and Mom had spent being town mother in a dirty smock, and David had spent being All-American boy with heart of gold and ambition to match, I turned out to be a human being who couldn't cheat a customer out of two cents on a pound of hamburger but could screw the fat, plain daughter of Dad's only employee—something no one could laugh about.

Mom collected claims. Little wrongs and slights we had to make up for. Little gifts and favors for which we were indebted to her. Guilt and gratitude were my daily bread and I ran errands for her, delivering her bouquets to pay for being born—bouquets that drove Dad farther and farther into her debt. "Compliments of the Wallace Grocery Store."

Mom kept records on all the flowers she sent to prospective or paying customers, and all the times she went to bat for David or me with Dad or our teachers, and all the times she gave in to our demands. Dad and David begged and cajoled and teased for a week before she agreed to let David use the car, and when she finally gave in, she marked it down as a debt they both had to pay. When first David and then I left to go to college, and later to enlist, we knew that in leaving her we were incurring a debt we could not repay just by returning.

We all wracked our brains trying to think of ways to repay Mom for what she had been through, for what she had done for us. I delivered flowers and helped her straighten the house. David won popularity contests and brought home school honors to lay at her feet. One Christmas Dad gave her a diamond ring to go with the wedding band he had given her when they were married—something Mom had always wanted, something Dad couldn't get wholesale. For a while after that we had fresh flowers at every meal, random cuttings jammed all together in a vase. Mom cleaned up the house and took special pains preparing the food Dad brought home from the store—salvaging half-rotten potatoes and wilted lettuce. Dad would tease Mom at dinner and Mom would be flustered and pleased, and David and I would look at each other and laugh, not knowing how to act.

But after a while Mother went back to stacking things away in the closets and throwing the food together. Maybe the stale meat and bruised vegetables discouraged her, or the house got her down. Maybe she had known all along that the flower arrangements weren't very good. Dad would come home nervous and irritable, and Mom would throw dinner on the table, and we'd sit down and start eating without hardly speaking to each other and Dad would leave the table and go to the bathroom to throw up. "What did you say to him, Greg?" Mom would ask and she'd mark it down in my account.

I bet Helen collected like that. A little string of virtues. Every boy she dated without kissing, every kiss she gave without meaning it, every dance she danced without feeling it. Stringing them like beads to count and caress and lovingly examine at night and to wear like a collar of virtue by day.

Bunny collected souvenirs. Her memory box she called it—a cedar chest containing the little silver megaphone she got as cheerleader, a wooden gavel with her name on a silver plaque she had received as president of a club, pictures of people she had met, snapshots of herself in all the places she had been, the football letter of an old boyfriend, a blue ribbon she had received in a declamation contest, clippings of favorite poems, an ashtray from a summer in Arkansas, the ankle chain I gave her, a hair ribbon from her best girlfriend, movie stubs from our dates, programs from dances, plays, football games. I guess she still has the program from the U.S.O. dance. A crushed corsage. A torn dress. A bastard child.

David collected triumphs. Every honor he ever won. American Legion Citizenship Award. Best All Round Boy. Class President. D.F.C. Good Conduct Medal. I bet he remembers every girl he ever went with. I bet he has the best kept logbook in the A.A.F. I guess I've collected some myself. Ruby Watson, Bunny Jensen, Lisa Burto, a Jap plane, and a thousand goddam seashells.

I believe that rescue will come. That is what the signal meant. There was someone out there and they were telling us to hang on. Maybe they were saying, "The war is almost over. Hang on a few more days and we'll have the goddamnedest search for the missing you ever saw." We will not be forgotten. Before the victory celebrations are begun the lost will be recovered. In the elation of victory a great nation will not lose sight of those who are missing.

Even if my country did forget me, the men I flew with won't forget. They won't just go home and hang up their uniforms and file away their logbooks. Not after all we've been through together. Not the guys I ate with and slept with and flew with. Not after all the hours we spent together in the ready room, waiting, playing acey-deucy, talking about girls. Not after I told them about Helen. Not after I showed them Bunny's panties. Not after I shared my brandy with them, gave them Lisa's address. Major Ebaugh gave his word. Captain Willett promised.

David will want a full report on what happened to me. He'll search the records to see if I was picked up by the Japanese. He will fly a personal search through the Pacific for me. As soon as the war is over. He'll have to finish what he is doing first. David would never leave a job half done. And he'll wait until he is mustered out so that he won't be conducting personal business on government time. Then he'll have to go home to say goodbye to Mother and check the books at the store. David is very thorough. But David will come if I just have patience. And he will find me if I just hang on.

Mother will ask that I be given a gold star on the church Honor Roll, but they won't do it. They are very accurate at church. Harry Watson will be determined not to do it even though he hopes I never come back. But Mother will be unable to resist hanging a gold star in the window and that'll make the other mothers mad.

"Why should she get a gold star?" they'll ask. "She still has hope that Greg may be found, but I know my boy will never come home." And as long as they talk people will remember that I am missing.

Helen cared nothing for me. I know that now. She only went with me because I was in uniform. She wrote me only because it was the patriotic thing to do. But when she heard I was shot down and missing in action she must have at least felt pity. When she dances with other men she must remember that she went to the hangar dance with me and kissed me under the arch. When she goes to the park, or hears a band play, or feeds the birds she must sometimes think of me.

She has the letters I wrote her. She'll read them once again before she destroys them. When she wears the sweater or sees the stuffed bear I gave her, she will be reminded of me—if only for the time it takes her to pack them away. She has my high-school ring. She can't throw it away and she'll have to wait a decent period of time before she returns it to Mother. Until then, I will be remembered.

And Lisa? How long will she remember? When Willett tells her I am missing, presumably dead, will she then forget? Or will she remember as long as Willett is around? In the dead hours when there is nothing to say and nothing more to do will they talk of me?

"I hope he was a better flier than he was a lover," Lisa will say.

"No, he wasn't much of a pilot either," Willett will say. "I'm sure the poor son of a bitch is dead. Better pilots than Greg have been lost in weather like that. Maybe we'd better do it once for him, huh?"

But maybe her husband won't get back either and every day she'll go down to the bay and stand in the wet surrounded by litter, her hair blowing in the wind. And as she watches for her husband's return she will also watch for me. And people will say, "Look at that woman. She must be waiting for someone lost at sea." And my story will get around.

Even if her husband does come back he'll ship out again. His kind always does. And she'll go down to the bay to watch him sail, and to feel close to him while he's gone. Standing there, hearing the gulls cry and the sounds of the boats, she will remember me and watch for my return. And people will say, "There's Lisa, waiting at the harbor, watching for her men."

Sister Mary Martha will kneel in her garden praying for salvation, and for those who are lost. "Look at your knees," they will say. "You are hurting yourself." And at night while the others sleep Sister Mary Martha will weep for her sins and for those who are lost. "You must be quiet," they will say. "You are disturbing the others." And as long as she prays they will talk of me

Bunny Jensen will try to deny that she ever knew me. But every time she hears a plane fly over the house, every time she hears the telephone ring, every time she puts on her panties, every time she looks at her child she will remember. The more she hates me, the more she will remember. The more she wishes me dead, the more she will wonder if I am alive.

As long as I am remembered by anyone, anywhere, there is hope. It will take time, that is to be expected. And they will be looking for Kee, too. He too has hope. We can hold out, Kee and I. Indefinitely. We have food. We have shelter. We have our work to do, improving the island, and we have this book.

And if they have written me off—a sigh for poor old Greg, a few cheap tears, a drink to my memory—this book will be a witness against them. A witness that they were wrong—that I did not give up, or panic, or languish away, but that like a man I lived, and learned, and built, and expected, and hoped, and waited, and waited—this book will be a testimony against them—that in their indifference, their lack of faith they betrayed me.

There is always sound on the island. The wash and lap of the waves. The irregular dripping of water, snapping of branches, buzz of insects, thud of falling coconuts. The wind in the trees makes a soughing like the sound of breathing, whispering, running feet.

Sometimes I am startled by the groaning and shrieking of branches being rubbed together by the wind, like the sounds of women in love and childbirth. At night when it is still, I have heard, carried on the wind, a strange chattering, like the cries of migratory birds or the tongues of the enemy.

Our own voices sound strange to us and we go for days without speaking, communicating whenever necessary only by gesture. "Come. Look. Eat." Then when we can endure the silence no longer we burst into speech, and I am startled to find that Kee is speaking to me, babbling really, about fishing, or bananas, or how lonely and homesick he is, with tears in his eyes. Sometimes I am surprised to find that without meaning to I have begun talking, catching Kee by the arm and trying to describe to him what it was like to come back from a mission and cut the throttle and feel the plane settle to the deck, how before saying goodnight Bunny would put on fresh lipstick, smile at me, and then give me one final light but exuberant kiss, or how Ruby had a rough place across her back between her shoulder blades where she never washed.

Sometimes Kee follows me about for hours and I know that he wants to speak but is unable to do so. Sometimes I walk with him, wanting to share yet unable to find a way, reluctant to break the spell. Sometimes at night by the fire when we can endure the silence no longer we shout and whistle and laugh, beating rocks together or pounding the trees with sticks driving out silence until we become drunk with sound. Too excited to sing, Kee chants or yells his war cries or whatever the hell they are. And sometimes I shout the songs we made up on the carrier.

> I'm too young to die in a bloody PBY,
> I don't want to go to sea in a smoking SBD,
> It's no fun to play in a crowded PBJ,
> But give me thunder for my guns,
> And whisky for my brew,
> And I'll always be faithful in my trusty F4U.

Or Willett's favorite song:

A faithful flier is a liar.
He gets drunk when he can't get higher,
He loves a whore when he can't get lower,
It's acey-deucy when he's choosy
And a hag with paint when he ain't.

We chant and roar until our voices are gone and then silence rolls back over the island like a cloud, shutting us off, crushing us, and we huddle beside the fire watching each other in fear.

At times I think I hear someone calling my name. "Greg." Never Gregory or Lt. Wallace, just Greg. Always I stop to listen. Sometimes waking up at night and sitting upright. And I think that Kee hears it too, because when I look across the fire he is watching me. But the call does not come again. My name is never spoken twice.

Spoken. That's it. Not called or shouted but spoken. Not a question or command, but clear, distinct, matter of fact. Spoken the way you speak the name of someone you know and see often. The voice is masculine. Not a deep voice but resonant, full, authoritative. But not a voice I recognize.

Today a perfect still came over the island. As though the wind and the waves stopped and the birds and insects became silent. At first I thought I had gone deaf, and then that I was dying. I was terrified and I hid in the thicket and waited for I did not know what, and all I could hear was the pulse beating in my ear. Then it passed. Once again the island came alive with sound. But I was afraid. I couldn't move. I couldn't think. I remained where I was, even after I saw Kee walking around unaware of what had happened. I don't know what I was afraid of. I never once thought of the enemy.

I love the sky. Open. Blue. Spreading down to the edges of the sea. Trimmed with lacy clouds, touched by the gold of the sun. Sprinkled each night with stars.

I love the clouds in all their variety. Fleecy and light. Heavy and rumbling with power. Lofty and calm. Low and boiling with rage. Slipping across the sky like puffy ballet dancers. Wisps of angels' hair and mares' tails. Faces of friends, scenes of home, mountains of ice cream, huge blimps and aerial icebergs. Necklaces of sunset, curtains of dawn, thin sheets of rainbow, halos about the moon.

When I look up I know that the world is good and that peace and beauty are natural to man. When I see the open sky I have hope. Our help comes from the sky.

NOTE TO SURVIVAL INSTRUCTORS: *Memory*

Pilots should be warned that memory will deteriorate during periods of forced idleness and that habits of concentration formed during flight training must be rigorously maintained even if such exercises are of no immediate use. For example, I try every day to run through the take-off and landing checklists and emergency procedures just for the skull practice.

shoulder harness—locked
tail wheel—unlocked
auxiliary electric fuel pump—on
fuel tank selector—main
mixture—automatic rich
cowl flaps—closed
landing gear—down
wing flaps—50°

arresting gear—down
gun switches—off
gun charging knobs—safe
hatch—open and locked

If a plane comes, I will not have forgotten how to fly. If not, I am keeping my mind active and occupied. Even so I fear some deterioration. Certain memories are so persistent and so real and yet I cannot remember what they mean. Last night as I was sleeping, or as I was going to sleep, I thought of a river side street—dark and wet with a taste of mud in the air. Three steps down to a door that was old and weather-beaten with a small glass window that was steamed over. A Christmas tree hung over the door, but it wasn't Christmas. Inside it was small and noisy, filled with smoke and stale air. I was sitting in a booth that was old and stained, its bottom barnacled with lumps of chewing gum. There was a red candle for atmosphere. J.N. was carved into the table and something else. Maybe the outline of a woman's figure.

There was a woman sitting across from me. A middle-aged, loose-lipped woman. Did she smoke? I believe she did—lipping the cigarette. It must have been a bar, because we were drinking. We kissed across the table but I couldn't hold her against me and she wouldn't leave with me. "You're drunk," she said. "I'll take you back to the base, honey, before the M.P.'s pick you up."

Was it a dream or a memory? Where was it? And who was she?

A smell came to me today, familiar yet obscure, bringing with it a whole set of sensations and memories—the dusty, cottony smell of automobile seats and sofa cushions, with the sour rank smell of urine and spilled beer, and a trace of cool, spice-like hand lotion or face soap. I believe Kee has experienced the same thing, for more than once I have seen him walking about sniffing the air.

Sometimes I will be walking about the island with no thought at all of home, and something—a sound or smell—will bring it all back to me. The way Bunny smelled of girl and sweat, cotton and wool, candy and Cokes. The cigarette and whisky smell of Lisa or the sour sweat and strong soap smell of Ruby. The taste of Helen's lips: small, stiff, but smooth with lipstick, sweet with mouthwash. Ruby's hair was stiff and coarse like pubic hair. Bunny had a mole on her smooth silky thigh.

I can remember a woman's breast—lumpy and not well rounded or contoured. The nipple was dry and I can remember the little brown flakes and the newer and pinker skin underneath. And there was a hair on the breast—a short blond hair, slightly arched, and lighter at the root end. And stiff, as though it had come from a clipped moustache. But it wasn't my hair. And whose breast was it?

There are times I can't remember Helen's face, but I can remember how fragrant she was. Everything about her was perfumed. I remember the way she looked at me when I came to her birthday party carrying a bouquet of Mother's flowers. "How nice," she said. "Did your mother grow them?"

I remember the very different way she looked at me when I came to the sorority house and for the first time she saw me in uniform. "You look nice," she said, and I knew she meant it. I knew she was looking around to see if the other girls had noticed. I remember how she watched through the glass of the closed doors as I walked away for the last time.

I turned to look back and saw her standing there, her face soft, touched by my disappointment, and I paused for a moment, realizing that if I had a few minutes more I could take her in my arms and kiss her; feel her lips yielding against my lips, her thighs pressing against my thighs, hear her whisper "yes" she would wait, "yes" she would write, "yes" she would be mine. And I realized that she had felt none of this until the door was locked and the sorority house was closed for the night. I walked away promising myself the biggest drunk and the ugliest whore I could buy.

There is a name that comes to me sometimes. Coy Lee Masters. I will be looking out to sea or gathering coconuts and suddenly, for no reason at all, I will say, "Coy Lee Masters." But I don't know anyone named Coy Lee Masters. Maybe it is someone Helen mentioned in one of her letters. Maybe it's just a name I heard somewhere and have remembered, the name of a football player or movie star. But there are times when I can hear his voice. A young voice and rather high-pitched, tight with anger. "Liar," he says, over and over. "Liar. Liar. Liar."

I try to picture what such a person would look like. Black oily hair, sharp dresser, sports shirt and pegged trousers. A handsome, swarthy face with long sideburns. Thick hairy forearms. Probably a football player. But I can't remember anyone like that.

Sometimes I remember a face, but it doesn't go with the name, and I can't place it although it seems important to me, even familiar. But it is so distorted out of its regular features that I cannot recognize it. It is like a face in a nightmare—angry, horrible, full of revulsion and sickness. The face is swollen and red, the almost colorless eyes are hard and bright, the stiff lips are pulled back from the yellow teeth as though they were screaming hot, bitter words. But the words do not seem to be directed at me, and it is not the face that sometimes speaks my name.

And I remember someone waiting for me. Waiting in the rain. Standing under the movie marquee, a suitcase at her side. The sign was very bright with red and blue letters and there was a large still photograph of a dog wearing a skirt. But I drove past and turned the corner as though I hadn't noticed. And I was afraid. Afraid of her, afraid of the car, afraid of being seen. Who was she? What did she want?

There is something in the water. On the other side of the reef. It is not Kee because he is gathering coconuts and he does not see it. Something large, struggling in the water.

Could it be a man? It's big enough for a man. But what would a man be doing here? What does he want? Why has he come here? There isn't enough room for three people. Not enough food. It would endanger us all.

We have our lives here, a measure of safety, a bit of comfort. We have arrived at an accommodation. We have reached an understanding with regard to need and responsibility. We don't want anyone else. Another person would change everything, destroy harmony, upset the balance of nature. The island would be different. Things wouldn't be the same any more.

Yet, I am a moral man, troubled with scruples, bound by ethical considerations, theories of fair play. I cannot deny help to someone in need even though he be the enemy. I cannot refuse food to someone even if we must all go hungry. I cannot decide the death of one so that two may live.

But what if it's a woman? We could use a woman. Someone to sleep with. To cook for us, make us clothes, tend us when we're sick. But a woman—a woman would change things. One of us would have to go. Would have to be made to go. And one of us would have to stay to protect the woman, improve the island, raise children, and accomplish our mission for being here. But which? The strongest? The craftiest? The deadliest? The one best suited for survival—not only the survival of himself but also of the woman and their children? The one trained in cultural values and military discipline? The one most capable of adapting to circumstances and environmental change? The one who keeps the records?

It is likely that because of my education and cultural background I am most worthy to survive and most capable of producing and training children who can survive on this island. Yet the very training that makes me worthy of survival handicaps me in any contest of selection. I have been taught since childhood that it is wrong to strike first or without warning. I am incapable of pretending friendship or hiding my true feelings. I have been taught the virtue of fair play and I cannot rely on tricks or ambush. I have been taught the primacy of reason, and if Kee cannot understand why I am best suited to survive then I am lost because I am unable to—

It is gone now. Whatever was struggling in the water has disappeared. It must have been a large fish. Kee goes on eating coconut as though nothing had happened.

NOTE TO SURVIVAL INSTRUCTORS

I am dying. I have had severe stomach cramps for several days and I believe it is appendicitis. There is no remedy on this island and little hope that I can survive it. Kee has been very good. He has brought me food and water although I cannot eat, and he stays at my side to show his concern and to brush away the mosquitoes.

Kee is frightened. Afraid that I will die and leave him alone on the island once again. I have tried to reassure him. There was a light out at sea. A signal. And it sent a message to us. Help will come if he will only hold on a few more days.

Kee sits beside me trying to keep me alive by his will, but there is nothing he can do. Yet it is a comfort to me to have him here. I used to think that I would want to face my last minutes alone but I know now the horror Kee must feel. After I die he will face life and death alone. When he gets sick there will be no one to bring him food or water, no one to keep the fire going, no one to call to in the darkness, no one to know what he suffers, no one to care if he dies. I have tried to share my hope with him—that if he can survive a few days more help will come. There is nothing more I can do for him. I have nothing else to give.

I have asked Kee to place these pages and scraps of bark in a safe place so that the Allies may find them. With the time I have left I will try to sum up the lessons the island has taught me so that my life here is not completely in vain. It is my hope that the lessons I have learned will be of benefit to others.

1. I was not trained to live for long in an environment such as this. I was not given the tools for survival. Dad pretended that life was a friendly game where you tried to take more than you gave, and all you needed to win was a good joke and a pawn to trade for something better. Mom thought life was an unkempt garden where one spent all day pulling weeds in order to gather a random bouquet

of stunted and faded flowers before sunset, and all one needed to live was patience and resignation. In school we were taught that life was a grab bag of surprises where everyone received according to his gifts, and the best gift was a big hand. In church we were told that the world was a chest of earthly treasures where each was rewarded according to his goodness and all that was required was polite speech and a grave manner. In survival training we were told to get out of the plane alive and to hold on until rescue came.

Life is an endurance test and the only rule is to survive.

2. Insofar as circumstances permit, pilots should attempt to ditch rather than bail out in order to save wreckage and contents of the airplane. If they must bail out every effort should be made to save the parachute or any other materials that may be used for survival. Out of my parachute we could have made clothing, bedding, signals, and shelter. Out of the shroud lines and harness we could have made snares, nets, fishhooks, and slingshots for killing birds. With the material comforts a parachute would have given us our lives here would have been far different.

3. The best hope for survival is in work. Instead of hiding in the jungle and waiting for rescue I should have gone immediately to work. It is impossible to fit oneself to the jungle. This is an inhospitable island, perhaps uninhabitable. If man is to survive here he must build a wall against the ugliness and rawness of nature. He must eradicate the insects, make clearings in the jungle, and build a shelter against sun, rain, wind, flies, and mosquitoes.

4. There are no rules of conduct, no principles of survival. The only law is to live. In order to survive such circumstances as war, isolation, nature, one must be com-

mitted to life. And the meaner and dirtier that life is, the more the survivor must devote himself to it.

5. I have been unable to discover any meaning for my life, or any purpose for which I was left on this island.

Kee left me this morning, although my condition was not much better. When he came back he was very excited and asked me to follow him. I explained that I had appendicitis and was unable to move and unlikely to live. Still he insisted that I go with him, pointing to the sky and crying, "Malihini huruhura." The enemy has come.

Although I was in pain I followed him, climbing up on the mound to see. Out to sea the sky is black and everything is still. I do not yet know what it means but a definite change has occurred. There is no wind and the birds and insects are silent. Even the ocean is quiet, but there is a storm out at sea. The clouds are dark blue, almost black, with streaks of green underneath and pockets of dirty yellow. There appears to be lightning in the clouds and the air is electric.

Kee is trembling with excitement and I feel excited also. Like that first combat mission after days and months of training monotony and routine flying. Scared stiff—but more than that a kind of excitement and wild good cheer. A sense of danger but also a feeling of purpose, that now it's all going to mean something. And over all—anticipation and hope. If you can only get through this you will be a different person and everything will be changed.

Maybe this is what they were trying to tell us. That they could not pick us up because of the impending storm, but would return after the storm passed. If not, ships running before the storm may discover us here. Or float planes may be forced down by bad weather into the lagoon. Crates of food, clothing, and medicine could be washed up on the beach. Radios. Weapons. Lifeboats. A storm is coming, and if we can but survive it, everything will be different.

I must put the book aside now, as a few drops of rain have begun to fall. They are scattered, but very large and they fall with a hiss. Gusts of wind are tearing at the trees. I must put the scraps and pages in the little cave and cover them with leaves. I will pile stones before the cave, both to protect the book and to notify the curious that there is something within.

Kee is begging me to go to the shelter and we must pick up dry wood to keep the fire going through the storm. There will be discomfort in the next few hours, perhaps danger, but we will survive to see a new and better day.

The island is a scene of unbelievable devastation. Branches, whole trees have been blown down. The vegetation has been uprooted, torn, shredded, blown into piles and tangles, leaving clearings and one swatch through the jungle as though a giant scythe had neatly sliced through it. Our cultivated trees have been blown down and in our clearings are piles of brush. All our work has been destroyed, all our efforts erased. The pool is filled with debris. The fruit has been stripped from the trees and pounded into the earth. We have been unable to find anything to eat. Not so much as a green coconut. Only by luck did Kee find some small fish that had been washed up on the beach and baked in the sun.

How many days the storm lasted I don't know. Three, perhaps four or five days have passed. It was impossible to tell, as there was no day or night, only darkness and wind and rain. The shelter blew away in the very beginning. We tried to hold it together with our hands but we could not stand in the face of the wind and whole sections of the shelter would blow away at a time. When there was not enough shelter left for both of us, Kee took coals from the fire in coconut husks and went to find a better place. I stayed, holding what remained of the shelter together to save the fire, but the wind increased and the rain flooded the ground. The fire went out.

I called to Kee, hoping that he could hear me. Hoping that he had found a safe place for himself and his fire. I could scarcely hear my own voice. I tried huddling against the trees, hiding in the rocks. I couldn't breathe because of the wind and rain and I thought I would drown. I tried to find the cave so I could take the book out and put my head inside where I could breathe, but it was impossible to see anything or to walk without being blown down.

How long I struggled like that, crawling and sliding along the ground from shelter to shelter, I don't know. There was water everywhere and I could hardly tell whether I was on the island or in the lagoon. I feared I would be blown out to sea. I called for Kee to come help me but he did not answer.

Then I saw a tiny flicker of light. Kee's fire. How he kept it going I don't know, but I knew my only chance was to find him. I stumbled and fell in the darkness, was blown down by the wind, knocked down by falling branches. I groped my way, falling over debris, bumping into trees, recognizing nothing. At times I would lose sight of the fire and almost give up hope.

Then I found him. Trees had been blown against large rocks, and by crawling under the tangle, Kee had managed to keep his fire alive by sheltering it with his body and feeding it coconut husks and bits of wet wood.

I crawled under the trees beside him and we huddled over the fire—cold, wet, cramped, our stomachs scorched by the fire, afraid to move or to sleep. We closed our minds to all thought of time, of food, of pain, remembering only to feed the fire and to endure. Then it was over. The wind died out. The rain stopped. We lay exhausted and shivering in the mud, watching the sky as the clouds thinned and parted and the sun appeared. Water still dripped from the trees like rain.

Slowly we emerged from the shelter, scarcely able to move because our joints were stiff and our limbs swollen, weak with hunger and exhaustion, numbed by the violence of the storm and the discovery of our own impotence. For a time we stood clinging to the uprooted trees waiting for strength to return to our feet and legs, waiting for our senses to accept the devastation of the island. But we could not rest for long. Hunger drove us to hunting for undamaged fruit or roots or seeds. Kee found small fish that had been blown or washed up on the island.

The book is safe but some of the scraps are wet. I write carefully for fear of smearing.

Spent day scratching in mud and clay looking for roots, seeds, anything to eat. Kee found one of the animals we had thought earlier were rats. Apparently it had drowned. They are edible.

Nothing today. Handful of seeds. No rats. No dead fish or drowned birds. No fruit. Not even green. Sick. Tired. I lay down beside Kee and cried. I'm not ashamed to say it. I cried. Not for fear, or self-pity, but because of the hunger and weariness and the hopelessness of it all.

I think Kee felt like crying also. He didn't talk or sing or try to comfort me. He fed the fire a stick at a time, and when it was hot enough, he turned his back to the fire, lay down on the wet ground and pretended to sleep.

I wasn't prepared for this. To die in combat, yes. To be killed by my parachute, strafed in the water, burned alive in the cockpit. Lost at sea. To die for my country. For a friend. Because of a mistake. But to die like this—naked and unknown, digging in the ground like an animal, grateful for roots and bark.

We know now there is no safety on this island. We were fools to believe we could survive here. Another day without food and we will be too weak to search for it any more. We were fools to believe that we could sustain ourselves here until help comes. We are totally at the mercy of nature. We are defenseless against another storm. We must get off this island or die.

We deceived ourselves that there was a signal from the sea. It must have been a star standing low on the horizon. If it was a signal it must have been the enemy tormenting us, trying to drive us to insanity and suicide. If it was a message from a friendly sub then the sub must have been sunk.

No one knows we are here. No one cares. We can only hope that a ship has been blown off course and will pass nearby, or that a plane tracking the storm will fly overhead, or that something to eat will wash up on the beach.

I have written this while strength lasts as a lesson to others. There is no salvation on this island. There is no hope but rescue. Beyond the horizon of the brightest day is the beginning of the end.

I wish I could see Mother one more time. Walk up behind her in the solarium, where she's arranging flowers "Presented in memory of Gregory Wallace, who gave his life for his country."

"Hi, Mom, what's for supper?" I'd say. She'd be so embarrassed. Because of the memorial and the gold star in the window. "It's all right, Mother," I'd say.

But she'd feel she had to explain. "It's not that I wasn't hoping you'd come back. I just wanted to do something for you."

"It's all right, Mom," I'd say. "I don't mind. Really."

Then she'd look down at the memorial she had planned for me. "It wasn't much, I guess," she'd say, poking at the flowers with stiff hands to make them stand straight and open. "It's the best I can do."

"They're fine, Mom," I'd say. "Just fine."

"No," she'd say, giving them another pat or two. "They're ugly. Did you know that?"

"Yes, Mom, I knew."

"And you've been ashamed of them. All these years you have been ashamed."

"Mom. Mom. I was never ashamed of you. It was having to deliver those goddam flowers. 'Compliments of the Wallace Grocery Store.' Having to pretend I didn't know what people were thinking, having to pretend to you that the flowers were beautiful and people were grateful to get them. That's why I tried to steal a box of candy for Helen's birthday. Because I was ashamed to take her a bouquet and I was ashamed to tell you that they were ugly and that everyone laughed at them."

"I knew, Greg. All along I knew and I knew that you knew. And I knew the reason you went on delivering the flowers and pretending to me was because you loved me. And every day that you have been away I have made a special arrangement just for you. People laugh at me, Greg. But they remember my boy."

"I'm home now, Mom," I'd say, throwing the flowers away. "You don't have to arrange flowers any more. And no one is going to laugh at us again."

I'd like to see David, tell him how I shot down that Jap plane, how I was the first to attack the carrier, how I held on here clinging to hope, keeping a log for others to use, following instructions. "Have you seen Helen lately?" I'd ask. "And oh yes, David, about the grocery store. You can stick it up your ass."

And Helen. Call for her once more at her sorority house. She'd be so surprised when she saw me. Clean, tanned, in dress uniform, wearing my ribbons, and maybe a decoration. She'd run down the stairs and kiss me and I'd take her out to dinner and dancing. Bring her back to the sorority house in my own car. Walk her up to the door where Miss Manning and all the other girls are watching. "I've lived through hell, Helen," I'd say. "And I lived for one reason. To come back and tell you something. You didn't give me so much as a kiss when I left. You didn't make much of an effort writing to me while I was gone. But you pulled me through because I wanted just one thing—to come back here and say, 'Fuck you, you faithless bitch.' "

I'd like to look up Coy Lee Masters, whoever he is, and buy him a hamburger and a beer and ask him how I lied. I'd like to buzz Bunny's house one more time and then land right out in the street. Neighbors and kids would run out in the yard to see what had happened, and Bunny's folks would come out on the porch, and then Bunny would come out, too. She'd be wearing a pink skirt and sweater and a jaunty hat, and carrying the baby.

"I've come for you, Bunny," I'd say. "Get your things."

"I don't need anything," she'd say. "Not now. Not if I have you." And she'd kiss her folks goodbye and run and jump in the airplane. I'd give it full throttle down the street past the houses and trees and neighbors, and pull it off the ground and head up into the sky, with Bunny hanging onto the baby and hanging onto me like she'd never let go.

I'd like to take Lisa a pair of nylons. A piece of ass is worth that much. Even an old piece like Lisa. And go back to that place where they keep Ruby. Sit on the stone bench with her in the corner of the wall until she recognizes me. Then I'd tell her why I couldn't take her away, and why it was best that she give up the baby, and that they would let her out if she would just stop thinking about it and stop pretending that she was someone she wasn't.

But they don't care. Kee and I are missing and presumed dead. David is a realist. He's seen too much killing to be sentimental or to hold out hope of survival. He knows how big the ocean is and how small a man looks in the middle of it, how slight the chance that we'll ever be found. He never had much faith in me anyway. "Mom, why should I have to take Greg with me just because he can't drive?"

David will tell Mother to give me up and she will hang a gold star in her window and ask the government to ship my body home. Helen will marry someone else. Girls like Helen are meant to marry. Where else can they be safe? Lisa will forget she ever knew me. Women like Lisa are not cursed with memory. Bunny will deny me. In the face of her own heartbreak, surrounded by memories and souvenirs of our moments together, in the presence of my child she will deny she ever knew me. Ruby will sit in a barren corner of the wall and pretend she's in a garden of children and flowers. Willett won't care. "As far as I'm concerned any MIA alive after three days is named Jesus."

They'll write me off just as they did Major Ebaugh. They won't stop to give me a chance. They'll go right on with their lives, pulling hope out of my grasp.

After two days we received a message that a destroyer had spotted a pilot, believed to be Major Ebaugh, in the water. We all yelled and ran up to Air Plot to listen. After that nothing. For days, nothing, while we waited. Slowly the word seeped through the Task Force, slipping from ship to ship. The destroyer had thrown him a line, but after two days in the water he was too weak to hold on. The destroyer wouldn't stop because we were in enemy waters. There might be submarines. They just rolled him over and kept going.

Two days in the water in a Mae West. Praying and hanging on. Kicking off the sharks. Watching for a plane, a ship, any kind of help. Half blind from the sun and salt water. Afraid to sleep. And then he sees something. A ship. By that time he doesn't even care if it's a Jap ship, just so they see him. But it's one of ours and he's almost out of his mind for fear they won't see him. But they do. Slowly they alter course to come alongside. They get so close he can see them waving. The poor bastard probably cries when he sees them crowding the deck watching him, shouting encouragement. Major Ebaugh, the leading ace, the best navigator, the best pilot in the squadron. The line hits the water, close enough for him to reach but there is no strength in his swollen hands. The ship won't stop and he watches the line running through his grasp, his last hope disappearing through his numbed fingers.

I bet the poor bastard prayed and cursed trying to close his swollen hands, trying to hang on. Then with the last measure of strength in him he gripped the rope, winding it around his hands, holding it to his chest, biting it with his teeth. But the ship wouldn't stop and the line rolled him over like a cork and slipped free.

Scuttlebutt said he didn't make a move after that, but lay face down—dead in the water. Not even trying to raise his head. And what was he thinking? Give 'em hell, boys? Remember Pearl Harbor? It's better to save one poor bastard from the sea than to splash six Japs?

Scuttlebutt said as he lay there, bloody foam streaked the water. As though maybe he had bitten off his tongue or lip. Or some said maybe his heart had burst. But it wasn't his heart that burst. And it wasn't blood he tasted as he chewed off his tongue. It wasn't salt water that stopped his breath as he lay face down in the water. It was despair. There is no hope.

NOTE TO SURVIVAL INSTRUCTORS: *The lagoon*

The lagoon looks peaceful enough and there are fish in it that could easily be caught by hook or net from a boat. But pilots should be warned that lagoons are deceptively dangerous. It is impossible to walk in the lagoon without shoes because of the coral and sharp pointed shells. There are also sting rays, sand sharks, and moray eels. Some of the shellfish have poisonous stingers.

~

We have found food. We discovered some of the rats nesting in a pile of debris in a clearing, and by setting the brush on fire we were able to drive them out and to kill two of them with clubs—an old grizzled one and one that appeared half grown. Spitting them on sticks we held them over the fire to burn off the hair and to cook them.

The animal is not really a rat. Its body is long and thin and it has a straight hairless tail. It is about the size of a possum and is probably some variety of that animal. The skin on the old one seemed tough and hard to chew, but our teeth are loose and our jaws weak from disuse. The flesh of the younger one was especially sweet and the skin was tender. Probably we could roast the young ones in their skin. There is very little flesh on the animals but it is all edible—tongue, brain, skin, liver. The intestines can be cleaned and wrapped around a stick and roasted over the fire. It is meat and there is strength in it.

As soon as we have rested and regained our strength we will go hunting again. If we can find a way to catch or trap the animals we can stay alive. For a little while anyway. Until the fruit comes back. Maybe we can catch some of the animals alive, breed them, have a steady and reliable food supply. That would give us a little time. Until the next storm. Maybe help would come before then. Or maybe, if we could eat regularly, get our strength up, we could build a shelter strong enough to save us from the storm. A shelter of logs, or even rocks maybe. With a chimney for the fire and a place to store dry wood, and emergency food and water. We would be safe then. We could live here indefinitely.

~

We are too weak to chase the rats down, and although they are not fast they are agile, and once they get in the brush they are impossible to catch. Our best chance is to outthink them.

The rats' safety is in the dense vegetation. The reason we could not catch them earlier was because it was impossible to run them out of the brush. By burning off the grass and brush to cultivate the land we eliminated some of their nesting places. The hurricane tore up more of the vegetation. By burning the piles of debris we will once again create clearings where it is possible to catch them. Also we can set snares and deadfalls along their runs, and when we set the debris afire we can chase them and kill them in the clearings or run them into the traps set along the trails in the brush.

I explained my plan to Kee and demonstrated how to make a simple deadfall. He can do it but he is impatient and wants only to hunt. Nevertheless I put off the hunting until we had set up some traps. Then, taking torches from the fire, we went to hunt. In burning the third brush pile we found four of the animals. They darted out so quickly that we were both taken by surprise. However, Kee threw a rock, breaking the hind leg of one of the rats. That slowed it enough that I hoped we could catch it alive and use it to breed others, but Kee dove into the brush after it and killed it before I could stop him. By the time I got to him he was sitting on the ground, proudly holding up the kicking rat by the tail.

I explained to Kee that he shouldn't have killed the rat, that it was more valuable to us alive, that we should have eaten the rats caught in the traps and kept this one for breeding. But all Kee could think of was that he had something to eat. Since he wouldn't listen to me, I thought of refusing to eat any of it to demonstrate that he was wrong to kill it. However, the other rats eluded the traps and the smell of cooking meat was so overpowering that I took my share. We pulled the rat out of the fire, tore it apart and ate it, burning our lips and fingers. But when Kee grinned and winked, pretending what a big hero he was for killing the rat, I ignored him.

Had no luck today in flushing out more of the animals although we burned off a lot of brush and debris. Nor have we found any of the animals in the traps. However, in poking around in the ashes we did find a nest of little ones that had been burned alive. These we ate whole.

Both of us have been troubled with cramps and abdominal pains, but I believe this is because our stomachs are not accustomed to solid foods, and also because we chewed up the bones. There is nothing wrong with eating the rats and as soon as our stomachs have adjusted to this rich diet we will regain our strength.

We must not give up now. We must make ourselves strong so that we can build a shelter that will withstand the wind and protect us from the storm. It is our only hope.

1. First priority must be to endure. To eat whatever is necessary to give us strength. To do whatever is necessary to stay alive.

2. Second priority must be given to preparing a shelter against disaster. At whatever price we have to pay. Present good must be sacrificed for future safety.

3. Third priority will be given to watching for signs of rescue. Our past suffering, our present plans, our future safety will be vain and without meaning if there is no deliverance from this island.

I have neglected to write in this book, since we have been busy hunting, which has been good. It has not rained since the storm and everything is so dry that we can be assured of getting meat by setting a few fires.

So preoccupied have we been with hunting and setting traps that it wasn't until today that I discovered a tree on the beach, half covered with seaweed and debris, washed up by the storm. It is a large tree and of a kind different from any found on the island. For a while I squatted beside the tree and studied it, but there was no mistake. The tree did not come from this island. It was brought here by the sea from somewhere out beyond the range of our sight and it has much to tell us if only we can figure it out.

I was so excited that my hands trembled, and I waited for a while to calm myself, for fear that in my excitement I might destroy or overlook something important. Here was our first glimpse beyond the limits of the island—our first message from the unknown and forgotten world.

Calming myself as best I could I began carefully to lift away the debris, pull back the tangled seaweed, and dig away the sand. Kee came to watch but I motioned him to stay back. I did not trust him to be as careful as I must be.

At last the tree lay naked before us, stripped and cleaned of the deposits from the sea and the storm. I motioned Kee over and he squatted beside me as we studied the tree. "Do you know this tree?" I asked. "Kee, merkans?" I asked. "A friend of Kee's?" But Kee looked at the tree, his face very grave, and then he shook his head. He did not know the tree. "Ku-see," I said. "Beyond. Over the horizon. Merkans," I said. "Merkans ku-see. Friend from over beyond the sea."

"Merkans," Kee said, reaching out to touch the tree. But I grabbed his hand lest he should destroy some evidence, and shook my head. He was puzzled, but I explained to him that the tree was special and must not be carelessly handled.

The rest of the day we squatted beside the tree studying it, having forgotten about hunting. It is a large tree, thicker than three men and longer than four. It is very solid, with no soft or rotten spots on it. Some roots and three large branches are intact. The roots are broken as though the tree had been uprooted and the limbs are torn as though leaves and smaller branches were stripped away, perhaps by the wind, or perhaps by the sea.

The bark is not only rough but also thick, and it has not been damaged by either the storm, rocks, or water. The texture is pebbly, almost grainy, with dark outer ridges that are almost black, and lighter inner channels of tan, pink, and faint traces of green. The bark has a sharply bitter taste, although part of this might be attributed to the salt sea. No resin has been found on the tree.

I have been greatly troubled by the irregular markings on the tree—knots, holes, and scorings. There are three large knots—protuberant, crested, and conical, and positioned in a most intriguing way. It is possible that nature might have formed such a geometric design but that is a most unlikely conclusion.

The two holes in the trunk are regular in shape, about

the size of the forefinger, very deep and straight, as though bored. It is impossible to discover their origin, but it is clear that the tree did not grow this way, that the holes were caused by something foreign to it, and that to the best of my knowledge no land or sea borer bores such a large hole, or bores in a straight line.

There are white markings on the trunk that I at first took to be paint or whitewash, since the markings can be scraped off and have a faint lime taste. However, I now believe the markings to be dried bird droppings.

There are certain impressions on the left center limb which I first took to be scorings by land insects or sea creatures. Further study has raised a question in my mind, however. One of the scorings is three vertical lines with horizontal markings, bearing some resemblance to primitive representation of human figures. The center figure is smaller, and the whole design can be interpreted as a mother and father holding a child between them, a letter from some unknown alphabet, or a crude rendering of a P-38.

Another marking is a deep, saucer-shaped hole with a shallow line tailing from it. It can be interpreted as a pot with a handle, a fish with large broad fins such as a sting ray, or the male reproductive organ.

Following our study of the tree we made a hasty survey of the debris on the beach, with the result that we found no bottles, metal scraps, or war materials. A badly deteriorated bit of matter was found that might have been a piece of oil cloth of a fragment of rotten leaf. The matter had dried and disintegrated at a touch. Driftwood was found, with a stain that might have been an oil stain.

CONCLUSIONS

1. There is no clear evidence that the war is near or even that there is a war.

2. There is other land nearby. The tree came from somewhere and the condition that it is in bears evidence that it was not long in the sea.

3. The land must be both large and fertile to produce a tree of this size, and in all probability it contains fruit-bearing trees, although this tree may not be one of them.

4. Such a land would offer greater safety and opportunity to us but as we have no way of getting there we must wait for someone from that land to come for us.

5. It is not certain that the land is inhabited, but a large area of fruit-bearing trees almost certainly would be.

6. If the pictograph represents a human family, then the inhabitants would be a primitive, matriarchial society that practices circumcision of the male sex. If the pictograph is instead an alphabetical symbol, then the inhabitants would be an advanced, language-making culture that could give and receive signals. If instead, the pictograph represents a P-38, the island is known to the A.A.F.

7. The two regular holes appear to be manmade because of the regularity of the entrance and the straightness of the shaft. This would indicate a primitive but tool-making society. However, the holes could be bullet holes, which would be proof of civilization.

8. The size of the tree illustrates the severity of the storm.

9. The meaning of the tree is that our best chance of survival is to build a secure shelter of logs and rocks and wait for help to come.

NOTE TO SURVIVAL INSTRUCTORS: *The signs of the coming storm*

Pilots should be trained in the identification of the coming storm. Survival depends on early recognition, physical preparation, and mental resolution. In knowledge is power. We are not afraid of that which we understand. Pilots who are trained to recognize the storm, who know what to expect, are physically and mentally prepared for it, are most likely to survive.

1. At the time of the coming of the storm there are dark and unnatural events. The sun turns dark at midday, the earth trembles, the sea becomes calm and turns the color of bronze.

2. The insects become hushed and still and only the swarm flies are out. The small animals lose their fear of man and each other and stand in the open watching the sky. The birds disappear.

3. In man there is a rising expectancy, an electrifying awareness of excitement and danger. The hair rises on the back of the neck and the pulse quickens. It is a time of destruction and desperation, a time of change.

I have made a complete and thorough study of the island, looking for the best location for the shelter. The place where Kee and I found safety from the storm was my first thought. It was a known and proven refuge. However, what has worked in the past is not always the best answer for the future. This shelter is too important to make any mistakes. It must be right.

1. It must be safe. Not only against the storm but against dangers that we do not yet know of. If we have

a refuge, a place of sanctuary, we can deal with the other problems of the island.

2. It must be accessible, open at all times, and available to both of us wherever we might be.

3. It must be comfortable, so that we can remain in it for long periods of time, taking refuge before danger comes, and remaining safe after danger has passed.

After studying the island for almost two days I have found a near perfect spot near the center of the island; it is easily accessible, high enough to be safe from flooding, and protected on three sides from the wind. It is far enough from the trees to prevent them from being blown down on the shelter and yet close enough that the trunks can be rolled to the shelter and used. But best of all there is a natural rock ledge large enough for us to get our heads and shoulders under. By extending the shelter with additional rocks along the sides, covering them with heavy logs, a cross-hatching of lighter logs, then leaves and earth, we will have a shelter that is both safe from the storm and waterproof.

The ledge is so perfect for our purpose, so conveniently located that one could almost believe it were made for us. However, there are some foreseeable problems.

1. The floor is rock and will be uncomfortable for long confinement.

2. There is scarcely enough room for the two of us and since we must keep dry wood under the shelter also, we must lie the whole time on our sides.

3. The height of the roof will not permit us to sit up or move about so that we must go out into the storm to relieve ourselves or else foul the shelter.

4. The only opening will be at the entrance at the opposite end from the ledge. This will also have to serve

for ventilation and a chimney for the fire, so our heads will be in the opening and our feet in the safest and most comfortable place in the shelter.

5. Since the shelter will be infrequently used, some means must be found for keeping it clean, in good repair, and free of snakes.

6. Explaining the plan to Kee. It will take time to build the shelter, and it will require hard, sustained effort on the part of both of us. More discipline than Kee has as yet demonstrated. Because he has food he has forgotten about the storm. Because he is comfortable he thinks he is safe.

Today I led Kee to the rock ledge and demonstrated how a shelter could be built, although he was impatient to go hunting. I showed him how he could build two rock walls at right angles to the ledge and cover the enclosure with logs, leaving only enough space to crawl under. I demonstrated where we could build a rock or log windbreak to keep the wind from blowing directly into the opening. I lay down in the space to show how we would be safe and comfortable. I smoothed out a patch of earth and with a stick drew a picture of what the shelter would look like from the side and asked Kee for his opinion.

I explained that it was impossible to survive another storm like the last one without shelter. "Malihini huruhura," I said, which in his language is supposed to mean destruction, enemy, evil, or something like that. "Great storm," I said, pointing at the sky.

But Kee played dumb. When Kee does not want to do something he pretends not to understand a word I say. I took his arm and pointed at the sky. "Great storm," I said. "Malihini huruhura." But Kee looked at me and winked as if to say there was not a cloud in the sky, and of course there wasn't. There has been no rain since the storm and the sky has been clear but hazy. But the storm will come again and the shelter must be ready.

That is the difference between primitive man and civilized man. Maybe in spite of my training in meteorology I am not able to read the weather signs as clearly as Kee, but I know that there is a storm out there. Kee can see a hurricane only when it is on the horizon. To Kee the storm is the past and he thinks only of filling his belly today. To me the storm was a warning and I worry about a shelter for tomorrow.

I must make Kee understand. It will not be easy, but the man who sees the danger is the one who must make the greatest effort to avert it. The ability to see into the future carries with it the duty to prepare for whatever the future holds.

To understand Kee I must remember that he is a primitive man—honest, forthright, dependable, but untrained in discipline. He has never been taught to sacrifice today's good weather in order to be prepared for tomorrow's rain. I don't know how to reach him. I could perhaps play on his fear, his superstitious awe of the "malihini huruhura." Intimidate him. But is that what I want? A fearful companion, or perhaps a servant who prepares for his own future only because I tell him to?

Maybe when I first discovered how small the island was I wished I were alone here. But I know now that we are a team. To survive here we have to work together as a team. I must gain Kee's trust and I must educate him to our future needs. I must make him a full partner in work and responsibility. What I want is a teammate, an equal who can share not only the hopes of the island but also its burdens.

This morning I went to Kee and explained again about the need for the shelter. I explained it simply and directly because if there is to be trust between us then we must be honest and open with each other.

"Kee," I said. "You have your bird of hope and I have my bird of hope. I know that if we hang on a big bird will come from the mali ku-see, from beyond the horizon, and will see us here with its eye and circle over the island and flap its wings, and afterwards a ship or a flying boat will come along and take us away like a big hand.

"Do you read me, Kee?" I asked. "Are you getting the word?" Because Kee was listening. He was paying attention. But he was watching me like I was trying to snow him. The way farmers sometimes used to watch Dad—knowing he was getting to them but not sure how he was doing it.

"Kee," I said. "The malihini huruhura came once and it can come again. We were lucky the first time. Very fortunate. Merkans malihini huruhura. Friends of the storm. But when the Great Storm comes again we cannot hope to survive it. Certainly not both of us. You, me, together? No. Not without a shelter. A pukaru. Kee, we can no longer sit on our ass and wait for the big bird to come and the big hand to get us out of here. We have to go to work. Build a shelter. Work," I said, pretending to build a pile of stones. "You, me, go work. Build big shelter—pukaru—before malihini huruhura comes. Got it?"

But Kee put on his stupid native act. All eyes and ears.

Waiting to hear the rest of it as though I hadn't even started. "Dammit, Kee, if you're going to have anything you're going to have to work for it. Can't you see that? I can't do it all for you. If we're going to live here we're going to have to build a pukaru. A shelter. I can't move the rocks and logs by myself. I'm going to have to have your help. Now, dammit, are you going to help me or not?"

But Kee had lost interest and wanted to go hunting. He got a torch, but I took it from him and threw it back into the fire. "No, Kee, we are not going hunting today," I said. "We are going to build the shelter and you have to help me. We can eat whatever is caught in the traps."

But Kee got another torch and went off to hunt. "Goddammit, Kee, we have to build a shelter. Can't you see that, you stupid bastard? I can't do it by myself. You're going to cause both of us to get killed."

I tried to stop him but I couldn't. I ran and checked the traps, thinking that if we had caught something in the traps he would be satisfied with that and consent to help me, but there was nothing. I ran after him again. "All right, Kee," I said. "You win. We'll hunt and build both. Okay? You help me work and I'll help you hunt. Is it a deal?"

But Kee didn't even want to discuss it. He went on setting the brush afire and I tagged along after him trying to tease him into a good humor. "Come on, Kee," I said. "We're civilized men. We can compromise. I'll meet you half way. You scratch my back and I'll scratch yours. Okay?" But he wouldn't listen and I wouldn't give up and we got no work done on the shelter and killed nothing to eat.

There is no point in continuing this way. At times today I thought of abandoning the shelter completely. Let the storm come. But that is stupid. I would be destroying myself as well as Kee and all we have worked for. And what is fair? Greater knowledge implies greater responsibility. Special training makes one especially responsible. We must survive in order to preserve the experiences and learnings that give our life on this island meaning.

Tomorrow I will work on the shelter alone. It will not be easy, but there are things I can do and when Kee sees my work, when he understands what I am doing, he will help.

Kee was a little stiff this morning, but I went on as though nothing had happened and when he saw I wasn't going to interfere with his hunting, he loosened up enough to invite me to go with him. But I couldn't. There was work to be done, and I began the search for the stones with which to build the side walls of the shelter.

Flat, smooth stones are best and the larger the better, since the fewer used the fewer holes will have to be chinked to keep out the wind. I found many rocks. However, several of them were so large that it will take both of us to move them. The rocks are dark gray or black, and probably volcanic. They seem heavier than those at home. Except for the porous rocks. These seem lighter.

I will begin the walls with the rocks I can move, and will locate and burn down the trees we will use for the roof. Then Kee will see what I am doing and offer to help.

Kee caught nothing today. Or if he did he ate it while I was working on the shelter.

Work is going well. I have both walls started and one wall almost completed. This morning I went hunting with

Kee and we killed two rats, both of them young and tender. Kee was excited by this success and wanted to continue hunting, but I insisted that we stop and eat. Actually it didn't take much persuasion, because we have had almost nothing to eat for the past several days except seeds and shoots.

After we had eaten I got Kee to go with me to the shelter and I lay down between the walls with my head under the ledge to show him how the shelter would work. I thought when he could see the shelter he would understand and want to help, but he had already closed his mind to the shelter and hardly looked.

I showed Kee that I wanted him to help me move a large rock to the shelter. This would have almost completed one side. Kee did it but he acted as though it really pissed him off to have to do what I've been doing for the past several days. It took us a lot longer than I thought to get the rock to the shelter and then it would not fit. Of course Kee just wanted to roll the rock up to the wall and quit but I couldn't do that. I worked and worked with it, but no matter how we placed it the rock left a big gap in the wall, too big to be chinked. I tried to explain to Kee what the problem was, showing him the gap in the wall, but he was in no mood to listen, and there was nothing to do but say to hell with it and roll the rock off to one side.

I felt I had to explain to Kee why I couldn't use the rock after all the work he had done but you can't talk to him when he won't listen. He just looked at me as though it were all my fault and didn't listen or try to understand. I'm afraid it's going to be even harder to get him to help me again.

I don't blame him for feeling frustrated, but what the hell does he know about frustration? I have built the walls only to have them fall down because there was no one to help me. I have found perfect rocks that I couldn't use because I couldn't get them out of the ground by myself. I have had to stop in the middle of everything to go find Kee and beg him to help me. But I can't give up now.

Went hunting again with Kee and we were able to kill one rat, so I can count on his help tomorrow. Kee is fair-minded and when I help him kill food, he helps me build the shelter. It took him a while to get over the frustration of working most of the day on a rock we couldn't use, but when he found that it took two of us to successfully kill enough to eat he was ready to cooperate.

"No work, no eat," I told him. "You help me build, I'll help you hunt. Half the kill is mine, half the shelter is yours."

It's a fair arrangement, but it's slow as hell. Every time I begin to get something done I have to stop and go help Kee hunt. I have gotten enough rocks to complete the walls even though I had to use smaller rocks than I wished in order to move them by myself. All that remains is putting the rocks in place and laying the logs across them and that will take both of us. Once that is done I can finish it myself.

Building the wall is hard, tedious work, as sometimes we must try two or three rocks in one place and try each rock several times to get the best fit. And because Kee cannot understand what we are doing but just goes through the motions, I have to stop each time and explain to him how I want it to go. And he is always dropping them before I am ready. Every one of my fingers has been mashed and I have had three nails torn off. The rocks are so heavy it's all we can do to lift them into place and if Kee lets go at the wrong time or turns the rock the wrong way I could lose a hand.

Kee is strong enough but he has no idea of what we are doing and he wants to drop the rock wherever it's easiest to put it. With any other man I would have been through long ago, but Kee is so careless and clumsy and every time he mashes a finger he wants to quit. Twice I had to stop him from quitting yesterday and he was so angry I decided I had better give him today off.

I hate to bully Kee, but this work must be done and if I let him quit every time he mashes a finger we will never finish. When he tries to leave I step in front of him and say, "No, Kee, work." And I stay in front of him and keep repeating it until he goes back to work.

Kee is larger than I and probably stronger but I refuse to fight him. When he becomes angry and shoves me I keep my hands at my side and say, "Merkans. Friend." But I do not get out of his way. He knows he either has to knock me down or go back and work. I realize I am taking a chance but I don't believe he would ever hit me.

Kee is gone. We were finishing the walls when a rock slipped and fell, catching his hand. His hand was pinned and Kee was in pain but the rock was so heavy I couldn't lift it by myself. I ran to get a limb to use as a lever but there was nothing close by. I found one big enough but it was old and rotten. I found another, which was broken but still attached to the tree. I pulled and twisted on it all I could but I couldn't tear it loose. By the time I found a limb and got back, Kee had somehow gotten his hand free and he was gone. All that was left was a smear of blood on the rocks. A lot of blood. He could be badly hurt.

I don't know what to think. I looked around for him. I called his name. I thought maybe he had become sick and had gone back to the pool to get a drink or lie by the fire, but I can't find him anywhere. What has happened to him? What is he thinking?

Did he think I dropped the rock on purpose? Intentionally to hurt him? Did he think I ran away to leave him pinned to the wall to die? Did he, like a native, go off to suffer in silence and alone? Could he think I wish him harm? Could he be hiding from me in the jungle like a wounded animal? Is he one of those superstitious savages that can make up their mind they are going to die and do it?

If I just knew how badly he was hurt. Maybe he just mashed his finger and went away to hide his pain so as not to appear unmanly. Maybe he's just waiting to regain self-control before he comes back to the shelter. Maybe the pain made him sick and he just went off to lie down for a while. Maybe he wasn't hurt at all. Maybe he just worked his hand free after I left and went off to hunt. He's pulled that before.

But it looked like his hand was really mashed. What if he's really hurt? What if he has passed out from loss of blood? Maybe he's calling me to come and help him. Maybe he's dying. And I am alone now. Alone on this island. With no one.

I haven't heard anything, and when I called he didn't answer. I could go and look for him. But maybe he wants to be alone. Would he think I was trying to interfere? Would he think I was tracking him down to hurt him some more? But if he is really hurt maybe I could help him. But what could I do; I have no training, no medicine, no nothing. But I could clean the wound, maybe bandage it, if he would let me. If he would trust me. It would hurt a little but maybe he would understand that I'm not trying to hurt him, that it gives me no pleasure to cause him pain, that sometimes you have to hurt in order to help.

At least I could comfort him. If he could move I could help him to the fire. I could bring him food and water. I could brush off the flies so he could sleep. I could stay at his side until he is better again, or until—he is dead.

Maybe he is already dead. If so I must go and find him. Bury him. But I have no tools. Nothing to dig with. I could bury him at sea. Put him on the other side of the reef. Perhaps attach a message to him some way so that if he is found—

But suppose he was only playing dead? Suppose he thinks I was trying to hurt him? Suppose he thinks I was looking for a stick not to free him with but to kill him with? Suppose he is lying in ambush, waiting for me to track him down?

We quarreled some over the work. We exchanged words. We both said things we shouldn't have, made faces, threatening gestures, and spat to show contempt. We even shoved each other a little. But how could he think I would deliberately hurt him, try to kill him over something as silly and childish as that? If he could just understand that there was nothing personal in my anger, that I was just trying to get the job done. For both of us.

The truth is, I don't know what he thinks. He risked his life to save me, yet sometimes he doesn't even seem to like me. Sometimes he seems afraid of me. I don't know if he trusts me or not.

1. I will carry on as though I had not noticed his injury or absence, and show no hostility or fear. This will indicate my innocence.

2. I will keep the fire going. This will prove my interest in our mutual safety.

3. I will go hunting and try to find fruit or seeds. Half of what food I find I will save for Kee as evidence of my good intentions.

4. I will go to bed as usual, as though nothing had happened, as proof to Kee, if he is watching, of my lack of guilt.

5. When the night is at its darkest I will move to a different spot away from the fire so that I will not be caught off guard.

So near. We were so near to finishing the shelter. So close to safety. So close to our dream of security.

~

David,

Kee has not returned. For a day and two nights I kept the fire going. I listened for his call. I climbed the mound and called to him. I do not know what to think.

It was an accident, David. The rock would only fit one way. Kee couldn't see this although I had demonstrated how it should go. Kee kept trying to put the rock in ass backwards although I kept telling him, "No, no, no." But he wouldn't listen and I couldn't gesture, because it took both of us to hold the rock. We were both sweating and our hands were slippery, and when I tried to wrench the rock around the right way so it would fit, it slipped out of my hands and caught Kee's hand underneath.

I guess I was angry at first that the rock fell. I was trying so hard to finish the wall and it was Kee's stupidity that caused the rock to fall. Then I saw the pain on his face and realized his hand was caught. I grabbed the rock but I couldn't lift it by myself and with his hand caught he couldn't help, and every time I shifted the rock he would yell in pain. The only thing I knew to do was to get a lever to lift the rock. What else could I do? There was no way I could tell him what I was going to do so I just left. I don't know what he thought. I don't know how he got his hand out. I don't know why he ran away.

David, I have my faults. I know I have hurt people but I didn't intend to. I'm not cruel or sadistic. You always thought of me as your mean kid brother. You thought I hated Dad. You thought I deliberately did things to hurt him. I never hated him, David. I loved him. I just hated to see him fawn on customers, to play the fool, to stick people who were supposed to be his friends. God, how could you love him and watch him do those things? See him demean himself that way?

Mother always thought I said things to him at the store and that's why he came home so upset, but I never said anything to him. I couldn't hide my feelings, that's all. So when he was dealing with the customers I would go down the aisle where I wouldn't have to watch and I would try not to hear. Or I would go hide in the stock room until he came looking for me, calling me lazy because he pretended I was trying to sleep. But he knew, David.

He knew because I was there the day Mr. Dockery came in to pay his bill. That old squinch-eyed man, his teeth discolored by tobacco, the corners of his mouth stained with juice, throwing the money down on the counter in that insolent way he had. "I'm paying this bill, Wally," he said. "But I'll never trade in this store again. I'll drive the sixteen miles to the A and P if I have to get a box of matches. But at least I'll know it's a full box.

"You know why I ain't coming back, Wally? Because you're a chiseler. A nickel-and-dime cheat. You ain't even got the guts to be a crook. Just a little sneak cheat. The last hamburger I got here was mostly oatmeal and the milk was half water. So here's your money. Every last penny. Count it out, you tricky son of a bitch, because I don't ever want it said that I beat you out of a red cent."

And you know what Dad did? He stood there and giggled. He said, "Now, Mr. Dockery, ha ha, this can all be straightened out. I'll talk to Harry about that hamburger. I've told him before, ha ha—Greg. Where's Greg? You haven't been putting water in the milk have you, Greg? I told you—I'll straighten it out, Mr. Dockery. If there's been a mistake, I'll straighten it out. You see, my boy here hasn't been working for me long. Now, David, he knew the business, but Greg here—ha ha—I have to keep my eye on old Greg."

And he counted the money. Every penny. Having to get down on his knees and pick up some from under the counter. "That's correct, Mr. Dockery. You're paid in full. Ha ha. Yes sir, if you'll just give me another chance. I haven't spent as much time in the store lately as I should have. I haven't been feeling well, and I've kind of let things slide. Harry's worked for me a long time, but now Harry, ha ha, he don't always—If you don't think this bill is correct, why—Gregory, did you make out Mr. Dockery's bill? You better take another look at this and be sure you didn't—"

I know he was my father. I know he did what he did to provide us with the house, and the car, and a college education. I know he did it for us. But if he had just once acted like a man. If he had slapped old man Dockery's face. If he had thrown him out of the store. If he had said, "Yes, I cheated you because you're such a stupid old fart. Now, pick up your damn money and don't ever set foot in this store again."

But to try to place the blame on me and Mr. Watson. To jump on Harry because he wasn't mixing the oatmeal into the hamburger good enough, when everybody in town knew it was mixed. To take his spite out on Harry because Harry had to take it, because Harry had been working for him so long he couldn't hardly quit. To kiss Mr. Dockery's ass and beg the old fart to come back.

You know what he said to me when it was all over? "He'll come back. He's not going to drive sixteen miles just to get a loaf of bread. Not that old tightwad. See, that's why I had to pretend it was you. To give him a chance to come back. He'll come in some day and say 'Your kid still watering the milk?' And I'll say, 'No, Mr. Dockery, I've got him filling up the watermelons.' Like that, and we'll both laugh and it'll be all over. Mr. Dockery's a good customer. Got a lot of mouths to feed."

I couldn't respect him after that, David. I tried to but I couldn't. And no matter how I tried I couldn't laugh at his jokes or hide the way I felt. That's why I hated working in the store. That's why he pretended he thought I was lazy.

And Ruby. You thought I used her. You thought she was so innocent. Just because she was a little strange. Just because she talked about being a nun all the time. You never saw her dancing naked or looking at herself in her bedroom mirror. You never saw her spread out in the back seat of a car. You thought I took advantage of her because she wasn't right. David, she wanted to get pregnant. She wanted a baby. She didn't care anything about me, she was just using me. You always acted like I took advantage of her. David, she chased me.

I used to walk down the alley behind her house on the way home from the store. She would always beg me to play with her. Offer me chewing gum to play with her. I didn't want to play with her. I felt silly playing games with a girl. And what did I want with her damn chewing gum? But I felt sorry for her. No one else would play with her and her dad was always at the store. She was always alone. So I'd stop to talk to her. And sometimes I'd play with her.

The games she played—I was always some mean guy who tortured her and did evil things to her, and then something bad would happen to me, and I'd be dying or drowning and she'd save me and nurse me back to health, and I'd be so grateful. I would follow her around like a pet monkey and throw myself in mud puddles so she could step on me, and kill anybody who tried to touch her.

One day it was raining and we had to play in the house. I didn't want to go in the house. You know how Harry was. All the time he'd worked for Dad none of us had ever been in his house. But Ruby begged me and said she'd give me a Coke. But then when I got in the house I was supposed to pretend I was mean and make her stand out in the rain. Then I became ill and she was the only one who could save me so I let her come in out of the rain and she gave me the Coke as medicine.

When I finished the Coke I figured I'd better get on home, but first I had to thank her for saving my life. I was supposed to get down on my knees and kiss her bare wet feet. I was just a kid, David. I didn't know anything about girls. Mom and Dad never told me anything. I was just going to pretend to kiss her feet because you remember what Ruby looked like. But she was wiggling her toes like she was ticklish so I kissed her feet just to tickle her. She wiggled her feet some more and it was kind of funny so I kissed her some more. I kissed her on the ankles and she had goose bumps all over her. You remember how fat and white she was. I kissed her just to make her get goose flesh. I thought she was laughing until I looked up. You should have seen her, David. Her face was all twisted and she was moaning and wiggling, and she started pulling at her clothes and saying, "Mother of God," and things like that.

I didn't know what to do, David. I was scared. No one told me girls were like that. I tried to get away from her but I couldn't. She kept pulling at me. I didn't want to hurt her but she was so big I couldn't get her off of me without hurting her so I just lay back and—

When it was over she cried and prayed and wanted me to kneel and pray with her when all I wanted was to get away, get out of the house, wash off the smell of her, never see her again.

I was scared, David. I was so scared I ran all the way home. If I had just had someone to talk to, someone to tell me what to do. I tried to avoid her, I took the long way home so as not to pass her house, but she would follow me around at school. "Greg, when are you going to come play with me?" I tried to ignore her but she wouldn't let me. I asked her to leave me alone but she wouldn't. I thought maybe if I was mean to her—I went back to see her after school. I abused her, David, I said she was a tramp. I called her dirty names. I even hit her. I couldn't help it. She was so fat and meek and servile. And then when I hit her she began to cry. I'd never hit a girl before and I really hurt her. I was afraid she would tell Harry. I started patting her and begging her not to tell. She started trying to save me, and we did the whole thing over again.

Even while I was doing it I promised myself if I got away from her I would never go back again no matter what. But when I didn't go to see her she would send me notes. God, you should have seen them. Wild, crazy things. Once during a school holiday she sent a note to the store by her dad. "Ruby wanted me to give you this."

I almost died on the spot. You know how Harry was about Ruby. How he dared anyone to make fun of Ruby or act as though she were anything but perfectly normal. You remember what a fit he threw when one of her teachers said she needed special help, and how he had her sit at the front of the church so everyone could see what a fine girl she was. I knew he wanted me to tell him why Ruby would send me a note but I couldn't think of anything. And I knew if she sent me another one he would read it.

I was trapped, David. I hated going back to that house, being in her room, but I had to. Each time it was worse. the games got longer and she got wilder. She wouldn't let me leave. I would have to fight her to get away before Harry got home. I didn't realize then that she wanted to have a baby. I didn't realize she wanted her father to catch us. I think I was a little relieved when he did. At least the worst had happened. I think I already knew she was pregnant.

I never intended to hurt her, David, I swear to God. I even tried to run away with her so she could keep the baby, but I couldn't. I even sneaked the car out of the garage, but I knew Dad would have the cops stop us before we could get across the state line. It wouldn't have worked anyway. I know a lot of it was my fault but I didn't mean to hurt her. It was because no one ever told me about girls like that, and there was no one I could talk to. It was an accident, David. Just as it was with Kee. I didn't mean to hurt him. I've never wanted to hurt anybody. Not even that Jap.

David, I've never told this to anybody, but I was the last man in the squadron to score a kill. There was a lot of kidding about it because some of the guys were already aces and we had lost several planes and three pilots ourselves. It bothered me some, I mean, what the hell, but I was doing my job—escorting the bombers, flying CAP, making strafing and bomb runs. I got a few Nip planes in my sights and I know I hit one, but I didn't see it go down so I didn't claim it.

Then one day we were vectored out to intercept some bogeys closing in from the east. By the time we reached the area, planes from another carrier had broken the formation, knocking down five. My division climbed to 24,000 feet and circled back looking for stragglers through broken clouds.

Captain Willett spotted something, yelled "tally-ho," and winged over. I followed him down to keep his tail clear. The Jap must have ducked into a cloud, because Willett went in after him and I veered off to catch the Jap if he cut back out. But they must have gone straight through the cloud because I didn't spot either of them.

I started to climb for a better look when I saw something low on the water. I dropped down for a closer look, and sure enough it was a Jap Oscar low on the water and headed for home. He didn't seem to have spotted me, and with the altitude I had I knew I had him bagged so I cleared my tail and threw everything to the firewall.

I was closing fast, thinking how the guys couldn't kid me any more and how good that meatball was going to look painted on my fuselage, and the bastard hadn't even spotted me yet. Then I knew something was wrong. Either he was setting me up for a pal who had me bore-sighted out of the sun, or he was hoping I'd overshoot and be easy pickings. I looked at the sun, blinked and looked again. Nothing. I cleared my tail. Nothing. The son of a bitch was low and alone. An easy kill. I cut the throttle for fear in my eagerness I'd overshoot. I was going to do this slow and by the book, leaving no chance for mistakes.

I switched on the gunsight and charged the guns. I was almost within range. Then I knew what it was. The poor bastard was either wounded or low on fuel. He wasn't thinking about dropping a bomb or being a hero for the Emperor. He was just trying to get his ass back to his home base. Just trying to escape, and he didn't have a prayer. Just hoping that one of his buddies would come to his rescue or that I would run out of ammo before his plane fell apart. Or that I was too chicken-hearted to kill.

I checked the sight ring and fired a short burst for range, watching the tracers lace into his tail. He knew I was there now for certain and I hoped he would ditch or try to evade, but he still held his course, either unable to maneuver or paralyzed with fear.

I checked the sight ring again. Within range and closing. A no-deflection shot. I cleared my tail and fired a short burst that smoked him. I pulled up and fish-tailed so I didn't overshoot and I was right on his wing tip. I was so close I could see blood splattered on the canopy and red streaks running out of the holes in the fuselage, and still he held the plane in the air, nursing it back home.

I thought of Pearl Harbor. I thought of Wake Island and the Bataan Death March. I thought of how the bastard had shot up the Task Force and then tried to sneak home. I thought of how he had machine-gunned my buddies in their life rafts or hanging from their parachutes. I thought if I killed him maybe the war would be over sooner. Nothing helped.

I aimed at his wingroots and held the trigger down until the plane blew apart. I didn't feel elated the way I thought I would. I even orbited, hoping to see a parachute or life raft. Nothing. My fuel was running low and I had to get back to the carrier, but all I could think about was that poor bastard all alone, hoping to sneak back home. Then he spots me closing in behind him and he's too wounded or the plane is too damaged to jink and all he can do is hold it in the air and watch me close in and hope that by some miracle I will let him nurse the plane back to the base. And then he feels my slugs tearing into the plane.

I'm not a killer, David. I know that now. Everyone had me convinced that I used Ruby, that I deliberately hurt Dad. But I know now that I couldn't intentionally hurt them, just as I couldn't strike Kee. But I have accidentally hurt him and it was my responsibility to go to his aid.

I cannot live here alone. Even if by myself I could finish the shelter, even if I could survive the storm. I could not alone face the horror and despair of this place. Therefore I am going in search of Kee, to help him if I can. It may be that he cannot understand that his injury was an accident. It may be that he cannot trust me to help him. It may be that his code requires that he exact some measure of revenge. It does not matter. If we cannot live together then I am prepared to be the one to die, because I cannot kill.

I am placing this book in a safe place in the cave with a pile of rocks over it and a cross made of sticks to invite curiosity. This I have done so that this book will be placed in your hands if I do not return. If by some chance this book is found, if by some miracle Kee is discovered alive and I am not, forgive him for my sake. He did not understand.

~

NOTE TO SURVIVAL INSTRUCTORS: *The cross as a signal*

There are three reasons for using the cross as a signal or marker.

1. It is obviously manmade.

2. It is one of the easiest forms to make and can be tied together without nails.

3. Association in the discover's mind will cause him to think that it is a grave or holy place. The superstitious will avoid it, the religious will excavate it.

~

I have found Kee. When he did not return I went looking for him to pledge my help, softly calling his name so as not to surprise or frighten him. I thought he might be hiding in the jungle and I searched through it for hours without a trace. I thought I had looked everywhere and was beginning to fear that out of pain or desperation Kee had drowned himself. And then it came to me. Kee had gone to the tree.

It was almost dark when I got there and I could not see him, but I knew he was there. I could smell him. The smell of sickness and dried blood and clotted pus. And I could hear him—the shallow breath, the low moans. He was lying beside the tree and his hand was placed on the trunk, resting on the three knobs or protrusions. He had not run away for fear or anger after all.

In his pain he had sought out the tree. Perhaps because it spoke to him of home, childhood, work and play—of climbing and swinging in its branches and making love beneath its shade, a tree from his grandfather's village, his mother's garden, a tree of memories, of commonplace things. Or maybe he turned to the tree because it was a voice from beyond and spoke to him in strange words of far-off places and secret dreams, of caves and rivers, mysterious valleys, hidden treasures, forgotten worlds. Perhaps the tree spoke to him of purpose, of plans bigger than his life, greater than the island, and he lay down beside it in supplication and placed his hand on the tree in petition or submission. Or maybe he lay down in the lagoon because he was feverish and placed his hand on the tree to keep his wound dry.

I called his name softly so as not to startle him. "Kee, I have come to help you," I said. He raised his head and looked at me and I do not know what it was I saw in his face—fear, shame, a plea for help—all that and more. But I saw no anger there. No hatred. I don't know what my own face was showing. Pity perhaps. Or maybe the same thing his face was showing—pain, and fear, and shame, and a plea for help.

"California," I said.

"California," he said, trying to smile.

Slowly I sank to my knees beside him and held out my hands. "Show me your hand, Kee, so I can help," I said. At first he hid his hand. And I said again, "Show me your hand, Kee, so I can help." Carefully he raised his hand. He held it out to me.

I turned away. I turned away quickly, but not quickly enough. The hand was crushed. Bits of bone protruded through the swollen flesh and a thick yellowish putrid fluid oozed around the bones. Red streaks ran up his arm and knots had formed under his armpit.

"The reason I didn't come sooner was because I didn't know. I didn't understand," I said.

"California," he said, so faintly I could scarcely make out the word.

Kee was so weak from hunger and fever that he could not support himself. But I knew I had to get him to the fire, to food and water as quickly as possible. As gently as I could I picked him up, being careful not to touch his hand, not to look at it. As gently as I could I dragged and carried him, stopping several times to retch. When I got him to the fire there was no food, but I put him in the pool to ease the fever, and making sure that he would not slip in and drown, I went in search of food, of course finding nothing in the darkness.

When I got back to the fire, Kee seemed to be stronger and the fever had diminished. As there was nothing else I could do I sat down by the fire and tried to rest, dozing from time to time.

Something woke me, and when I looked up I saw Kee crawling toward me, his head and shoulders seeming to float above a layer of fog, his hand extended. His eyes were rolled back. His mouth was open. "Kago viti ruke," he said. "Help me." The night was dark and wisps of ground fog lay under the trees. In my stupor I thought it was a nightmare and that when I tried to run I would not be able to move. "Kago viti ruke," he said, placing the hand on my leg. "Help me." It was no dream but I could not run.

I thought I would be sick again, throwing up the sour, bitter, stinging water, but there was nothing left in my stomach. I looked down at the hand, trying to see it objectively, trying to think what to do. I'm no doctor. I have had no training. There are no instruments. No bandages. No medicine. Gently I placed my hand about his wrist, turning the hand toward the firelight. Several of the small bones in the hand were broken. Three of the fingers were crushed. The index finger was the most severely damaged—badly mangled and almost disjointed. The bleeding had stopped, but the hand was infected and the flesh had swollen until the skin had split. The hand is useless. Our plans are ruined. The shelter will never be completed.

Not knowing what to do, I held his hand gently under my arm and talked soothingly to him hoping he would sleep, hoping that daylight would bring answers, and healing, and hope.

"What will be the end of us?" I said. "What will we do now? What are the sounds of rescue? What are the signs of hope? And who can help us? The food has failed. The shelter has failed. The storm will return. There is no luck in which we may hope. There is no plan on which we may rely. There is no one to save.

"Why are you here?" I asked him. "How did you get here? Why did this happen to you? What is your secret, Kee? Where is your hope?"

Thus did we spend the night.

Morning brought no healing, no hope, no answers. Morning brought increased sensibility, heightened perception. Morning brought the sight of broken bones, the smell of rotting flesh, the taste of vomit and bile, the sounds of moans and pleas for help. Kee held out his hand to me and begged me to help. There was no one else to do it.

1. I sharpened a stick by rubbing it against a rock and hardened it by charring.

2. With the stick I carefully opened the wounds, draining them by gentle pressure, washing them in fresh water, and sucking out the poison.

3. I took a rock and split it to get a sharp edge. I honed this edge as best I could with grinding and chopping.

4. Taking the sharpened rock, I heated it in the fire and amputated the forefinger by chopping away the flesh from around the broken bone.

5. With hot coals I burned the wounds to stop bleeding and prevent infection.

6. With clean leaves I bound the hand to keep out dirt and flies and to hold the bones in place until they knit.

7. Taking the severed finger, I buried it in the coals and stirred until it was thoroughly charred to avoid contamination and to prevent it from being dug up by ants and rats.

Kee watched the whole time. Sometimes he came close to fainting but he never took his eyes off me. Not watching my hands or what I was doing to him but watching me, studying my face.

I don't know what he saw there. I haven't been trained to hide my feelings or to pretend emotions that are not real. I couldn't help it that in his nakedness and suppurating flesh he was repulsive to me, that every time I spat out the poison I gagged until all I could do was shudder. It was only natural that I was pleased that the rock worked, relieved that it neatly severed the flesh. Where would he be if it hadn't worked? And if he saw satisfaction in my face that I had done a competent job that is nothing to be ashamed of. I did the best I could. Maybe others could have done better, but I was proud of what I did. Proud I had been able to do it. And that's what he saw in my face. Not cruelty. Not pleasure. And I felt shame because of what I saw in Kee's face.

What was it I saw there? It wasn't hatred or even anger. It was resentment that I was whole, that he was dependent on me, that to help him I must cause him pain. And there was shame that he was hurt and helpless, that I had seen him so, that his need made prisoners of us both.

Kee is asleep now and seems to be resting. I must go hunt food so that he will regain his strength. I am responsible now not only for the health and well-being of myself but of two men. He who is strongest must bear the burden of both. As long as there is food Kee will eat. As long as there is strength in me, he will live.

NOTE TO SURVIVAL INSTRUCTORS: *First aid kits*

First aid kits should include:

1. General anesthetic
2. Surgical knife
3. Sterile probe
4. Sutures

Have been unable to find anything to eat. Handful of grass seeds. Some bark that gave us both cramps. It rained today and there is the beginning of fruit on the trees. If we can only hold on for a little while there will be fruit again. And after the fruit—the storm?

I have been unable to kill any of the rats that appeared to be so numerous after the storm. There seem to be few of them left. The storm, the failure of the fruit, and our hunting and burning of their nesting places seem to have thinned them out. I am afraid the island is large enough to support only one man. Yet, when I return to the fire empty-handed, I find Kee watching me in disappointment, perhaps even contempt. But I am whole, therefore the responsibility is mine.

Kee seems in less pain but he is very weak. I must find him some meat, even if it means burning down the whole island to flush out the rats. He is very restless. When I wake up at night he is watching me, but when I sit up he pretends to be asleep. Last night he appeared to be hiding something in his hand. But what could it be? Food that he has discovered near the fire and does not wish to share?

This morning while hunting for food I came upon the shelter. The stain of Kee's blood is still upon its walls and it seems not to have changed in any way. It will stand for a long time—long after we are gone—a kind of monument. Anyone who comes to the island will see it and catch a glimpse of the size and glory of the dream we had—a dream of safety. Of refuge.

For a long time I poked about the shelter, studying it, trying to figure ways of finishing it. But without Kee it is impossible. We huddle naked beside our little fire, impotent before circumstance, powerless to alter fate, peering blindly into the darkness about us.

If only we could call down a Jap float plane, cause it to land in the lagoon, we could overpower the pilot and gunner and I could fly us to safety. At least to another island. An hour in the air would be enough. Half an hour would be enough. If we could only climb up to five thousand feet for one look to fix our position and plot a course to the nearest island.

If only we knew some words of Japanese or had a Jap flag. Some Jap symbol that would call a plane down. What would a Jap want that he would land in the lagoon to get? He might land to investigate our fire, or the reason for the clearings on the island. More likely he would just radio a report. There is no way to call down a Jap plane and no one to save us. Only our own desperate devices. But I will not sit here idly watching Kee die, wasting away myself. I will do what I can.

Could kill nothing today but found some wild potatoes that I took back to the fire to share with Kee. But when I got there Kee seemed to be hiding something in his hands. I thought it was a bit of food he was holding out on me while I shared everything with him, and I caught his wrists and forced his hands apart. I am surprised that I had not noticed it before. Had not smelled it. Pus oozed around the rotting leaves I had wrapped about his hand.

No one ever told me how to live without hope, how to live with continuing horror. No one prepared me for this. All they ever said was, "Hope for the best. Look for the silver lining." They never told me where to look when there was no hope, no silver lining. In school they said, "A man who won't be beat, can't be beat." How did they reconcile that with a team that lost half its games and a school that operated along the path of least resistance? "Help your buddy," they said in flight training. "His life may depend on you." They didn't say what to do when you can't help. What to do when you can't heal.

I can scarcely bear the smell of Kee's hand. I can't bear to look at it. Yet I know that I am responsible for it because I tried to help him, tried to heal. Now I will never be free of that horror, that sickness and shame, until Kee is whole again.

I am no longer capable of lofty thoughts. I am no longer capable of exalted feelings. It seems incredible to me that I once laughed, that I once feared death, that I once believed in tomorrow. It seems incredible to me that I was once the master of a machine and had the controls in my own hands. That I could fly. That I could climb into the sky and loop and roll and glide. That I once believed I was the master of my fate and controlled circumstance. I know now that life is blind, without hope or meaning. My only wish is to die.

David, I can't last much longer. Kee's hand gets worse and worse and there is nothing I can do. I can't bring myself to examine it. I no longer care what people think, but you have misjudged me before, David, and in order to help you understand, I add the following.

1. What I saw outside the reef was a large fish, probably being attacked by sharks. It was not a man. No man could live on an island like this and watch another man die. If it had been a man I would have risked my life to save him as Kee risked his life to save me.

2. I did not have appendicitis. It must have been stomach cramps, due to eating wild raw potatoes. It has not recurred. However, there is a sore on my arm. At first I believed it was a jungle ulcer. I know now that it is cancer.

3. David, as you know, there is talk about homosexuality among groups of men who are kept in close association such as in prisons, ships, etc. I believe such talk is entirely without foundation as I have never witnessed anything of

the sort. Kee and I are naked but certainly there have been no such feelings between us. Kee saved me from the sea and I saved him from the island. We are responsible for each other. I have done what I can for him because he is a human being, and because I could not live here alone. That is all there is between us. However, I am unable to directly deny thoughts of homosexuality, since a denial would be construed as a clear admission of guilt. Please alter the text in whatever way is necessary to avoid misunderstanding.

4. The animals we ate were not really rats. At least not the kind we have back home. Their diet is vegetable.

5. Since the storm our life has been one of abject misery. Digging for grubs. Eating rats. We are naked. Covered with sores. Kee is dying and there is nothing I can do. What use is there, David? At least let us die while we are still capable of courage. Of decision.

6. What happened with Bunny was—I didn't hurt her. I was insistent but I didn't force her. I was very gentle. So gentle she cried. You know what she said? She said, "There was an emptiness in me that was never filled until you filled it." And I knew she wanted me to say something. That I was sorry. Or that I loved her. Or that I would marry her. But I didn't. I didn't know what to say. I took her panties to show the guys back in the barracks, and I left.

7. David, I wish you would check on my kill. It was an Oscar. I blew him all to hell, but I didn't have time to look for friendly planes to verify. I was running low on fuel. I had a good fix on the carrier and when I spotted it I had only a few minutes left. I got in the pattern and the LSO gave me the go around. Too high. I came around again knowing I had to make this one good. Knowing the engine

might quit with me too low to land on the carrier and too high to ditch without hitting the fantail. And I did make it good. I was in the groove and that LSO bastard gave me the wave-off. Someone hadn't cleared the barrier. I didn't have enough fuel to make another go around or to try for another carrier, and I knew I could hang a cable. I chopped the throttle, nosed over for a quick look, corrected, pulled the nose up into a full stall, hit hard and bounced but I hooked up and slammed to a stop before I hit anything.

I held up a finger when I taxied past the bridge to let them know I got a kill and I ran down to the ready room to tell the rest of the division. I was going to drop my parachute over a chair, hang up my Mae West and goggles, and say, "Scratch one Oscar."

But before I could say anything the LSO followed me into the ready room and read me off in front of everybody for taking a cut. When I tried to explain that it was come on in or ditch beside the pick-up destroyer and lose the plane, the Air Officer jumped me too, threatening to ground me. Hell, I knew they weren't going to ground me as badly as they needed pilots. I wasn't worried about that. But when I reported my kill he asked for verification, as though I had carried spectators with me.

"I didn't have time to look for any witnesses," I said. "He blew all to hell. What more do you want?"

He made a note of it. "We'll check the gun camera," he said. "I hope it was working."

I don't know whether they gave me credit for it or not, David. It was a cloudy day, and those damn cameras didn't always work. They wouldn't take my word for it because I took a cut. Hell, I saved their damn airplane for them. But you could check, David. I know I got him. I splattered the bastard all over the windscreen. I blew him all to hell.

8. David, I realize I haven't been much of a brother. I guess we were never close the way some brothers are. We never seemed to do things together. But we had some moments, I guess. Working together in the stock room. Eating grapes and snitching candy.

Remember the time I got lost at camp? God, I was scared. I'd never even been alone before and here I was lost and it getting dark. I could see snakes under every bush and I was so scared I just sat down and cried. Then you found me. You said, "Come on, Greg, or we'll miss supper."

I'll never forget that. You didn't make fun of me for crying or bawl me out for getting lost. And when we got back to camp and the counselors came running out to scold me and the other kids crowded around to make fun of me, you told them I had been looking for arrowheads and you showed them two to prove it.

I still got chewed out but I didn't mind because the other kids weren't gloating any more. They were envious. I never did know where you got the arrowheads, David, but that day you could have pissed on me and I wouldn't have said a word.

And the time you came home with your wings. God, I was proud of you. My brother, a pilot. I'll bet you were the first person in Wonder Springs to ever go up in an airplane by himself. I was proud just to stand in your shadow. I was proud just to have the same name and eat at the same table. I didn't even mind when you got the car and took Helen to the movies.

When you got home we stayed up the rest of the night talking. How sick Dad was and how bad he looked, as though everything inside him were caving in. You said that Helen was my girl and the only reason you went with her was because there was no one else in town. You said that all you and she talked about was me, and the reason you kissed her was because you might not see her again.

We talked about what it was like to fly. The chances of our ever getting in the war. You said they had assigned you to bombers and I decided I would try for bombers too, and maybe we could go on missions together looking out for each other. But whatever happened, when we came back home, we'd be ourselves, we wouldn't be Wallace's boys any more.

I was going to take over the store at home, and you were going to set up stores in different places. Clean, well-lighted stores. Organized. Efficient. And when people came in they wouldn't expect a pat on the back and the latest joke, they'd expect the best food, the fastest service, and the fairest prices. We talked all night, and not once did you call me "Walrus."

I am not a wicked man. I have faults. I have made mistakes, but I have done the best I could. If circumstances had been otherwise I would have been different. But what can you expect when you grow up in a place like Wonder Springs, where everyone knows everybody else's business. If Dad had let me have the car I would never have gone to see Ruby. Even if I had, Mr. Watson would never have caught us in his car, parked in his garage, the one day in his life he left work early to drive over to Westcliff to see the doctor. Surely Ruby must have known that.

But even that wouldn't have mattered if Ruby hadn't been pregnant, or if Dad had just had the guts to face things instead of promising to send Ruby to convent school and running all over town telling people he wouldn't hurt Ruby Watson for the world and that he was going to make it up to Harry.

If Mom had just talked to Ruby when she came to the house. Who else did Ruby know that she could go to? What other woman could she have turned to for sympathy, or advice, or whatever the hell she wanted. If Mom had just explained that she would have to go away, that she would have to give up the baby, that it was for the best but some day she could have other children.

But to give Ruby a suitcase of our old baby clothes, which she had kept all those years stuffed into a closet, and to send her out in the rain when everyone knew they weren't going to let her keep the baby. And you know what else Mother gave her, David? I swear it to God, she gave her a handful of flowers.

Ruby would have been all right if they had left her alone. Even sending her to convent school would have been all right. I think Ruby would have liked that. Even being pregnant might have been all right if they had explained why she couldn't keep it. If they had let her see it. But to just take it like that when she wanted it most.

And making me go see her in the institution. That was stupid. That was revenge. As though seeing me would help her when she didn't even know who she was. Sitting in the bare corner of the asylum wall, pretending she was in a convent garden. It was revenge pure and simple. Making me talk to her about Ruby when she never wanted to hear or think of Ruby again. As though I had made her what she was. As though I were the one who had always called her "angel" and had made her sit at the front of church, and had stood watching her fornication through the steamed-over car window. As though I were the one who had called her "whore" and "slut" and had stared at her nakedness, and had beaten her fat naked body, and had condemned her to live behind walls, and had taken away her baby.

Things would have been different with Bunny if it hadn't been for Ruby and the war. I had never known anyone like Bunny. When she laughed it was because she wanted to laugh, not because she wanted to make someone else laugh. When she gave you a flower or a kiss it was because it pleased her to give it, not because it pleased you to get it. When she talked it was because she wanted to listen and share and when she was silent it was because she wanted just to be with you.

I needed someone like Bunny to talk to, someone to share the excitement and adventure and the haunting fear that I might fail. When I made a bad landing it helped to know that she would share the failure. And on those rare occasions when my instructor felt obliged to compliment me—"That wasn't too bad, Wallace, we may teach you to fly yet"—the triumph was doubled by sharing it with Bunny.

But there was a war on and no one counted too much on tomorrow. There wasn't time for holding hands, and writing poetry, and walking in the moonlight. Bunny was an everyday girl and I wanted a weekend wife.

Ruby taught me that girls weren't sugar and spice the way Mom and the other old ladies pretended. I knew they didn't want to get married just so they could cook and clean house and change diapers. After Ruby I knew that what girls said and what they did were two different things, and I wasn't interested in what they said. And being in Primary, I couldn't get married.

After that incident on the porch I didn't call or go to see Bunny for a while. I should have apologized or sent her flowers or something. I really wanted to see her again but I kept remembering what a mess Ruby had been. And when Bunny called to say she thought she had a little something in the hangar, I should have tried to help her work something out, but I was tired of being blamed for everything and I just couldn't go through that again. "Tough luck, baby," I said. "I've got a war to fight."

But I did try to do something just before I shipped out of Primary. I called that football player, whatever his name was, the one with the sideburns and wavy hair who thought he was Victor Mature, and told him that Bunny was knocked up and that he should marry her for the good of the service. And after I got to Intermediate I wrote her that when I got my wings and commission I would be able to marry her, and if she hadn't already married the football player to let me know. But she never answered the letter. I never knew if he asked her or if she married him. I've never known if she kept the baby, or even for sure that she was pregnant.

I never really got over Bunny. If it hadn't been for the lousy war—If there had just been time—If they had sent me to an Intermediate base way off from any place where I would have had time to think, time to realize what Bunny meant to me, what I had lost. But they sent me to an Intermediate base near Helen's college. And Helen was delighted to see me. Helen admired my uniform. Helen ran down the stairs to kiss me. So I wrote Bunny offering to marry her if necessary and got squared away to accept Helen's attentions and to win my wings.

But Helen wasn't there waiting the way Bunny had been; Helen never seemed to understand about flying. When they laid out the target with all my hits on it and all the guys whistled and groaned and Captain Slack said, "My God, it's Eddie Rickenbacker"—I was so excited to tell Helen I got lost and almost missed the bus. But when I got there, Helen was with some girl and I had to wait almost an hour, and all she could talk about was how her friend had made the sorority. I thought of Bunny. How I wished I could tell her. How happy she would be. How she would understand, and cling to my arm, and smile, she would be so proud. And how I would make love to her or go down trying.

I asked Helen to wait for me, to write me because it was important that there should be someone to care, someone to come home to, but Helen wouldn't promise and when I shipped out she wouldn't even kiss me goodbye. I can't tell you what that did to me, David. The girl I had asked to marry me wouldn't even kiss me goodbye. Why? What had I done? David, I treated her like a princess. Mother could have gone on any date with us and not been embarrassed. Was Helen afraid of what Miss Manning and the other girls might think? Was she frigid? Was she in love with someone else? Was she just teasing me, stringing me along?

If Helen had kissed me goodbye, if she had just promised to write I would never have looked at a whore like Lisa. But I was feeling rotten about the way Helen had treated me and I was lonely my last night in the States, and Lisa was lying beside me on the bed telling me how long it had been since she had seen her husband. And I thought, "What the hell? It's a long war and this may be the last pussy you'll ever get."

I know my life wasn't all it should have been, but I was as good as my training. How was I to know there were girls like Ruby? No one told me what I should say to Bunny. How could I understand a girl like Helen? The only thing Mother ever said about sex was that nice people didn't do it, and she and the other women I knew pretended in spite of marriage, children, and double beds that nothing like that had ever happened to them. And Dad and the other men huddled in the store and winked and smirked and talked like sex was a trick you played on a girl, and only on a girl you didn't love. And if you left her pregnant and desperate you were a real winner. "Shall I carry Harry or hari kari?" And they all snickered, elbowing each other, as though flesh did not record consequence and pain.

No one told me that people making love abused each other. No one told me that that wasn't the end of it but only the beginning, that a brief victory over a girl was a lasting debt. No one told me how to keep from being used by Ruby after I had used her. No one told me what to say to Bunny after I had played a trick on her. No one told me what to think of Helen, who didn't do that kind of thing.

No one ever told me about war and loneliness and fear. How could they let me go off that way? As though war were an elaborate game? As though all the dancing and shouting, all the movies and parties, music and tears, all the drunkenness and loneliness, brief affairs and lasting goodbyes were without consequence and pain? How could Mother not have known? How could you be silent, David? How could Dad have forgotten? How could he and his Legion buddies have pretended that war was a practical joke played on women, superior officers, and the French police?

How could they have made hardtack, hobnail boots, and 40-8 boxcars glamorous? How could my instructors have pretended that I was destroying machines—ships, airplanes, tanks? There was a man in that airplane, David. A human being. And he wanted to live, Mother. He wanted to go back home, Dad. Back to his father and mother and the house and the town—And I kept punching holes in his wings and fuselage, splattering blood and chunks of flesh on the canopy.

Why didn't someone tell me we would be left in the water to chew off our tongues, left on islands to eat our hearts in despair? How could Dad forget that men scream and bleed and cry for their mothers? How could Dad forget that a man's bones shatter, his guts explode in tangles, his eardrums burst and his eyeballs pop from his skull, his hair sizzles and his skin curls and fries?

It wasn't all my fault. If things had been different I would have been different too.

My God, a boat. We have found a lifeboat. My God, it's like the answer to prayer. Not a Jap float plane but something just as good. With a plane we could get off faster, higher, but the boat requires no fuel, it will carry us longer, and it's safer. My God, it's even better than a plane.

I was just sitting beside the fire with Kee, too despondent even to look for food. We had reached the end of the flight deck, flaps down, throttle open, and it was fly or die. There was no other way to put it. I decided to climb the mound for one last look around for a ship or something on the horizon—not out of desperation or curiosity, but as a matter of form, something I ought to do.

And I saw it. A lifeboat. Riding low in the water but still afloat. There was no doubt about it, but still I wanted Kee to see it, to verify it. I did not want to believe too easily. I did not want to be fooled by false hope. I dragged Kee halfway up the mound for a look at it and then we had the same idea. The sea was running high, and if we didn't get the boat over the reef the waves would knock it to pieces against the coral.

Because of our weakness it took us a long time to get out to the reef and then I thought we would never be able to get the boat over the reef, because it was heavy and half filled with water. The waves kept knocking us down and pulling us about, and both of us got bad cuts on the coral and Kee hurt his injured hand.

But we got the boat into the quiet water of the lagoon and just held on to it, gathering strength to push it ashore. It was almost dusk by the time we got it to shallow water, and we were too weak and exhausted to beach it. But we grounded it and it's safe. I have gone back twice to check it and tomorrow we will beach it and examine it for repairs. It was damaged some by the reef.

But we have a boat now. The means of escape is in our hands. Into our darkest day has come salvation. It's like a miracle. It's like the answer to prayer. Not what we asked for—a Jap float plane—but something just as good. Maybe even better, because in our weakness we might have been unable to overpower the pilot and gunner, or on the verge of landing safely behind our lines we might have been shot down by our own guns. And we didn't know how to call down a float plane.

It is almost as though there were a Purpose, a Design in this world that saved me from the air only to be thrown into the sea, that saved me from the sea only to be cast away on an island, and has now presented me with the means of escaping this island and finding safety.

The remedy for all our troubles is at hand. We can get off the island, escape hunger and the storm, find safety and medical attention. In our hands is the means of escape. At last fate is in our own grasp. We are not dependent on the caprice of rescuers, or the ability of searchers. We can decide our own future, and whether we live or die it will be because of our own action.

The lifeboat is about two and a half times the length of a man and perhaps an arm span in the beam. It does not appear to be a regulation naval craft, but neither does it appear to be a civilian fishing boat. It is perhaps a lifeboat of a type with which I am not familiar. It contains no food, medicine, survival gear, life jackets, signaling equipment, or oars, although it is fitted with three oarlocks on each side. Two of these have been damaged, either by rust or crushing against the reef or perhaps the side of a ship.

The wood seems to be pine, although I am not sure they use pine in boats, and it appears to be quite old. The bottom is covered with barnacles and things, the paint is completely gone below the water line and above the water line remains only in protected areas. It appears to be a dull reddish brown, a kind of barn-door red gone to mud, or tin-can rust that has been wet—but this color may be due to exposure and fading. As a result of the pounding on the reef the boat has sprung a leak in the bottom.

In addition to the oarlocks the boat seems to have been equipped with a sail, as there is a bracket near the center of the boat and tie-downs on the gunwale. All traces of the sail and mast are gone. If there was a hand line around the outside of the boat it is also gone. If the boat had a rudder or centerboard they are also lost.

On the left side, the boat has been damaged near the forward oarlock and sections of it have been torn away, either by gunfire or abrasion against the reef. On the opposite bulkhead there is a dark stain that can be scraped off with a fingernail. It could be a blood stain or perhaps old varnish. However, it has a salty taste, which would indicate blood, and this would seem to be consistent with the conclusion that shellfire caused the damage to the opposite gunwale. However, the salty taste could be the effect of long exposure to the sea and salt spray.

The boat seems to be equally pointed at both ends, but at what I believe to be the stern there is a barely perceptible marking. —r —f——. This is definitely not an Oriental marking; therefore the boat belonged to one of our allies. At least it would seem so. The r presents a problem, though, since it is definitely not an s such as USS or HMS and it is not a capital letter. However, it is possible, due to the deterioration of the paint, that the r is not really an r at all but what remains of a 4. The marking could then be —4 —f——. Perhaps a serial number, or a model number, or even the year the craft was built. However, that solves nothing.

We have been unable to find a button, a scrap of cloth, a mark, or scratch, or clue to the identity or fate of the people in the lifeboat. Only a dark stain that might be blood. What can it mean? That no one was in the boat? Did it break loose during a storm? Was it thrown overboard during a battle? Or was it launched by desperate men who were machine-gunned, blown up, burned, or drowned before they could reach safety? Or was it occupied by desperate men who faced day after day of endless waves, and hunger, sun, and thirst, until one by one they slipped from the boat into the relief of darkness and death? Where did the boat come from? How far? And did they see no ships, no island, no planes?

For some reason I can't explain I expected to see something when I climbed Nellie's Tit for a last look. Not eagerly, or fatally, or desperately, but somehow I knew it would be there. I don't know what I expected. A submarine perhaps, come to take us off the island. And when I saw that it was an empty and half-sunken lifeboat I was disappointed. But the lifeboat could be better. These are Jap waters. The submarine could be spotted by a Jap patrol and depth-charged. Instead of being trapped on the island with no food we could have been trapped on the bottom of the ocean with no air. But with the lifeboat we have the means to escape.

Or maybe when I first saw the boat and knew that it was not big enough to be a submarine, I thought it was a dead man floating in the water and I was happy, because a dead man would cause no problems and yet he would be a message from the world. There would be labels on his clothing, markings on his shoes. His manner of dying would tell us something about the war and the state of the world. Did he die of hunger, disease, suicide? Was he shot, abused, neglected?

And he would be carrying some kind of identification. Perhaps a billfold with pictures—wet but not ruined. A picture of his wife in a sun dress standing beside the car with a baby in her arms and a dog at her feet. Pictures of other women in tight little bathing suits, shorts, sweaters, low-cut blouses, filmy nightgowns. And a letter, still legible, from a girl back home who went to the movies, and ate banana splits at the Ice Cream Parlor, and hamburgers at the Hamburger King, had picnics in the park, drove a car down the main drag, and went to sleep between clean sheets thinking of her lover, holding her pillow tightly to her soft naked breasts.

And when I saw that it was not a dead man, but an empty boat with no bodies, or buttons, or scraps of cloth, I was disappointed. Yet the boat is better, for it too is a message from the world, a letter of hope, a picture of escape. The boat is damaged but it is repairable, and even in its damaged state we found it afloat.

I believe Kee is disappointed in the boat. I tried to explain to him its promise, the hope it gives us, but he is in pain and worried about his hand. Because he is so concerned about the needs of today, food and medicine, he cannot see the promise of tomorrow, cannot understand that this is the greatest day in the history of the island—the day of our deliverance. Escape from naked and utter need.

First priority must be given to Kee's hand. I fear for his life if I do not stop the infection and get him off the island soon. When there was no hope that he would ever get proper medical attention, I could not bring myself to torture him further, to probe and pick at his wounds. But it must be done, and now that there is a chance that the additional pain might save his hand or even his life, I can do it.

Secondly, we must regain our strength. This means meat. But now that we have the means of escaping the island, we no longer have to worry about tomorrow. If necessary we can burn down every tree to get meat; we can kill every animal. Those we cannot eat we will cook and take with us in the boat. It is no longer necessary for us to reserve something for the future. Our future is not on this island.

Then we must repair the boat, and outfit it with a rudder and some kind of sail. The sail can also serve as a shade. Since we will be naked we must have some shelter from the sun. If we can find any coconuts we can use the oil for protection, carry fresh water in the shells, and use them when empty for bailing the boat. Kee will be impatient to begin, but we cannot afford any errors. We will have the stamina for only one escape attempt. Therefore we must be wise in choosing the direction of our escape.

Since we do not know the direction of the nearest island, our shakedown cruise should be a circle about the island. We will build a big fire on the mound, and using it as a point of reference, we will circle the island looking for other islands close by and observing the direction and velocity of the wind and ocean current. This will extend our range of vision by several miles in every direction, and moving into new territory increases our chances of being discovered.

If we sight another island we will return, get the fire and the book, and make our escape. If we do not spot land or surface vessels and do not appear to have been sighted, we will decide in which direction our best opportunity lies, bearing in mind wind direction, the drift of the current, and the direction from which came the signal on the horizon, the man struggling in the sea, the lifeboat, and the tree.

The last few days have been the happiest of my life. Even cleaning and disinfecting Kee's hand did not destroy our joy, as it seemed to relieve the pressure and pain in his arm and I believe the infection is stopped. The operation, the lifeboat, and the steady diet of meat has done wonders for Kee. He is so grateful. He is always at my side and is willing to do anything I ask. I believe he understands now what the boat means to us. We have worked together with a single will, a single purpose, a single hope, gathering food and repairing the boat.

I have tried to spare Kee the heavier work of piling the brush around the trees to burn, chasing the animals, and moving the boat, but he is eager to do his share. Sometimes I think that if we had only worked this way on the shelter we would have completed it and been safe from the storm. But that is wrong. If it had not been for Kee's hand we would have built the shelter and put our trust in it. Thinking ourselves to be safe here we would have destroyed the lifeboat and squeezed out our lives in the dark and narrow shelter. Imprisoned by our fear.

There is a purpose to our lives. There must be, even though we may not always see it. How else can we explain this island, and our presence here, and this means of escape placed in our hands? Our lives do have meaning, and I cling to that thought. In purpose there is courage. In purpose there is faith. Purpose robs pain of its possession, labor of its degradation, hunger and nakedness of their shame. Life lived with purpose is life filled with hope.

We have prepared a big signal on the mound to serve as a reference point for us and also as a signal to any passing ships or planes. In a moment I must put the book aside in a safe place until we return. At dawn we set forth to find our way off this island. This was not paradise. One does not need hope in paradise. In paradise one does not wait.

Dear Mother,

The boat is ready. I am beginning the journey that will bring me back to you. If for some reason I should fail, this letter will be found and placed in your hands.

I didn't tell you before because I didn't want to hurt you, Mother, but the time has come to speak the truth. Your flowers were ugly. People laughed at them. They laughed at you. They pitied me because I had to deliver the shabby, ill-assorted bouquets. You always pretended you did it for the store, for Dad's sake. He hated them. They embarrassed him. The sickly funeral-parlor smell of the house made him ill at his stomach. You thought I upset him, that I made him sick. It was the flowers, Mother. And you.

My childhood was an unhappy one, but you could have been my savior, Mother. I wanted to be liked and respected the way David was, but you made me deliver your bouquets. I wanted to be admired by nice girls like Helen, but you gave me a bouquet of stinking, sticky flowers for her birthday. I wanted to be free of Ruby. The sight of her made my flesh crawl. You could have saved me, Mother. You could have helped Ruby when she came to you. You could have put your arm around her and talked to her like a child. But you gave her junk that meant nothing to you and was worth nothing to her, and sent her away.

If you get this letter, Mother, it is because I am dead. But don't weep, Mother. You still have David. He's the one you really always cared for.

~

The boat is lost. We scarcely got it over the reef before we started shipping water. With our added weight the boat rode low in the water and we could not bail fast enough. Kee was unable to paddle and I couldn't paddle and bail both.

Kee was frightened before we even got over the reef, but I couldn't turn back. I knew it was risky in the leaky boat but a single glimpse of another island would have been worth the risk. So I kept paddling with the makeshift oar, trying to keep the boat head on into the waves, while Kee did nothing, frozen in fear, bailing a little when he had to.

If I could have caught but a single glimpse of another island I know I could have made it, even if I had to swim.

But riding low in the water we could see nothing but the tops of the waves, our view poorer than the one we had on the island. We were making very little headway, floundering in the waves, and in desperation I stood up for a better look, a sweep of the horizon. I saw nothing and the boat wallowed, took a wave broadside and sank from under us.

I tried to save the boat, as we were a long way from the island for swimming and I thought Kee could hang on to it. If we could have gotten it back to shallow water we could have repaired it and would have had one more chance. But the boat was too heavy for us to turn over, too heavy for us to tow. We clung to its side for a while preparing ourselves for the long swim back to the island.

I decided to go first, since I was the strongest. Also I had taken bearings and Kee could follow me, as we could not often see the island over the waves, or even the smoke from the fire, and I knew before we got back it would be dark. I began slowly, saving myself, sometimes having to tread water and wait for Kee so that we did not become separated. I was unable to help him in the water, but I knew I would have to help him over the reef and I stayed in sight so he would not give up.

Once we had gotten over the reef and into the shallow water I pulled Kee through the lagoon and he fell on the ground and gave up. I sat for a moment beside him to catch my breath, but I could not quit. The island was dark. Not a flicker of light from the fire, and I knew that I had to find live coals and get a fire going or we would be totally destitute without even a fire for comfort, without a fire for light.

I crawled up the mound and knelt in the dark, sifting through the gray ashes, searching for a single red spark. At first I did not believe it, fearing it was some trick of the imagination, some flicker of the optic nerve that had been burned by the sun and salt water, and now, strained and tired, was staring into the gray ashes in the darkness. I wished that Kee could see it, that he could verify it. A ruby no larger than the end of my little finger. I dared not touch it to be sure for fear I would extinguish it.

Feeling in the darkness for leaves and twigs that had escaped the fire, I knelt in the ashes and held them to the spark blowing gently with my breath. There was a flicker and then a tiny flame. I clawed at the ground trying to rake up fuel for the fire, calling Kee to come and help me, but he did nothing. I wished for clothing that I could feed the fire. I wished for the book so I could add its pages and scraps.

I got the fire blazing bravely enough that I could leave it for a moment, stumble down the Pillar of Hope in the darkness and gather firewood, calling Kee to help me. When I had a strong fire again, I took a torch to start another fire beside the pool and went to look for Kee.

Kee still lay where I had left him—naked, wretched, shivering, shriveled from the water, looking less than a man but without the patient endurance of an animal. Taking him by the arm I led him to the fire, gave him some water to drink, and tried to comfort him.

Sitting with Kee beside the fire, listening to him moan and suck his wound, I knew the darkest and most bitter moment of my life. We seemed lost and forgotten, our lives of no consequence to anyone else and no pleasure to us. The rats are gone and most of the birds. Many of the fruit trees have been burned or are dying. The jungle is gone, the grass is gone, and we have lost the boat. All we have left in this world is the fire and the book and each other.

And one thing more. Something I discovered as I choked and splashed in the sea, promising myself to quit if after five more strokes I didn't see land. I could not give up, even when I wanted to, even when what I was going back to was what I had just run away from. Something brought me to the island, something prevented my escape, something was leading me back.

There is more to life than chance. Life is cruel, but it is not a mockery. I know now that there is a meaning in our life here, a purpose beyond our understanding. I know that it was wrong for us to try to escape our fate, to try to evade our reason for being here. That is why the boat was lost. I know that we cannot save ourselves, that rescue is our only hope.

Our lives are not without consequence or hope. Beyond the limits of our sight and hearing was rescue all the time, while we struggled and made our futile plans of safety and dreamed of escape. All this time rescue has been out there, just beyond us, trying to be known.

Sitting beside Kee in the dark, I told him of the hope that is in me. I told him of the promise that Major Ebaugh made—that he would never rest until every member of his squadron had been accounted for. I told him that Captain Willett will go to see Lisa and they will have to talk of me. And even if he tells Lisa that I wasn't much of a pilot, and even if Lisa tells him I was a twenty-second man, and even if they laugh at me, they will also have to say that I am missing.

I told him that Mother will hang a gold star in her window and will adorn the church with flowers in my memory. But even that won't satisfy her for long, and as soon as the war is over she will insist that my body be returned home so that she will have a grave to decorate and tend and border with flowers. And in searching for my body, they will find us alive. That one day David will appear out of nowhere and say, "Come on, Greg, or we'll miss the victory celebration." And he won't make fun of our tears or bawl us out because we are naked and dirty.

That Sister Mary Martha was praying for me, that Lisa was watching the harbor for my return, that Helen waited by the flight line. I told him that Bunny remembered, and that as long as she hates me I am alive.

Already I am beginning to hear the sounds of rescue. A quiet, plaintive sound. Not harsh or insistent or restless. Like the sounds of early morning in city streets. Like the sounds of a woman stirring in her sleep. Or the rustle of the wind in a wooded park. Already it is raining out at sea, and by morning rain will be falling again on this island. The grass will come back, the jungle will grow again, the trees will bear fruit, and for a little while we will be saved. If we can persevere for a few days we can endure. I will dig in the ground. I will hunt in the sea. But I will survive. And I will keep Kee alive also. The fate that brought us to this island, that spared us from the storm and sea has provided food if we can but find it.

Sister Mary Martha, pray for us.

Patient Helen, teach me patience too. May I watch for rescue as Lisa watches for her men. As long as Bunny remembers hatred, as long as Ruby remembers shame, may I remember hope.

Major Ebaugh, you who have navigated the chartless sea, plotted the starless night, computed the secret and invisible wind, help me to plot my course aright.

Low ceiling all day. Limited visibility but no rain. Only low ragged clouds and fog. If a plane were to fly over, even very low, the pilot would not see us. Even if he were searching for us. A convoy could pass just beyond the reef and we would never know it, could not see it.

Socked in. Unable to get out. Unable even to see out. And then toward evening I saw a hole, an opening through the clouds, and I could see through the low gray scud to piled cumulus at 6,000, up to a high, thin stratus at about 20,000 feet and beyond that—blue. If only I could get up there above the clouds, up where I could see, could move—

Hunted seeds, dug for roots, scratched for crabs and small fish under the rocks and coral. Got a coral spine in my hand. Found barely enough food to keep alive, but there is the beginning of fruit on the trees. In a few days, with another rain, there will be fruit to eat, and then the birds will come back and there will be eggs. A few more days and I will have pulled us through this time. Scratching in the ground for both of us. Saving the best for Kee. Looking for tidbits to tempt him into eating, to keep him alive.

I have heard that primitive, superstitious men can make up their minds to die and then lie down and do it. I fear for Kee because he has no interest in living, or even eating. He would starve before he would look for food. And even when I find the food for him I have to tease him into eating it. Kee must have medical attention soon if he is to live. And out there somewhere, gathering its strength, is the storm. We must get off the island.

Gold-star Mother at my graveside. Weeping at my tombstone. Happy with a grave to tend. Hidden in beauty. Entwined with ivy. Smelling honeysuckle and lilacs. Tasting roses. Mother, there is no one there.

Mother among the flowers. Picking bouquets. Marigolds for memories. Daisies for laughter. A rose for each sunset. A poppy for each friend. Tulips for happiness, pansies for joy, lilies for—"Who are the flowers for, Mother?" I asked her once. And she handed me a lily. "For my little boy."

Gold-star Mother at my graveside. Digging in the ground. Cutting. Pruning. Pulling up by the roots. How is one to abide faded asters? What can be done with petunias that wither and larkspurs that turn brown? What is one to do with roses that fail to bloom?

Youth is a blighted paradise and hope is the canker worm that lays waste the roses. Mother, I am dying here.

Patient Helen, surrounded by friends, waiting to receive. Careful not to be too happy or appear too pleased. Patient Helen, unwrapping each treasured surprise. Careful not to appear too eager or to tear the pretty paper. Patient Helen, searching through the ribbons and papers for one gift more. "Greg, did I misplace—Oh, of course, the bouquet. How stupid of me. What did I do with them? They were just lovely. How sweet of your mother to think of it."

Patient Helen, sitting beside the fireplace. Listening to "Moonglow" and "It Had To Be You." Careful not to be taken in by their sentiment. Remembering the hangar dance and a kiss in the park. "Let's not go yet, Greg. There's lots of time for that. Let's just sit here and talk about home. It seems so strange to go to the store and not see your father. I felt so sorry for your mother. And for David, of course. David was always so close to his father."

Helen in waiting. Holding my letters in her lap, neatly arranged in the order of their writing and contained with a pink ribbon. Patient Helen, careful not to cling to memories too long or remember too much. Fingering the letters. Waiting to drop them one by one into the fire and let the flames silence my cries for remembrance, my pleas for her faithfulness and love and the occasional token of a letter.

Hold the letters tightly, Helen. Patiently put them away again. Buried out of sight beneath slips and bras and cotton panties. Careful not to see your name written with such love and care, careful not to think of the unfulfilled longings, the sweated dreams, the aching loneliness held by that thin ribbon of pink. Helen, I am waiting here.

Deliberate David, who never took a cut, never got caught pilfering from the store or screwing Mr. Watson's daughter, searching through the records, tracking down Gregory's whereabouts, discovered that good ole Greg damaged a wing on a Yellow Peril, was put on report for buzzing a girl's house, laid Bunny Jensen and hung her panties in his locker, was unable to satisfy a San Francisco whore, let Major Ebaugh chase after a Jap alone with darkness closing in and visibility down to zero, took a cut and was almost grounded, lost an airplane and shot down one Jap, unconfirmed.

Bad ole Greg. Shows little sales leadership or managerial skill. Not worth saving. Let him rot into the jungle. And David closed the book, gave up the search, and went back to brown-nosing in Washington, hot after the men with the suction. Not caring that Greg clung heroically to life, sending messages for help, or that he kept Kee alive when there was no one else to feed him, and gave him hope when he no longer cared enough to lick his own wounds. David, I hope still.

Lisa of the whorbor. Sitting by the seaside. Listening to her seashells. Watching the ships come in. Examining all the faces as she searches for her men. Looking for a husband, or a lover, a stranger, or a friend. Rigged for victory celebration in a cheap seaside hotel. One dark room. One window overlooking an airshaft. The city's noise. The ocean's smell.

You remember, don't you, Lisa? You said, "There's nothing out there I care to see. If I see the ocean I think of my husband and how long he's been gone. If I see the city I think of all those people making a buck and having the time of their lives."

You remember, don't you, Lisa? You asked me if you were my first woman and I said no. I said I was usually better than that, that it must have been the liquor or the excitement of going off to war. You held me close, and said it didn't matter, and you cried.

We said goodbye in the lobby with the desk clerk looking on. Stiff with embarrassment and regret. I gave you what money I had. You gave me a bottle of brandy. "Thanks for everything," I said. And I promised to look for your husband, to go to CINCPAC if necessary to get him shipped back to the States. "I'll write to you, Greg," you said. I asked if I could see you when I got back, remember, Lisa? You wouldn't promise, but you said you would watch for my ship.

How many ships do you watch for, Lisa? How many men? Will you watch by the harbor until all your men come home? And those who see you waiting, watching for your men—do they call you constant Lisa, faithful wife, with a heart as big as the sea? Or do they call you Lisa of the whorbor? Sea bitch. Easy lay.

Ruby Watson wanted to be a nun. A sister of charity, a child of innocence, an everlasting bride. To sit in a convent garden surrounded by flowers that cannot wither and children that cannot cry. Behind a high stone wall that shuts out the chaos of a world that cannot care and the madness of souls that cannot fly. Meager. Impoverished. Loved.

But Rudy's convent was loneliness and the world was within her wall. Her heart could not always care and her soul could not always fly. Her flesh was pimpled and milky white, her glands were swollen, her tongue was raw. In devotion she plastered her face with ointments and examined her skin. In meditation she studied her body in the mirror, pinching her flesh. In penance she goaded her kidneys and whipped her bowels. Because there were no children to play with, she played with Greg. Because there were no flowers to roll in, they rolled on the floor and the back seat of the car.

And when Ruby saw her father's face framed in the car window, twisted in horror and distorted by the steam on the glass, she thought it was God's face. And when her father sent her away, she thought it was God who rejected her. And when they took her baby she thought Ruby Watson had died.

But for Gregory Wallace and for Sister Mary Martha she lives in a convent with happy children and fadeless flowers, surrounded by high walls that shut out shame and dreams of flight. Sister Mary Martha, I hold onto your prayers.

Major Ebaugh, the best navigator in the squadron, who said he would rather rescue one of his own men than to splash six Japs, who promised he would not accept relief or rotation as long as a single one of his men was missing and unaccounted for, who plotted our course to the target, who read the wind on the waves and reckoned our return, became lost in darkness, disoriented in low, ragged clouds, desperate as his fuel and time ran out, ditched at sea and was never recovered, chewing off his tongue in despair. But every man in the squadron believed in that promise. Counted on it. Every man swore to back him up. Major Ebaugh, I watch the skies for your return.

Captain Willett was a liar. All that talk about women. Lies. How he laid them and left them without memory or regret. Lies. All lies. Willett shot a Jap pilot as he was trying to bail out, blasting him back into the burning cockpit. Willett strafed a lifeboat full of desperate, waving Jap seamen. Willett called Joe Cunningham a coward for aborting a mission when his engine overheated, and on the next hop, Joe refused to turn back when his fuel ran low and was lost at sea. Willett cared for no one but himself. All that talk about looking for survivors. Lies. All that talk about being my friend. Lies. All lies. All he cared about was Lisa's telephone number and Helen's address.

Bunny Jensen hates my guts. Because I humiliated her, and tore her dress, and bruised her arms. Because after I had hurt her and defiled her I couldn't find the words to stop her tears or remove her shame. Because I hung her panties in my locker, buzzed her house, left her number on the wall by the barracks phone. Because I told that football player she was pregnant and convinced the son of a bitch that I was going off to die in the war and that he should marry her to save her from the whorehouse.

But you can't forget me, Bunny. Not as long as you hate me. Not as long as you love my child. As long as you hate me you will remember.

I may be lonely but I am not alone.
I may be lost but I am not forgotten.
I may be missing but I am not dead.
I may be hated but in that hate I live.

It was before dawn when I first heard them. They were very high and still a long way off and their drone was barely audible above the wind and the waves. I looked at Kee across the fire. He appeared not to have heard; he was still asleep. Quickly I built up the fire but the whole sky was overcast. Not the faintest glimmer of a star. And the sound was growing more distinct.

Still I wasn't sure. I stepped across the fire to awaken Kee and saw that his eyes were open. He had heard it too. "Listen," I said, cupping my hand over my ear, my voice trembling with excitement. "Hear?" But he made no sign of listening, or even of having heard me. "Mali ku-see," I said. "Something from the sky. They have come, Kee. They have come." Not even his eyes seemed to move. Apathetic. Beyond caring. Doing nothing.

I caught him by his good arm. "Fire," I said. "We've got to build fires. Big fires that will punch through the overcast. We've got to get the message to them." And when he didn't move I caught him by the arm and pulled him to his feet.

He was surprisingly light and so weak that he tottered. His eyes were dead, without interest, and the sound was very loud now, the lead planes almost overhead. "Wood," I said, giving him a shove. "Get wood." And I ran to the Pillar of Hope to start a signal burning there.

Desperately I worked trying to keep three fires going, regularly spaced and in a triangle so that they would not appear accidental, or the camp fires of natives. And as fast as I could, I set other fires.

Dawn came. Gray and overcast. The damp wood smouldered and the smoke hung below the heavy clouds. And still the planes came over at broken intervals. Flight after flight. South by southeast. Very high. Over the clouds, and our signals were not reaching them.

At last they were gone and the sound of them passed. Our fires still burned slowly and a pall of smoke hung over the island. They had not seen us. Our only hope was that they would pass over again on their way back from the attack, and that the sky would clear.

But the ragged gray clouds hung low in an unbroken ceiling as far as the eye could see. I watched the sky. I ran from one place to another looking for a hole in the overcast, a sign it was breaking up, praying for a wind to move it out of the area. The sky did not change.

I fell on my knees and cried in frustration. I pounded on the ground. Soon they would be back if they were coming back. I went to look for Kee and found him huddled by the tree that had washed up on the beach. He had let his fire go out. Catching him by the arm I dragged him back to the fire and put him to gathering wood. I got the fires going again and then set fire to as many trees as I could find that would burn, knowing that Kee would not last until the fruit was ripe. We need rescue now.

I was so busy setting fires, my ears filled with the crackle of the flames, that I did not hear it at first. A single plane. Above the clouds. West by northwest. A single plane returning from its mission. Much lower now but still above the clouds and we could not reach it.

I began to shout. I knew it was madness but I could not help it. I shouted and waved my arms although it was impossible for me to be heard or seen. I ran up to the Pillar of Hope and back again. I cursed, I promised, I cried. Hope was just above the clouds. Not over five thousand feet. And we could not reach it. Could not make ourselves known.

I don't know how long I shouted but when I stopped and fell exhausted the plane was gone. I lay on the ground hoping for other planes straggling back to their field. Nothing. The sky was like lead, shutting out everything. The fires crackled. Smoke and ashes sifted down, filling the dead and heavy air.

Time passed. I wasn't asleep. I must have been in a state like Kee's. I no longer cared that the fires were burning out, that it was getting dark, that we had not eaten all day, that Kee might be dying.

And then I saw him. He sat down beside me and held out his hand. His rotting, oozing hand. Held it out to me as though it were my problem. As though I were responsible for his stinking, filthy wounds. Threatening me with it. Punishing me with his sores.

I hit him to drive him away. I shoved him down the hill, but still he crawled back. Holding out his hand. Begging me to do something. I will never be free of that horror, that shame as long as Kee is alive.

I turned away so that I did not have to look at his eyes. So that I did not have to watch him crawling up the hill with one hand. But he came up behind me and put his hand on my shoulder. I turned and he found it as hard to look at me as I found it to look at him. It wasn't blame I had seen in his eyes. It was shame and guilt. He dropped his head and put his hand behind his back. He just wanted to be close to me. But he could no more ignore the hand than I could. "Show me your hand, Kee," I said. "Show me your hand and I'll try to help."

I led him back to the fire and examined his hand. In my ignorance I had made two mistakes. I had not cut the finger cleanly at the joint but had left the shattered bone so that the wound stayed open and raw, and I had not cauterized the wounds deeply enough to stop the infection. Remembering these two things I went to look for a sharp, heavy stone. I put the stone in the fire and looked at Kee. He tried to look at me but couldn't. "Nuka biru," he said. "It's okay."

When the stone was burned clean I put his hand on a log, holding it steady with my knee. Kee held my ankle with his good hand and closed his eyes. He was gripping so tightly that my foot hurt, but I didn't care. Taking the rock in both hands I brought it down with all my might on his wrist. Kee screamed and kept on screaming. His hand had not come off but was flopping loosely as he held his arm to his chest. Blood spurted in his face and ran down his chest. I grabbed his arm, trying to finish the job before the shock wore off, before he bled to death. But Kee wouldn't let go. He curled over the hand, protecting it, completely out of his senses while his life was running out on the ground. I tried to pull his arm free but could not and so I hit him with my fist. I hit him and hit him until he was limp and I grabbed the arm and held it on the log with my knee and I chopped and chopped until his hand came off.

I dropped the rock, so weak I could not hold it. I thought I would faint. Blood was everywhere. But I had to stop the bleeding. Gripping his arm in both of mine I thrust it into the fire. His eyes blinked open and his mouth was wide but no sound came out. He didn't hit me or fight back. He knew what I was doing and why. He understood. Only his arm moved, twisting and writhing as though it had a life of its own while I lay on it with all my weight trying to hold it in the fire. I held it until the hissing and bleeding stopped and then I turned the arm loose and crawled away hoping to die.

Kee is quiet now but he is not asleep. His eyes still watch me but they are dull and lifeless. His face is swollen and covered with blood where I hit him but I have not washed it off. I have not even washed the blood off myself and my hair is matted and my hands are sticky. But I cannot leave him now. I cannot live here alone. If Kee dies a part of me dies. If I have killed Kee I have killed myself also.

NOTE TO SURVIVAL INSTRUCTORS: *Survival kits should include a bone saw*

Kee is better. There is a little fruit. Still green, causing stomach cramps and diarrhea but there is something to eat. We will live for a while but I do not know why.

Why did I ever come here? Why couldn't I have died cleanly, quickly over the Jap carrier like a hero? Why couldn't I have drowned in the ocean, quietly, silently to sink down into death without horror and shame? What good is there to hang on? What purpose to survive? Why did I come to this place to die? Why here?

Once I saw a light, very dim and very far away, but it seemed to be blinking a signal to me, a signal I could not understand. Was it just the fading light from a strange and distant star that was sometimes interrupted by a cresting wave?

And once a stillness came over the island. The wind stood still. The leaves were motionless. And I hid as though some awful thing was near. What did it signify? And the voice I hear. Are my ears so hungry for words that my brain manufactures them? Or is there a message for me?

A lifeboat crossed miles and miles of ocean to come to us, only to sink when we tried to use it, without a single clue as to who built it, who used it, who damaged it. Was it a gift? Or was it a grotesque joke? An insanity?

I saw something in the water, not just floating or swimming, but struggling in the water. But what was it? Was it a fish being attacked by sharks? Was it a man splashing and calling for help, bringing news of the war, and hope for rescue? Or was it something from the depths, a sea turtle or octopus, splashing for a moment at the surface, and then diving again to the bottom?

Was the tree just an accident that means nothing? But it came from somewhere. It grew in some soil and bears the markings and history of those years if we could but read them. Kee goes to the tree for something. Because of superstition, or memories, or some secret understanding that I do not share. But what is it?

I went for a while to sit among the ruins of what we thought was to be our shelter. A pile of loosely fitted stones and we thought it was our refuge, our security from the storm. The very height and meaning of our civilization and cooperation and dreams of safety. But what does this pile of stones mean? That there is no safety? That a shelter cannot be made by men who cannot speak freely and openly cooperate? Is it a monument to man's folly? Or are the ruins of man's dreams the monuments of his spirit?

Where is our hope now? Where is our safety? Where is our purpose? Not in rock shelters to turn the storm. Not in rotting lifeboats to escape the island. Not in indecipherable messages from unknown sources.

There is a purpose for this island and a reason for our being here. There must be. Otherwise life is insane. A joke. An obscenity. If there is an island then there must be a use for it. If the ocean currents have pattern, if the winds move according to reason and measure, is it strange to believe that there is a Navigator charting and plotting our lives?

And if that Navigator had a chart of the ocean, our time of departure, a forecast of the weather and the winds aloft, could He not direct us by dead reckoning? And if He knew our destination could He not plot our course and vector us here? And if I was saved from the strike, from the sea, from the storm, from the lifeboat, is not my life a testimony of design and purpose? And if the island was placed here to lie fallow for years and years forming fruit trees and fresh water, waiting until we came to fulfill its purpose, and if we have been here months and months waiting to fulfill our purpose, is not that purpose rescue?

I never thought much about God because I never had time for anything that unimportant. Mother always had a God around to record her charities, water her flowers, and to look after her family, especially David and me. Dad had a good-natured God who liked to be coaxed and cajoled, and who could abide anything but shoplifters, failures, and people who wouldn't work for a living.

At church they had an Old Man who kept records and was very stingy with chalk or paste or anything else of His you might want to use, and punished you if you left food on your plate or talked back to your parents. At school they taught us about a God who wanted you to brush your teeth, keep your nails clean, not mark on your desk, and recite the pledge of allegiance from memory.

Ruby's God wanted her to die to herself that she might be good, and Sister Mary Martha's God wanted her to live in limbo that she might not be bad. Helen's God wanted her to be proud of her virtue, jealous of her treasure, suspicious of tenderness, afraid of love. Bunny's God wanted her football team to win, her true love to marry her, and her children to be happy and healthy above all others. The skipper's God wanted us to kill Japs, and Lisa's God created the city and the ocean and seventy-two-hour love.

I didn't need a God to kill Japs or to thank me for doing good. I didn't believe in a God who wanted men to hide from consequence or to live in shame and fear. And no one told me that there was a God who plotted lives, reckoned destinies, and saved from emptiness.

I know that there is a God, that He created me. It was He who rescued me from my mother's womb, He who lifted me out of the sea, He who saved me from despair. In His own time He will rescue me from this island. His name is the Rescue God, and above Him there is no other.

~

God, I know this island is just a speck in the vast ocean. I know it would be ignored by a ship, overlooked by a PBY. I know that its shape is ordinary, its value nothing, its history commonplace. I know that it does not merit notice or favor. But faith is a very small island.

I believe that You have noticed this island and that You have favored it above all others. You have provided the island with food and water so that it is habitable. You brought me here that I might record its use and purpose and You brought Kee here that we might know companionship, help, and mercy. You have given us fire that we might know warmth, and light, and contentment. You have given us the sunrise and sunset that we might know beauty and peace. You have given us the ocean that we might know mystery and power. You have given us the horizon that we might know hope, and the sky that we might dream of escape. Give us freedom, God. Get us off this island before we die.

~

NOTE TO SURVIVAL INSTRUCTORS: *Recognition classes*

Survival training should include classes in the recognition of God's purpose.

1. God's purpose is mysterious and puzzling. It is not easy to understand why God brought us here.

2. Pain and anguish are part of God's plan and signify that His purpose is being accomplished.

3. Accidents are the handiwork of God.

4. The history of this island is the story of God's purpose and the end thereof is rescue.

~

Kee is ill and very old. I believe he is older than I had at first thought. I believe that islanders are all very young or very old. Few of them appear middle-aged. They maintain a childlike innocence and irresponsibility for years and years and then become old and wise overnight.

Also pain and despair seem to have aged Kee prematurely. His face has deep lines, his eyes are hollow and vacant, his hair is ragged and gray. He has forgotten the words I taught him and is incapable of responding to his own name. "California," I say, trying to cheer him, to re-establish that earlier understanding. Kee seems to have never heard the word. Now I am no longer sure that was what he said. Did the word mean something to him? Or was he simply responding the way I had taught him?

Kee will not let me out of his sight, but follows me painfully and slowly wherever I go so that I dare not move except to seek food and then I can't go far for fear of exhausting him. No matter how I try I cannot elude him nor escape the sight and smell of his hand.

At night he sleeps fitfully, moaning and crying out in his sleep. And each time he wakes he checks to be certain that I am nearby. We bury his arm in warm ashes and this seems to help him some. I know of no other way to help him. I lie awake at night trying to recall, to invent some anesthetic. There is nothing. Therefore I tell him of the hope that is ours.

I tell Kee of God's purpose and why we are here. God created this island out of the stuff of the sea. Bits of the ocean floor, the shells and skeletons of sea creatures, the droppings of birds, the minerals and sands and seeds carried by the waves. And the seeds took root and began to grow—grasses, creepers, tiny trees. And the ocean brought other things to the island—other seeds, other fruits, tiny creatures. And the winds brought birds and insects and flying things. And all things grew together in a formless tangle of vines and bushes and leafy trees. Life and death without purpose.

And then the sea brought Kee here, and the storm brought fire, and the wind brought me. And at first we were lonely and afraid and we hid in the jungle waiting for the Task Force to come and save us. And when we despaired of rescue and longed only to die, God sent us a message—a star, low on the horizon, sending its message of hope. "Hold on. Accomplish My purpose. I am coming."

So we took hold on the island and began to give it form and substance, to learn its secrets, to find ease and comfort here. And God sent the storm to show us this was not paradise. Our work was ruined, our comforts were destroyed, all our plans for the future collapsed in fear.

Out of the storm God sent a tree. Where it came from, how it came, what it meant we did not know. We who had conquered this island and unlocked its secrets could not discover the message of the tree, and in our confusion and fear we determined to build a shelter that would make us safe from the great storm.

But confusion does not make men wise nor does fear unite, and all our labors together drove us farther apart. He cannot build a shelter who cannot fathom his brother's heart. The wall that rose between us was not a wall of words but a wall of suspicion and jealousy. Angry words were spoken, angry deeds were done, and in pain and blood did we discover our brother.

And God sent us a lifeboat to test us and it seemed that all our troubles were over. Together in our new-found understanding we would repair the boat, together in our new-found trust we would escape this island with its history of hunger and blood and loneliness. But understanding and trust were not enough. Escape was impossible. The lifeboat sank.

We barely got back to the island. Our despair was complete. There was no rest or comfort here. There was no safety. We could not save ourselves. We could not escape. Our only help was hope. Our only hope was the Rescue God.

As Kee finds comfort in our hope, I tell him of God's purpose for us. We must build signals as evidence of the eagerness with which we await His coming. We will turn the whole island into a great signal. Every tree will be a cry for help, every blade of grass will be a prayer. At His coming all the signals will be lighted so that all the island will burn in testimony to the presence of the God who comes to rescue. Our only voice is smoke, our only tongue is fire.

It is in the best interests of this island to please God.

It is natural for man to worship. The act of worship may be occasioned by scenic beauty, a sense of well-being, despair, loneliness, or lack of sexual intercourse. Every day I worship God and pray that we may be worthy and that He will hasten the day of our rescue from this island. But even as I pray I know that He does not expect us to sit idly waiting for rescue; therefore I work as I pray. Kee works with me in spite of his pain and weakness.

We no longer speak or have any need to. We watch the horizon for signs of the coming storm and we work. When I wake in the morning, Kee too is awake. When I begin to work so does he. We work side by side all day without speaking or touching, or even looking at each other, yet closer than we have ever been. United in a single impulse.

And as he works Kee sometimes forgets his pain. He is a simple man and to be happy must have a task. It matters not at all whether it is my task, or his task, or meaningful or senseless, so long as he believes he is getting somewhere and can see some progress. I believe Kee would die for progress. We work hard. Too hard. And we have too little to eat. But at night we look about us and see the signals we have made, great piles of brush everywhere, awaiting God's coming and the fire, and a kind of serenity comes over us which is better than food. Kee knows. We work with a single impulse preparing a testimony. And God must save us. He must come soon.

The wind seems to be shifting and the sky is dark with towering purple-green cumulus, but what does it mean? A seasonal change? But what season? What year? How long have I been here? My brain seems to have crystallized. My fingers are stiff and cramped so that I can hardly write. I watch the horizon for signs of storm.

Where is He? Why doesn't He come? What more is there to do?

God sets signs and wonders out to sea and posts them in the sky to warn us that the time is near and that only he who is prepared will be saved, only he who waits will be rescued. Let every vine, every leaf, every blade of grass give voice to His coming.

God, we thank You for this small island, unmarked on the charts of men but known to You.

We thank You for the fire that has given light to our darkness and we offer it to You.

We thank You for the coconut trees, and the banana trees, and the ones with the pear-shaped fruit that fed us and we offer them to You.

We thank You for the fruitless trees that kept the fire, sheltered us from the sun and rain, and gave the birds a place to nest and lay their eggs, and we offer them to You.

We thank You for the grass seeds and the knotted roots that sustained us when the fruit failed, and we offer them to You.

We thank You for the orangeweed that soothes the stomach and the bind root that binds the bowels, and we offer them to You. All belongs to You.

The island is ready, O God. The holocaust is prepared. Give us a sign, O God. May our signal be acceptable in Your sight. Amen.

It was still and the sky was as green as the water. There was a green pall over everything. Even Kee was sure of it. "Mali ku-see," he said, pointing at the horizon. "Hope," or "something from beyond." The sign of the coming of the Rescue God. I could feel it. I was so excited I could hardly breathe. I began to jump up and down and shout. I ran up to the Pillar of Hope to wait and Kee went with me. I watched as the clouds piled higher and higher and the sun turned dark and I knew. He was coming. In our excitement we had not set fire to the signals.

With Kee following I ran back to the fire. Seizing a torch, I gave it to him and showed him how he should set the signals afire. Every tree, every blade of grass. Kee wanted to stay with me, but I pushed him away and grabbing a torch for myself, I began setting the signals in the opposite direction.

I worked my way around the island setting fire to everything that would burn. I don't know how long it took. There were sparks and flames everywhere and the smoke was so thick I could scarcely breathe or see where I was going and I stumbled and fell, and rose again as long as I could keep going, slapping the sparks out of my hair and beard, and then I threw the torch aside and waded out into the lagoon to splash water over my smoking head and wait for Him.

Kee was already crouching in the water and we waded out even farther to escape the smoke and embers and to better see His coming. The sky grew darker and the wind rose, whipping the water into foaming waves so that we had to retreat to shallow water, and it blew the smoke far out to sea. And with a peal of thunder the sky split open and it rained. A torrent.

We crouched in the water waiting, scarcely able to see,

scarcely able to breathe in the downpour. First a deluge, and then a steady downpour that drenched the island. When at last the rain stopped mist hung over the island. Yet we had seen nothing. No sign had appeared.

Puzzled, we turned to look at the island. The signals had gone out. Quickly I ran to the nearest signal and dug through the ashes. They were wet and cold. I ran to another signal, and then another. We had lost the fire! I couldn't believe it. I ran from signal to signal. Surely somewhere there was fire. A spark. A still-hot ember. I guess Kee was following me. I do not know. I could only dig and dig. There was no fire.

I climbed up the Pillar of Hope. Nothing. I could see nothing. The sea was calm. Only a few cloud formations remained. The sun was breaking through the mist. He had not come. And all around me was the blackened wasteland of the island. Kneeling, I hid my eyes in my hands. I couldn't look. I dared not think.

Why hadn't He come? There had to be a reason. There is no luck. There is no chance. For every act there is a reason. For every misfortune there is a wrong. Something had displeased Him, therefore He had not come. Was it because of me? Was it because of Kee?

Behind me I could hear Kee. He was crawling toward me. I could hear him moaning. I could smell his hand. I ran but there was no place to run to. I hid but there was no place to hide. Wherever I went he was there. Fouling the island with his smell.

I ran until I could run no farther. I fell down beside the tree panting for breath. I tried to burrow under it, digging with my hands. And then I stopped. He was there and I could smell him. I picked up a rock and I hit him. "Go away," I said. "Go away." And I hit him, trying to drive him away and he would not leave. He crawled back to me and held out his hand. Accusing me with it. Punishing me with it. He lay on the ground and held out his hand. And I killed him.

It is quiet now. And dark. There is peace. I am alone.

~

If I die here, who will know?

If I am guilty, who will care?

If I have turned this island into hell, a jungle of errors and mistakes from which I cannot escape, who will blame?

If I have destroyed, who can give life again?

Who prepared me for this? Who taught me how to live without hope? Who told me the meaning of loneliness? In what school did I learn solitude? In what church did I discover grace?

~

NOTE TO SURVIVAL INSTRUCTORS: *Why God didn't come*

1. Because of conspiracy, an evil that corrupted my plans and prevented God's blessing. That is why there was no peace here, no understanding. That is why this paradise is a place of devastation. Because of them.

2. The best interests of this island are served by the survival of him who is best equipped to discover its meaning, record its purposes, and please God.

3. Under certain conditions affirmative self-defense may be justified. Thus is the world made safe for godly man.

4. It is better to injure a brother than to offend God.

5. God must come now because I cannot live here alone.

Dear Dad,

You taught me that war was a lot of laughs with drunken buddies and French broads. Well, laugh over this. I am dying, alone and forgotten. You always thought I was the lazy one, the one with no initiative. The one who would never do anything. Well, roll over in your grave, Pop, because I've got two kills and that's more than David can say.

That's right. Two kills. That Jap I caught sneaking for home after attacking the fleet and that Judas I caught trying to prevent my rescue from this island. I had known all along that he was different, not one of us, but I had tried to overlook it. I tried to communicate on his level. I included him in every plan for the island. I kept the log for him. I tried to educate him. I treated him when he was sick and brought him food. I overcame my natural revulsion in order to doctor his wounds. I did everything I could. I gave him the best the island had.

And he did nothing. In his perverse and underhanded way he sabotaged every dream I had. How can you build when there is no desire for improvement? How can you plan when there is no concern about tomorrow? No value higher than the demands of the stomach? How can you create a civilization with material that is contaminated? How can you escape desolation when obstruction is in the boat?

And when, because of him, I failed, was he contrite? No, he threw the failure in my face as though it were my fault. When I shared my food with him, was he grateful? No, he complained because I had not gotten more and wanted my share. And when, because of his need, I was forced to operate on his hand, and stop the bleeding, and suck the poison from his wounds, did he thank me? He held out his hand to me. As though his sores were my fault. As though I must share his pain. As though I must suffer his wounds.

I tried to run away but he followed. I tried to hide but he found me. I tried to drive him away but he would not leave. Each time I shoved him aside he came back. When I hit him with a stick he lay on the ground and moaned. When I hit him with a rock, he held out his hand to me. I hit him and hit him to make him hide his hand. To make him stop accusing me with it, stop punishing me with it, get it out of my sight.

I hit him until I could hit him no more, until his face was gone and only his eyes were recognizable. Still he clung to life, and still he held out his hand, motioning to me. Only he wasn't accusing me any more, he was reaching out to me. He wanted to tell me something. Putting down the rock, I put my ear where his mouth should have been. Nothing. He had no lips with which to speak.

"California?" I asked. "What did it mean? What was your secret, Kee? What was your hope?" And one eye slowly closed. Maybe he winked.

Why do men die trying to speak, Dad? For hours you lay silent, quietly dying. And then your eyes opened and you looked at me and your lips began to move, to form words, although there was no breath to express them. But I watched the lips as they moved. Slowly. Painfully. As though you had died and only your lips were alive.

What were you saying, Dad? Were you asking for your cronies? Your friends who hung around the store because you were always good for a laugh but never came to your room to see you die? Were you asking after Harry, your long-time and loyal employee, whom you had trained in trickery and deception, and who was now in charge of the store? Were you asking where was David, your first and best-loved son, while Greg never left your side? Or did you ask that I remove the flowers that decorated your sickbed, filling the room with the smell of gladiolas and death.

What were the words on your tongue, Dad? A curse? A cry for help? A plea for understanding? Something you had always wanted to say and never got around to? Were you trying to say you loved me? Were you touched by the irony that after a life surrounded by people you were going to die in the presence of an unloved son? Sometimes I think you were only asking for a glass of water and sometimes I think

I am alone now. I have subdued all. Why doesn't He come?

I know that there is a God.
That He created this island.
That He created me.
It was He who rescued me from my mother's womb.
He who lifted me out of the sea.
He who saved me from despair.
It was He who set a sign in the sky.
He who taught us with a storm.
He who warned us with a lifeboat.
In His own time He will rescue me from this island.
His name is the Rescue God and above Him there is no other.

As I had no tools for digging, I placed Kee's body in the ruins of the shelter and pushed the walls in on him. His final resting place. Perhaps that was the purpose for which the walls were built—a monument to human ego, a shelter from the storms of life, a sanctuary from the eye of God.

We were together for how long? And in all that time I never really looked at him. But as I bent low to hear his words, I noticed for the first time—Kee's tongue was twisted, and on the underside of his arm was a small round scar like a smallpox vaccination. And as he was dying I saw—was it because he was dying or had it always been there?—a light film over his eyes. Was that why he sometimes seemed to wink? I don't know how he could see. I believe Kee was almost blind. And the signal he would never admit—maybe it was the message from some ship. And the cloud on the horizon that he could not see—perhaps it was a distant island. And I was right all the time.

Was that what he was trying to tell me? That he was almost blind? That his visual judgment was impaired? Or maybe he was trying to tell me who he was, how he came to the island, why he clung to life in spite of all his anguish and pain. Was he trying to tell me how to live? Was he trying to say that rescue had already come? Was he a native or an exile? If he had kept the book would it be different? If only I knew that secret, if only I knew what his hope was, then I would have hope myself.

What do I really know of Kee? I know no more about him than I did the first day I came to this island. His name. That's all I really know of him. Kee Yop. Not really a name at all. More like the name of a harbor. There is a harbor in the Solomons called Kaiyot. Was that what he was saying, that he was from Kaiyot? And the other words? Hope. Something beyond the horizon. "Mali ku-see." There is a island named Milikazi. When he was pointing at the horizon and saying Mali ku-see was he saying that the island was in that direction? And nothing more?

Will I become like Kee? Blackened by the sun? Unfamiliar with the sounds of my own tongue? Unable to speak except in mumbles? Was that his last and final secret? That he was just like me until the horror and loneliness of the island turned him into a savage? That once he could speak like a man, and reason, and sing? That once he could fly? Major Ebaugh, who rescued me from the sea?

Oh Kee, if you were here now, if you could tell me where you came from, and why you were here, and what your hope was. If you could look at the sky and tell me what the signs were. Oh Kee, if you were here now you could keep the book.

I am alone and the loneliness is unbearable. At night I shiver in the dark. In daylight I try not to look at my skin, which is slack and running with sores, or my hands, which are like claws. At night I lie awake listening to messages I can't understand. By day I see signs and watch—expecting what? I can't see as far out to sea as I once could. There is a roaring in my ears, and when I look up I get dizzy. If rescue comes and my dulled senses recognize it, how will I signal without fire?

I sit on the Pillar of Hope with nothing to eat, yet I'm not hungry. I am starving but I can't eat. Sometimes I hear something above the clouds. Sometimes I see a distant speck. I wave my arms until I can no longer raise them. I shout until I have no voice. I am naked, and hungry, and sick. I have no fire. I wait for rescue because rescue must come. Even if I have no fire. Even if I am unworthy.

The truth is I don't like women. I always thought I did, but I don't like wives, and I don't like mothers, and I don't like martyrs, and I don't like sluts, so I guess I don't like women.

Helen would be a wife. Always out to make an impression on your boss and friends. At home, hard, her skin loose, her face oiled, her hair in curlers, but in public braced, polished, powdered, and combed. A picture of seduction everywhere but in her own house.

Bunny would be a mother. The moment she got the ring and the church's approval she'd turn off the siren and start warming up the milk glands. She endured my thrusting and stabbing because that was the necessary condition, and when it was done she said, "You filled the emptiness that was inside me." Already aware of the union of egg and sperm. Already content to be alone and contemplate her swelling belly. Already looking forward to the time when she would have no sex at all but would look like a soft and shapeless man. Comfortable. Doughy. Smelling of diapers and powder. Her belly bulging, her teats distended, content to serve.

Ruby was a loser. Happy only she was being used. Wanting to be carried off and raped. Wanting to get caught. Happy now that she is a martyr. Content to sit in a corner of the asylum wall and pray for forgiveness. Stripped of everything, even her name. Sister Mary Martha, suffering saint.

Lisa was a slut. Expecting me to hold off until she was ready. Expecting me to deny myself to please her. Expecting me to pay for the privilege. There was no husband in the Navy, no sitting by the seashore, no listening to seashells. She never wrote or watched for my ship. She never remembered.

In times past my life seemed a string of accidental events, but thanks be to God, I can see a pattern, a divine conspiracy that testifies to the greatness of the Rescue God.

1. I know there is a God.
2. That He created this island.
3. That He created me.
4. That it was He who waited in the rain beneath the movie marquee.
5. He who watched through the frosted window.
6. That it was He who waited in the house for the telephone to ring.
7. That it was He who struggled in the raging sea.
8. He who lived on this island and in misery held out his hand.
9. He who spoke my name. Sent a message of hope by an alien star. He was the silence who visited this island. He was the tree sent from afar. He was the lifeboat
10. Signals may be seen at greater distances than we can detect help. The sounds of rescue are sweeter than mother's milk. The Pillar of Hope is higher than the clouds of despair. The Grand Design that placed the island here and filled it with fruit and fresh water is wiser than the plans of men.
11. In His own time He will
12. His name is the Rescue God and above Him
13. God

Lt. Gregory Wallace 015323. My plane was hit while I was attacking a Jap carrier. I ducked into the clouds to avoid Jap cover. Became disoriented. Lost my bearings.

Bailed out. Have been here for many, many days. Course to target was 280. Launched attack from

harness—locked
wings—spread and locked
tail wheel—unlocked
rudder—6° right
aileron—6° right wing down
elevator—1° nose up

I've got to get back. Got to get off this island. What am I here for? To live. Right? God's purpose for me is to survive. Got to be tough, resourceful, wary. Trust no one. Expect help from none. Avoid obligations. Keep separate from that which is alien, subversive, inferior. Hope for rescue.

~

Log is beginning to rot away. Some words almost gone. Must make provision for keeping book safe until it is found. Without this book my life here would be without meaning. My thoughts unknown. My suffering to no avail. The sun has risen every day and I have lived each day the best I could according to my training, but only those sunrises, only those days recorded here will be known or remembered. To Kee this book was a mystery. Something magical. But the book is not a mystery, it is the only known. The only reality. It must be saved from the decay that corrupts all man's dreams and efforts.

1. The book will be wrapped in green leaves and left in the cave in the rocks.

2. Signs will be left, curious enough to attract the attention of the knowing, subtle enough to escape the eye of the unenlightened.

3. False messages will be left to discourage the uninitiated.

4. A pile of rocks will be placed before the cave.
5. A pile of bones will be placed on the rocks.

I have recorded here the essence of man's life and his duty. Truth, dear David, is not in reports and surveys but in these pages and in the stories of the survivors.

1. Our father, who is a cheat and a clown, but who in death discovers the secret of life and is unable to pass it on to us.

2. Our mother, who waits for us, weaving wreaths of flowers beside our tombstone.

3. David, our brother, sole surviving son. If David had died over Germany, we could have gone home. By saving his own life he condemned us to die.

4. Kee was our brother too. Kee, who is always with us, destroying our dreams of progress with his simplicity, our dreams of paradise with his wounds.

5. Helen, who snares us on a dream of innocence, laughs at our shabby gifts, denies our apprehension, and sends us away without a kiss.

6. Bunny, who smelled like an overripe peach, its flesh torn and bruised, who bears our stripes, rears our children, and is never marked by us at all.

7. Lisa, who knows us too well to be a wife, who loves us too well to be a whore.

8. Ruby, who incites us to games of glory and splendor and leaves us with memories of madness and dismay.

9. Major Ebaugh, who reckons time and wind, who plots his heading and marks his course and is lost in darkness.

10. Captain Willett, who shows us how to love without fear, how to live without doubt, how to kill without remorse.

11. Harry Watson, who teaches us how goodness corrupts and love destroys.

12. Sister Mary Martha, trapped in innocence and goodness and doomed to walls.

13. Gregory Wallace, who was the first to screw Bunny Jensen, who knocked up Ruby Watson, who shot down a Jap plane—get on his tail, get him in range, splatter him on the windscreen—who survives.

❧

There was no one named Kee Yop on this island. Only because of my training was I able to keep the plane in the air as long as I did. I saved myself from the parachute. I saved myself from the sea. I saved myself from the island. I invented Kee as an escape from loneliness so I would not lose my sanity. I was not afraid of him. I did not hurt him. I could not have killed him. There was no one else here. It is my hand that is missing. It is my wound that smells.

❧

Dear Sister Mary Martha, praying on your bench in the corner of the convent wall. Did you ever think that perhaps there is no forgiveness in this prison of deceit? Did you ever look over the gray walls and think that out there is innocence? That grace and meaning are beyond the sea?

Did you ever think that hope is a star that shines in the darkest part of the night, sending a message you can't understand? Or that rescue is an airplane that passes unseen above the clouds? Or that help is a lifeline in the hands of a dying man who has no strength to clutch it? Do you ever think that this life is madness, that this world is a prison, and that if you gave up hope you would be free?

Why do you weep, Sister Mary Martha? Is it because there is no gentle Jesus in your convent of stone? No statue of sweet Mary and her babe? Only streets, and walks, and walls.

Sister Mary Martha, the sun is dark at midday. The sky is black and green and the sea is the color of old bronze. Everything is hushed and still and even the sea is silent.

I tremble in excitement and expectancy. The hair rises on the back of my neck and my pulse quickens. It is the sign of the coming of the Rescue God. It is the beginning of a new day. It is the time of change.

Come malihini huruhura. Come Great God with lightning in your wings.

Afterword

Most readers don't take kindly to a change of pace. Accustomed to a favorite author's quirks and patterns, they settle back comfortably and look to the next Amanda Cross, the next Tom Clancy, the next James Michener like they look to the next package of Velveeta Cheese, confident of what they'll find and content to accept it for what it is. So, when an author who has established himself as a first-class storyteller shifts stylistic, chronological, and geographic gears, these self-same readers are nonplussed and unsettled, vaguely feeling that Their Author has somehow failed them. That Their Author may be paying them the highest compliment of which a writer is capable—to assume that they can cope with some naggingly troublesome ideas—most times never enters their minds. Such is the case with Robert Flynn and *The Sounds of Rescue, the Signs of Hope.*

Robert Flynn (1932-), a native of Chillicothe, Texas, and already a playwright of some note, made his novelistic debut in 1967 with *North to Yesterday*, a funny, sad, rowdy book about a handful of ragtag cowboys and the trail drive north that followed the Last Trail Drive. Well and good; Bob Flynn writes westerns. Then, in 1969, he published *In the House of the Lord*, a funny, sad, reflective novel about a minister whose ingrained sense of human compassion puts him at odds with his flock and his sect. Well, okay; Bob Flynn writes funny, sad novels about folk somehow out of step with their times. Whereupon he wrote *The Sounds of Rescue, the Signs of Hope* (1970), a thoughtful, complex, and singularly unfunny novel about a young Marine pilot shot down in the Pacific during World War II, and readers who sought to classify, pigeonhole, process, and homogenize him threw up their hands in defeat.

Why defeat? Because Robert Flynn is not a formula writer, and to try to make him into one is to do him and his work a flagrant injustice. He is a writer with things to say about the human race. That he constantly strives for new and better ways to say them speaks to his sense of his craft and says much about his respect for that hugely complex state that we call the human condition. His concern, as he says elsewhere in this volume, is with individuals "who discovered that their training as human beings was not only inadequate and flawed, it was false." His characters, to a person, find that they're not equipped to deal with the world that confronts them; the world isn't what they've been led to believe it is. To survive, either they or their world must adapt, and in the struggle that results lies their story. Such, memorably, is the case for Lt. Gregory L. Wallace, 015323, as he regains consciousness on the shore of an unnamed island somewhere in the Pacific.

It's important that Flynn chooses to site his hero on an island. We, as readers, are immediately at ease; we've been stranded there before. We've been shipwrecked with *Robinson Crusoe* (1719) and the multitalented *Swiss Family Robinson* (1812, 1813), and we've watched as they single-handedly turned the jungle into civilization; we've eaten smoked goat meat with the marooned Ben Gunn on *Treasure Island* (1883); and by all means let's not forget the most famous island of them all, Thomas More's *Utopia*

(1516), which gives us a model and a name for an ideal existence. Flynn has a long and honorable tradition to call upon—which is probably why he rejects it. Greg Wallace is no Crusoe, no Ben Gunn. He's a young, confused, and frightened American who's trying desperately to come to grips with the world as he's been taught it, the world as he wants to remember it, and the world as it actually is. His island, moreover, is no Treasure Island, dotted with wild goats and pirate gold. It isn't the Robinsons' island, happily equipped with a shipload of supplies a few yards out in the lagoon, and it's a far cry from Utopia. It's an island, instead, that throws Greg on his own resources, and how he responds gives Flynn his novel.

Islands have a way of stripping us raw. Surrounded on all sides by water, left with scanty food and the barest essentials of survival, we are inexorably compelled to confront nature, existence, and our innermost selves. Greg Wallace is no exception. He tries to live according to the dictates of his survival lessons, and constantly comes upon new circumstances that haven't been covered; nature doesn't cooperate and he comes close to destroying himself in his struggles to stay alive. He tries to establish first communication, then society with Kee Yop, his enigmatic native companion. Kee Yop doesn't cooperate, either, and, at last, frustrated beyond all reason, Greg kills his only neighbor in a fit of rage. He tries to keep his mental discipline by thinking of his superior officers and the models they set for him, only to have to confess that they, too, are grievously flawed human beings, lust-driven and tragically fallible. Like every good American boy of legend, he tries to get comfort from memories of his own past—memories of his storekeeper father, his flower-growing mother, his ambitious brother, his boyhood and adolescence in the small town of Wonder Springs, and the four women (one foolishly idealized and three only commodity) who touched his soul. And he has to face his shame, his embarrassment, and a growing sense of his own unworthiness. Greg's world turns inside-out as we watch, taking him from a defensive "I'm not at fault . . ." to a pathetic "Why didn't somebody tell me? . . ." and bringing him at last to a new, humbling consciousness of where he stands in relation to existence and to himself.

In a formula story, Greg Wallace would be rescued in the last five paragraphs, plucked from his island by a PBY and returned to a world of willing women and chocolate ice cream. Flynn, to his credit, leaves Greg to his revelation and us to wonder. Will Greg survive? We don't know. For that matter, we don't know that Greg is *alive* at all. Ambrose Bierce, in "An Occurrence at Owl Creek Bridge" (1891), has his hero escape from a hanging and work his way back to his front door and his family, only to be brought up short when his body reaches the end of the rope and his neck snaps. Sixty years later, William Golding has the events of *Pincher Martin* (1956) take place wholly in the last moments of a sailor dying on a bald rock in the North Atlantic. There is ample precedent for Flynn's having Greg die as he crawls ashore, thwarting his hope by killing him with salvation within his reach and leaving us with only the record of a hallucination. But, somehow, I doubt that he did. That kind of trick wouldn't play fair with the rest of us, who haven't the luxury of writing the world off as hallucination.

The Sounds of Rescue, the Signs of Hope marks an important stage in Robert Flynn's development as a novelist. It looks backward, to be sure, to *North to Yesterday* and *In the House of the Lord*, linked with them in its motif of the ill-equipped person in a world he never made. But it looks ahead as well, to the prize-winning *Wanderer Springs* (1987), which uses a middle-aged man's return to the small

Texas town of his youth to establish the sustaining, affirming theme of a person's arriving at a quiet, humbling peace with himself, his past, and his present.

The Sounds of Rescue, the Signs of Hope is not a book one can easily classify. It is not meant to be. It is a book of human strife and human flaws, and of the strength that comes from the genuine courage that acknowledges that strife and those flaws. The world may be torment and transience, but it still holds persons who press onward in the face of fear, and contradiction, and hypocrisy, and disappointment, seeking valiantly for meaning and truth. They know that the world has meaning, if only they can find it. They are outnumbered and outmanned, but their quest is noble. They are heroes.

Fred Erisman
Texas Christian University

About the Author

Novelist Robert Flynn, a native of Chillicothe, Texas, is rapidly claiming his place as one of Texas's major writers. His most recent novel, *Wanderer Springs*, was published to wide acclaim and won the Western Writers of America Spur Award as the Best Historical Western Novel of 1987. His classic trail drive novel, *North to Yesterday*, published in 1967, won a Western Heritage Award from the National Cowboy Hall of Fame and was named Best Novel of the Year by the Texas Institute of Letters. Flynn, a frequent speaker at conferences and colleges across the state, is also the author of *In the House of the Lord* and a short story collection entitled *Seasonal Rain and Other Stories.* His nonfiction account of the Vietnam War, *A Personal War In Vietnam*, is available from Texas A&M University Press. He is presently at work on a novel about Vietnam, where he was a war correspondent.

Flynn is novelist-in-residence at Trinity University in San Antonio, where he and his wife, Jean, make their home.